About the author

Patricia was born in the UK, and alone at age 27 emigrated to Australia.

There she married and had two children, obtained a Bachelor of Applied Science as a mature student and married again at age 71. Patricia wrote this, her first book, at age 73.

I would like to dedicate this book to my two children, Alexis and Fergus.

Patricia Ilich

MAYBE I'LL WRITE
MORE LATER...MAYBE

AUSTIN MACAULEY
PUBLISHERS LTD.

A CIP catalogue record for this title is available from the British Library.

ISBN 978 1 78554 580 1 (Paperback)
ISBN 978 1 78554 581 8 (Hardback)
ISBN 978 1 78554 582 5 (E-Book)

www.austinmacauley.com

First Published (2015)
Austin Macauley Publishers Ltd.
25 Canada Square
Canary Wharf
London
E14 5LQ

Acknowledgments

Thanks to Cai, my nephew for refusing to write my story for me and encouraging me to write it myself.
My darling husband Mike for his patience and guidance with all my many computer problems
My two sisters Victoria and Francesca for their help and advice.

Forward

Flying higher than most dreams,
Nothing matters on the bottom of the ocean,
Standing ground above the screams,
Clutching what's floating, on the ride to oblivion.

By
Kevin Francis, Lemongrass Café, Harvey, W.A.

Newspaper Report – November 2002 (extract)

"Fears are held for the safety of Donald and Susan Smythe who are three weeks overdue for their rendezvous in Brisbane. The pair were sailing their yacht "Brissibabe" from Sapporo, Japan, to Brisbane Qld. Last known contact was from Taipei, Taiwan."

Newspaper Report – August 2004 (extract)

"Asia Pacific Alliance Airlines Flight No. APA 300 disappeared over the Pacific Ocean on Tuesday and teams are searching the area last reported from the plane – no wreckage has been found so far.

CHAPTER 1

THE FIRST MEETING
Perth, Western Australia.

Early Saturday morning, September 5th 2008, thirty-five-year-old Fiona Campbell rang the intercom at the apartment of Peter Elliott. Fiona was dressed simply in a black sweater, tailored trousers and an unbuttoned jacket with her company logo "Global Geosurveys" embroidered on the front. She was carrying quite a heavy brown paper package along with her shoulder bag and had a worried look on her face.

Peter answered the bell with a sleepy, "Hello, who is it?"

Fiona answered with a slight Scottish accent. "Hello, is that Peter Elliott who used to live at 2, Holdsworthy Vista? My name is Fiona Campbell, from Global Geosurveys and I'd like to speak to Peter Elliott please."

There was a long pause and then the reply came back, "Who did you say you were?"

Fiona repeated her introduction and Peter then asked, "What do you want with me? It's Saturday morning."

"Yes, I'm sorry to be calling on you so early but I have to speak to Peter Elliott, it's about a plane that went down four years ago."

Again there was a long pause and then Peter said slowly, "Well, you'd better come on up – just push the door and take the elevator to the sixth floor, I'll meet you there."

Peter met Fiona at the lift and he beckoned for her to follow him into his apartment. As they came into the lounge area he turned to face her and asked warily, "Now what's this all about? My parents died in a plane crash four years ago."

Fiona stood unsteadily facing him and shuffled from foot to foot as she slowly and quite delicately delivered her opening line. "Yes I know… that's what I would like to talk to you about. May I sit down please? This package is quite heavy."

"Yes, yes," said Peter pointing to the white leather settee.

Fiona laid the parcel down and then sat back and gave Peter a worried look; she didn't know how this stranger was going to react to her news. Peter was not angry at this woman personally but had always been angry with the authorities, whom he felt had never dealt with the details of the plane crash correctly. He started with the questions straight away. "Did you come to tell me they have found the wreckage at long last? Would you like a cup of coffee, I was just going to make one for myself? You know we never had a formal acknowledgement of the plane crash and I had an awful job settling my parents' estate. It really wasn't good enough. The media went on and on about it for months, but nothing was found."

"Yes, I'd like a cup please, black and no sugar."

"So where did they find the wreckage then and are you the official spokesperson come to confirm what we all knew at the time? Bit late now! Sorry for being so abrupt but it really isn't good enough."

It was quite early and Peter's shock of unruly, and uncombed blond curls fell in a dishevelled tangle around his face. He surveyed the woman in front of him and felt sorry for her having to deliver bad news, what a job it must be to have to contact families of accident victims – especially so many years after the event, and probably knowing that the company had been very lax in admitting they had a plane down and taking responsibility for the obvious loss of two hundred or so lives. She looked very smart but not unduly fashionable; attractive, without being pretty, and her voice sounded controlled and steady. Peter handed her a steaming mug of black coffee as she started to tell him her news.

"Well I'm sorry to tell you that actually we haven't found any wreckage at all."

Before she could continue Peter put his coffee down and jumped to his feet, almost knocking over the coffee table and demanding, "Well, what on earth are you doing here then? Churning up people's memories and emotions, haven't we suffered enough? What do you want from me?"

Fiona took a deep breath and said calmly, "The plane **did** go down into the Pacific Ocean... and... presumably sank. There was no wreckage found, but there was one survivor." Peter held his breath and sat down gingerly on the seat opposite Fiona, his eyes wide with questioning emotion.

"What! Who survived?"

Fiona replied slowly, "Your mother."

"Oh my God, is she alive? Where is she, how do you know all this, and who are you anyway?"

Fiona replied steadily, wanting the story to come out slowly, "As I told you my name is Fiona Campbell and I am a surveyor with Global Geosurveys. We survey land for possible development and report to various governments. Four months ago we did a preliminary survey of Du Pont Island in the Pacific Ocean. In the course of this preliminary survey we came across a wrecked yacht, the 'Brissibabe' which had gone missing in 2002. There was a ship's log and a continuation of the log with subsequent writings – a report of events really, written by Sally Elliott."

"Oh my God," cried Peter. "So, is she alive, can I go to her, where is this island?"

"Well the truth of the matter is, Peter, we don't know if she is alive or not." Fiona then lifted the parcel next to her on the couch and handed it to him. "We had to submit the log to various authorities, the airways administration people, the police, the maritime authorities and some aircraft disaster investigation people, but at the end of that they took copies of the log and allowed us – the company I work for – to deliver the log to you."

"So, is my mother alive or not?"

"As I told you," Fiona quietly said, "I really don't know; no one really knows for sure. All you need to know is in the log, so please read it and if you have any further questions here is my card, you may call me during office hours for the next two weeks, after that I will be unavailable for a few months."

Peter looked confused and as Fiona rose to leave he took her arm gently and said, "Please tell me all you know, I have to know."

Fiona took his hand gently off her arm and started to make her way to the door of the apartment saying as she went, "I've told you as much as I can right now. I have a further appointment and I must go now – as I said, after you have read the log you may call me."

With that she called for the lift and as a last minute thought she warned him, "We have withheld all this information so far, but it is being given to the media on Sunday night. It won't take the reporters long to track you down and I think you will be inundated with the media trying to get your reactions, etc. I would advise you to clear out to a hotel or stay with a friend for a few days. Your life won't be your own as of Monday morning." And with that, she departed, leaving Peter stunned and almost speechless.

It was Saturday morning and Peter had arranged to meet a friend for breakfast in town. He rang Luke, his friend and made his excuse for calling off the meeting saying, "Luke I'm really sorry but something's come up and I can't make breakfast – it's a bummer I know, and I'm sorry, but I'll ring you when I'm free and we'll do it another day – can't tell you what it's about at the moment, will explain all later."

Luke was a little perplexed but agreed to call off the breakfast and made a note to ring Peter in the week and ask him what it was all about. Luke had been Peter's best friend since Art School and he had diversified from painting and gone into ceramics and then glass blowing. There was a very productive little factory in Fremantle he joined, and as Luke was very good at his job he was able to make a decent living from his designs and creations. Peter poured himself another cup of coffee, took off his shoes, put his feet up, and undid the parcel. There was a large hard-backed official ship's log and three notebooks, numbered 2, 3 and 4. He started to read the log first and got through the yacht's boring daily log, written by Donald Smythe, quickly skipping over what he obviously knew to be unimportant to him. Where the handwriting changed he

recognised his mother's hand, and with tears in his eyes
started to read.

CHAPTER 2

THE START OF MY ORDEAL –
August 2004

Well I know I shouldn't be doing this, and apologise for interfering with a ship's log – which I think is supposed to be sacrosanct – but I have no option – I think I need to record what happened to me and also what brought me here, and my finding the "Brissibabe". I'm writing this in case someone, hopefully finds it, and takes it back to the authorities – sometime. Where to start – I don't know. I've never kept a diary and I'm not much for writing letters – so please forgive me – dear reader, finder, rescuer, whoever you are – for my simple, plain English. First of all could you let my family – particularly my son – know that I am alive and well (or was, and at the time of writing reasonably fit and healthy).

My son is Peter Elliott, of 2 Holdsworthy Vista, South Perth WA. Australia 6000. So, I suppose I should tell you who I am etc. Well my name is Sally Elliott and I'm 72 years of age. I am reasonably fit and healthy for my age, but at the moment very sad and quite traumatised, but still grateful to be alive. I've always been lucky, (never so lucky that I could win the lottery) but playing cards with my husband or having a flutter on the horses – I could always beat him – other than that I've never been a gambler. However in this instance I have been incredibly lucky.

So what have I to tell you, dear reader? Well quite a story – as I'm about to relate. I am, as far as I know, the only survivor of a terrible tragedy.

Just a fortnight ago, Joe, (my beloved husband) and I were enjoying a lovely holiday in Japan, staying with a dear friend who lives in Osaka. (Can you tell him about me also please? His name is Taka Matahatsu and he lives at Matsugaoka Heights No. 203, Senriyama, Matsugaoka 6-29, Suita-Fu, Japan 565-0842.) I guess you'll have found the wreckage of the plane by now but here's the flight information as I remember it. We left Narita airport on Flight APA 300 flying Asia Pacific Alliance on Monday 8th December 2004.

About 2 hours into the flight the nightmare began. My husband and I were sitting in the seats where there is a gap in the seating, directly behind an emergency exit door – so we didn't have a seat directly in front of us and I think that was a factor in my survival. We'd had dinner and I must confess to having a small bottle of wine, followed by a nice cup of coffee. Joe said he wasn't feeling so good. He got up to go to the bathroom and I had taken my shoes off and was doing some sitting exercises (to ward off my chances of getting DVT). The airline gives everyone a little travel pack which has in it a toothbrush, a miniature tube of toothpaste, an eyeshade and a pair of cabin socks. The socks are just a long tube and fit everyone, I really like them as they do help to keep my feet warm. I had just put mine on when suddenly all hell broke loose. Without any warning the plane banked steeply to the left – then to the right. Everyone screamed, it was so unexpected. I pulled my seatbelt tight and, as I've done a fair bit of yoga, was able to tuck my legs under me, sitting cross legged – and then the plane started to sort of roll back to the left; and then, horror of horrors, started to drop – well plummet actually. I just curled up into a tight ball (which I can as I am quite slim and very small) and braced myself for the inevitable. I was terrified, both for myself and for Joe, he was still in the bathroom. I really wanted to unclip my seatbelt and go find him but that would have been impossible. People were screaming and the one or two people that had been walking around were being flung across the room like rag dolls, hitting their heads and bodies against the sides and top of the cabin.

I don't now, and never have, believed in God – but I have to say when terror has a grip on every muscle in your body – prayers, and appeals, and bargaining are the only thing on one's mind. "Please don't let us crash – please, God – I'll do anything, please don't let us crash – Oh my God, Oh God, Oh God!" and down we went. Everyone was yelling, and the dinner trolley had crashed into the seats behind me. Overhead lockers opened and various pieces of luggage fell out hitting people. The noise was terrible. Bedlam!

I really don't remember much after that – I must have blacked out, or been knocked out – but I jerked into life when cold, very cold water slammed into my body. I think the plane must have broken up and we were sinking fast. I had the presence of mind to release my seatbelt and I remembered someone once told me (if, in this kind of situation) to just "follow the bubbles". I really didn't know which way was up, and how or why I was in the water, but I did see bubbles and I followed them, stroking as hard as I could and holding my breath, for what seemed ages. I bobbed up in the middle of the ocean – I saw no-one else – and only bits of the plane sinking around me. Many bits and pieces floated away from me, out of reach, but to my surprise two orange lifejackets bobbed up along with two inflatable neck rests and a bottle of wine. I made a grab for the lifejackets and caught them by the ties – and caught the bottle of wine, which was actually only half a bottle and as I had nowhere to put it I stuck it down my knickers (for safekeeping). (I'm 72 – I don't wear those silly little thong things, but the good solid Bridget Jones type.)

I was screaming for Joe, my husband, over and over again, then sobbing and shaking uncontrollably whilst treading water to stay afloat. I tried to put a lifejacket on but with the long ties floating around I nearly strangled myself with it – and had the silly (hysterical really) notion that they'd find my body, "strangled and choked to death by a lifejacket"! After some time I did get the lifejacket sorted out and got it on, whilst hanging on to the second one. I realised then that my right leg and hip were really hurting but I couldn't see any blood so it couldn't be too bad.

It was starting to get dark, but I could see quite clearly that there was nothing nearby, no wreckage, no one and no land. It was no use swimming, where would I swim to – in which direction? Luckily the ocean was relatively calm and about a 2 metre swell was running but it was not rough. I couldn't see anything but sea, so I just lay on my back and sobbed and sobbed. It was getting dark now and I was scared, terrified actually. As the hours passed I contemplated the three ways I presumed I was going to die:

1.   I would be eaten by sharks
2.   I would die of thirst
3.   I would succumb to the appeal of seawater and just drink it and go mad

I think the third option held, if not the greatest appeal, at least the less abhorrent. I know I was more afraid of the sharks than anything else. Well darkness came and I could see nothing – which wasn't much different to what I could see when it was light, all I could see then was empty ocean, so it wasn't really much different – but actually it was, – there's something terrifying about not being able to see anything. It was a cloudy night and there was no light from the moon. It was dark, really dark, not even any stars that I could see. I decided to try and utilise the second life jacket and tied it to my legs and sort of lay back with my feet resting on the jacket. It wasn't comfortable and my leg and hip were still hurting but it was better than having the sharks nibble my legs as they were dangling in the water below the surface. I wasn't sleepy at all, just really sad, traumatised and terrified. I wasn't even hungry or thirsty – we'd had dinner just before the plane went down – and I had more than my fair share of a nice red wine. Eventually I think I started to get drowsy but was too scared and cold to actually go to sleep. I kept crying for Joe, over and over. After hours and hours I thought I heard a low, muffled sort of sound – I couldn't make out what it was at first, but then my befuddled brain realised it was the sound of surf – not crashing thunderous surf, but just a gentle shushing (is that an actual word?) As a pink dawn was breaking I could make out a shape ahead of me – I quickly realised it was a cliff face, not huge but the start of hills really, and I was drifting towards them – so I untied my legs from the second lifejacket and whilst holding on to the ties, tried to swim away from the cliffs in front of me. With the bottle of wine in my knickers, and only one leg really working well this was no easy task but when I was on the top of a wave I could see a long break in the cliffs. I kicked my way, with my one good leg, towards the break and although I was absolutely exhausted, pulled myself through the water in that direction. The tide must have been coming in as I certainly didn't have enough energy to propel myself through the water efficiently. Somehow I hit the sandy beach with a wallop as the waves dumped me and rolled me over. I lay on the beach in the half light and sobbed and sobbed again. I don't know if it was relief, horror, grief, but I lay there for ages as the sun came up, and I just lay there – wondering how I had survived and I couldn't feel any real injury, only a very sore and bruised I think leg and hip but my dear husband and everyone else, as far as I knew, had perished. Actually it had all happened so fast I don't think anyone would have had time to – what? I don't know, – pray, hold a loved one, write a note, – whatever, I don't know. So here I am on the beach. Is this an island or the mainland of which country? I have no idea. Let me see – we were about two hours out from Narita. My geography is not so good, but assuming we were on track – on the correct flight path, we should be near Singapore or Thailand – or were we further east into the Pacific – where I know there are thousands of islands?

CHAPTER 3

ON THE ISLAND

After writing the foregoing I think I want to address the rest of my writing to my son. I want to feel like I'm talking to him personally. I think this will help me get through this ordeal and whatever awaits me. I'll write a bit each day or so – or each week, as I feel like it – if I can – but I am hopeful that someone will come and rescue me – sooner or later. So, Pete – I'm talking to you now: – where am I? I don't know, all I know is that I've lost your dad and I don't know if I can bare that loss – we were so close as you know, he was, as they say, my soul mate. Apart from when I was in hospital, having you, and your dad was in hospital when he had his appendix out, we have never been apart – never, not for a night – I've never slept without him by my side. So back to what happened.

The waves had basically thrown me up on to the beach, and I more or less crawled, exhausted, frozen to the bone, from the waterline. I lay in a heap for hours just sobbing and calling out for your dad. Much later, when I was able to stand up, and stop shivering, I had a good look around me. Now I've read Robinson Crusoe, The Swiss Family

Robinson, and I've seen Tom Hanks in "Castaway" so I know the three most important things for survival are:

1. Water

2. Food

3. Shelter

So in a daze I forced myself to concentrate on survival. Hanging on to the bottle of wine had been a mistake, it had been a real nuisance, getting in my way, but although I wasn't thirsty I reckoned a quick drink wouldn't hurt, in the circumstances. So, as you know, Pete I'm 72 years old – if I die here, now – well it's not so bad. I've had a good life, done a lot, travelled a fair bit, and known real love – so if this is the end – well, so be it. Of course I'm missing your dad and you – and that will be a tragedy if I never see you again, and the rest of the family. So, I'll try and describe the place where I am and tell you how I managed.

There are hills here and the beach sand is sort of black in places, but not all over – and I think it's from an old volcanic eruption. There is one hill, way back in the distance, which definitely looks like a blown out volcano. It must be extinct – oh, Jesus, I hope it's extinct. Well I limped quite a way around the beach – cliffs at the back – still carrying the bottle and the two life jackets (I don't know why!) I think it might be an island – and after about a half a kilometre there was a break, back in the hills – and wonder of wonders a little stream – trickle really – seeping down the gap in the hills and on to the beach where it disappeared into the sand. I hobbled up the side of the stream to where there was a little waterfall – no, not actually a waterfall, more a drop in ground level really – about 20 cm from one level to the low beach level. I knelt down and took a tentative sip, to see if the water was drinkable. It was wonderful, cold, clean and I realised I was really thirsty. I put the wine bottle under the overflow and filled it up – yes I know I was watering down the wine but I had nothing else and I might just need the water for later on.

A little way up the stream I came to a water hole – a dip in the earth which created a sort of bath size water hole. It looked clean and free of any grooblies (mosquitoes etc.) so I waded into it and had a good rinse off (I've always hated the feel of saltwater on my skin – once dry) – and took my socks off which were soggy and an encumbrance. So I said to myself – Survival No. 1 item – water – found. Next, food. I wasn't actually hungry but I knew I would be, before too long. Well I could see coconut palms further up the beach and there were tons of old coconuts bobbing up and down in the shallows and plenty at high tide mark – but getting into one – well that was going to be a challenge. I had no tools, well nothing with me at all except the clothes I stood up in – being my underwear and a thin cotton dress. I've not been used to going around barefoot and my feet were going to be a problem – they were a little sore already from so much walking in only my stocking feet. I tried to remember how Tom Hanks got into his first coconut – I couldn't remember. I must think of a way to get into one. As you know, Pete I'm 72, slight of build and very small. I used to be 4ft.11 in – and that's what's on my passport – but in actual fact I'm shrinking as I get older – and your dad measured me about a month ago (he put a mark on the pantry wall) and we discovered I am now only 4ft 9in. I have a bit of arthritis as you know, so no real strength in my arms or hands – so getting into a coconut was going to be difficult. I can do most things that I need to do but opening jars and bottles are more difficult now-a-days than they used to be – that's old age for you. Luckily I'm not really hungry at this stage – so I decided to rest up until I felt more active and sleep was calling urgently. I found a nice clean spot under a grove of trees on the edge of the beach and just went out for the count. I don't know how long I slept (my watch has stopped) but when I woke it must have been late afternoon. Now I was quite hungry –

very hungry. (I don't think I have ever been really hungry before in my life.) I picked up a coconut and banged it against a rock, trying to get through the smooth outer coat and then the rough inner fibre and finally into the hard shell. I had nothing – no tools – it's impossible. I banged it against a rock, over and over but to no avail. I wandered up the beach, angry now at my futile efforts. I thought I should go exploring – off the beach, but I'm in my bare feet, so walking anywhere off the sand was going to be impossible. I'm ashamed of our human race – here on a beautiful pristine beach there's rubbish all over. Mostly plastic bits and pieces, odd bits of rope and a broken thong or two. I decided to look carefully now to see if I can find any unbroken thongs that I could wear to protect my feet. I found one almost immediately, far too big for me (I have very small feet) but I held on to it. Now I needed a left footed one and I might just be able to manage, but all that I could find was broken bits and pieces. Still I held on to the one right foot thong. As I walked on the beach the flat sand gave way to a rocky outcrop and covering one side, just under the water line, was a large bunch, gathering I suppose you might call it, of lovely large black mussels. Great, I thought, I love chilli mussels. I put down the lifejackets and the bottle of watered down wine and collected some dozen or so nice looking mussels, holding them in the fold of my dress. I needed something better to carry them and I remembered seeing further back, up the beach a broken plastic container and I thought that would do quite nicely to carry the mussels in. So I went back to look for it and got it and put the mussels in, also I plucked off the rocks, just under the water line, another ten or so. So I had food – mussels. Item for survival No. 2 food – no problem. Well not quite. I couldn't eat them raw, I needed a pan to cook them in, with water (that's easy) but then a fire. Oh Lordie, how do you make a fire – even if I found a pan – which is highly unlikely as pans don't float, and how do I open the mussels? Fire was going to be a problem too. I remember

18

Tom Hanks and the difficulties he had, and the raw bleeding of his hands as he tried to rub two bits of wood together. I couldn't do that. First I don't have the strength and second, my hands are soft and I just couldn't work them so hard that they would blister and bleed. (I'm a bit girlie like that!) I took the mussels, my one thong, my bottle of watered wine and still the two life jackets (I don't know why I was hanging on to them) and returned to the little stream. I laid the mussels down and then sat on a rock and just gave way to a fresh burst of emotion and frustration. I cried and sobbed for so long, but the instinct for self-preservation is very strong – so I took a rock and one by one bashed the mussels and ate them raw! Yuk! Slimy, rubbery, sort of metallic taste. The worst part was picking out the bits of shell. I just couldn't break one cleanly – anyway it got me through those first hours. Another burst of self-pity, crying and crying for hours and then an exhausted depression set in and I just wanted to curl up, and forget the whole thing. I drifted off into a restless sleep, haunted by nightmares of the plane crashing and calling out for your dad, over and over.

CHAPTER 4

FINDING THE "BRISSIBABE"

Next morning I woke to a pink hazy dawn and as I looked around me I couldn't help noticing only two things making any kind of noise, the seagulls screeching overhead and the waves washing up on the sandy shore. Other than that I couldn't detect any sounds at all – certainly nothing that would indicate any animals or any kind of civilisation. I couldn't see any signs of human activity either, no grass huts, no smoke, no buildings or jetties, nothing. I decided to take the bottle of watered down wine, and the one thong (hoping to find a partner) with me and explore further, leaving everything else by the stream. The beach was littered with rubbish and weed and I found some sort of wreck. I think it had been a very small, wooden rowboat of some sort, with a bit of a housing in the centre, which was all broken and distorted. I inspected it closely to see if I could salvage anything that might be useful. I could see part of the housing was metal, attached to what must have been a wooden wall, so I pulled and pulled to get the metal off the wood. I was thinking, this could be my pan for cooking. Eventually part of it gave way and I pulled it off. It was a corner piece and I thought, if I tipped it on its side I could put some water in and boil it over a fire – great idea. The metal wasn't too heavy and not too big so I was able to drag it back to the stream. So now I had water and mussels and a metal container to cook them in – all I needed now was a fire. I certainly wasn't going to do the Tom Hank thing, my hands are soft and I just couldn't work them to the point of blisters, and bleeding (I'm a bit girlie like that!) but I remembered a method I think I had seen on the telly years ago where you make a sort of bow and arrow arrangement. You put a piece of string from one end of a bendy rod to the other, then put into the string another piece of rod and then you sort of file it – well moving the bow backwards and forwards with a sawing action. The friction you need is made by the rod on top of another flat piece of wood – and on top of the rod is another piece of flat wood to hold the spinning rod straight. At the base of the spinning rod you put some dry material so that the heat caused by the friction is sufficient to make a fire. Well that was the theory as I remembered it.

Well, "theory" for me is where it stays. It took me hours to find the materials to do all this and then hours again trying to get it to work – which it didn't! Exhausted I mashed up another few mussels, had my supper and curled up in my little area under the trees and went to sleep. More nightmares!

Next morning the pain in my leg had abated so I decided to walk around the next headland (still toting my bottle and one thong) to what I discovered was another cove. If this is an island, this first side is quite windy and rough, but once around the headland it was a very different story. Calm and peaceful, and mostly detritus free. By the by, I decided to name my areas. I called my landing beach with the little stream and mussels, Windy Cove and this next cove, Peaceful Cove. (Not very original I know, but I think my mind is befuddled, due to my being so hungry!) I had a refreshing swim in the calm waters of Peaceful Cove, and then decided to explore further up the beach. There was a large rocky outcrop with lots of rock pools and most covered by seaweed. Normally I love exploring rock pools but I couldn't waste too much time as I need to look for food, quite urgently. At the back of the beach were coconut palms, sand dunes and lots of ordinary trees further back. Just exploring I wandered up the sand dunes and again came to a break in the dunes, and in between the dunes came to another little stream – well a gentle trickle really, but it was fresh water and tasted good. As I walked up the stream to see what kind of trees were growing inland I came to an amazing sight. I was about 200 metres inland from the beach, round a bit of a bend, following the stream and looking up a bit of a rise, maybe 4 metres above sea level was the hull of a boat. It was obviously a wreck with the back end all stoved in but you could still see it had been a yacht of some sort. There were no sails of course, and no mast – but you could tell where the broken remains of a mast were. There were guard rails still around the edge of the boat and the remains of a name, but I couldn't make out what it was.

The hull was mostly stuck in the sand dune, at a very drunken angle, with only the damaged back end showing – but I could tell it must have been a nice yacht, probably some 12 metres or so long. How it got there I had no idea, but from the look of it – must have been there a few years. It was faded fibreglass (I think) and all paint just about gone. I don't know the exact size, length or width, I'm not at all familiar with yachts, boats and sailing terminology, but it was obviously "living in" size – not just a "day's sail" size. I ventured up the rocks, which gave me a sort of stairway, and stepped on to the yacht, after tentatively tested the decking. It seemed strong enough to take my weight. Although the whole boat was sitting at a crazy angle I was able to walk on the deck – drunkenly. I know it was silly of me but I called out "Hello, is anybody there?" and guess what? No answer came the reply – ha, ha. The boat had a raised cabin with a door and there were hatch covers further down – all closed and looked in good condition. I tried the door handle and it fell off in my hand – but it opened the door. I stepped over a ledge, peered in and then took a step down into the cabin. It was a bit dark at first, but then my eyes adjusted to the gloom inside the cabin. There were items all over the floor but it was dry and very few cobwebs. There was a table and bench seating on two sides. Further down there was a small kitchen affair with a sink, cooktop and various drawers and cupboards. A door at the side of the cabin led to a very small bathroom/toilet and straight on from the kitchen was the bedroom arrangement – well just a double bed really, with cupboards and drawers around it. There were two small windows around the living area with thick curtains, closed. All must belong to someone, but to whom, and where were they? A bit spooky really. (Thoughts here of the Marie Celeste!) At one side of the cabin was a sort of office arrangement – drawers under a tilted table with maps and stuff for navigation. In the kitchen (I think it's called a galley when you're on a yacht) were lots of drawers and cupboards. I opened one of the drawers, which had a simple sort of locking device, and there were knives and forks etc. The next drawer down had plates, mugs, bowls etc. – even glasses. What had happened to it, and where were the owners? I didn't know, but I can't believe my luck. In the cupboards were tins of food and plastic boxes of stuff – all labelled so neatly. Tea, Coffee, Rice, Legumes, powdered milk etc., incredible. I checked out the tins of food and found a can of beans (God bless Mr Heinz) and greedily wolfed the whole can down, cold. (Stuff the raw mussels!) The bed looked really appealing, although somewhat dusty with cobwebs and dead moths. I stripped the bed and took everything outside and shook it all well. After I made up the bed again I sank gratefully on to, what felt at the time, like the most luxurious bed in the world – even though it was at a crazy angle and I rolled downhill into the wall of the room. Actually I felt a bit like Goldilocks – and half expected the three bears to come back home saying "and who's been sleeping in my bed?" (I think I was slightly delirious!) I fell into a deep, deep sleep but was tortured with terrible nightmares about the plane crashing and leaving your dad in the plane's bathroom. In my dreams I kept trying to get him out of the bathroom. I think I, subconsciously felt guilty for leaving him there. Oh, Pete I do miss your dad so much.

The next day I set to, to clean up the mess on the floor and on all the surfaces. It took me a long time as there were broken cups, and a broken jar or two (pickles or jam or something). I then tackled the fridge (which hadn't worked for years I think). There were dried up things in there I couldn't even recognise. Eventually I got everything out and put all the rubbish in a plastic bag (there was a roll of plastic bags in the kitchen cupboard). It was easy to clean the fridge then with water from the stream and plenty of detergent I found in the kitchen. After a while I had a good thought about the rubbish I had collected and thought some of it may be able to be used. I mean, not the broken bottles and stuff, but the dried up, mouldy food that had been in the fridge. Maybe some of the dried up food might be tomato, or capsicum or similar – and if dried up – could be reconstituted – planted and grown. I decided to separate the rubbish into two lots, one definite, hard unusable material, and one, unrecognisable vegetable matter. Also in a bin in the cupboard was the dried up remains of a sweetcorn cob and also a dried up pumpkin, or what looked like a pumpkin anyway. I took the bag of unrecognisable vegetative matter and put it to one side. It might just be I thought, that some vegetables would regenerate once in the warmth of the sun and with a goodly supply of water. Of course, I hoped that I would be rescued before any plants might produce something, but you never know, I was thinking ahead, that it might be months before anyone would find me. There was a dip in the dunes behind where the boat was lodged and I decided that would be my rubbish tip. If I can use the plastic bags that are on the boat I will not feel that I am desecrating the island with my tin cans and things.

I am alone, but I do feel that your dad is all around me. I believe the soul goes on and I feel he is helping me and keeping me company. I talk to your dad all the time; yes I know it sounds crazy, but I talk to myself as well. I get mad with your dad (unfairly I know) sometimes and shout at him for going to the bathroom instead of staying by my side and surviving with me. Sometimes too, I call out to God (whom actually I don't believe in) and ask him – "why me?

Why did I survive the crash and no one else?" Only the seagulls answer me with their argumentative squawking.

CHAPTER 5

GETTING ON WITH LIFE

The next few days were spent quite happily going through the boat and its contents to assess what could still be used, how much food there was, and what equipment was available. The best thing I found was a small gas lighter, for the kitchen gas rings (which actually worked, although I don't know how much gas is in the bottle) – and wrapped in plastic bags, in a plastic box, matches: boxes and boxes of matches, all dry and very usable – brilliant. (Sorry, Tom Hanks I wish I could have given some to you when you needed them so much!) One of the first things I used was someone's toothbrush (I thing I would never normally do, and I would never lend anyone my toothbrush – even your dad – toothbrushes are sacred – not to be shared!) I found some toothpaste and took a cup and went outside, down to the stream and got some water to clean my teeth – luxury! In the tools section of the boat I found a hammer, screwdrivers and all that kind of stuff. Now, coupled with a pointy ended knife I could attack a coconut. I collected four or five coconuts from the beach and took them back to the boat. I left them at the base of the rocks and excitedly collected my "tools". I was able first to get through the tough, smooth surfaced, outer wrapping, and then through the fibrous next layer. Now for the actual coconut. I think I was drooling at the thought of that lovely chewy flesh. I got a steak knife with a very pointy end and started to grind it into one of the three eyes at the top of the nut. After a bit of work I was through. I tilted the nut up and tried to drink the milk but could only get a dribble. I realised I would need another hole in one of the other eyes to allow air to get in. After a bit of a struggle with the second hole I was able to have a really good drink from the nut. Superb. It was beautiful, refreshing, and I know, – nourishing. Now I have to get into the nut itself. Not a problem I thought. I took the hammer and gave the first nut an almighty wallop. Far from breaking up, the coconut defiantly, shot off to the side of me and into the sand. A second wallop made it jump up and attack me, nearly knocking my head off. This was no good. "Come on," I said to myself, "think!" How do I make it stay still so I can break into it? After two more bad tempered wallops I realised it had to be stabilised so the wallop I give it will have the desired effect and not turn it into a missile. "Right ho!" I said to myself. "I can do this." So I got the recalcitrant nut and wedged it into the pile of rocks and stones at the base of the boat. Once lodged quite tightly I gave it another "death defying" wallop. At that it gave up and cracked into three pieces. When I opened it up I was quite surprised. The flesh was soft and white and creamy. When we've had coconuts at home – bought at the supermarket – the flesh had always been hard and crunchy. Anyway I went and got a spoon and dug into the soft flesh and almost purred like a kitten at the incredible smooth, soft flesh… wonderful, what a treat. Yum. I started singing:

"Don't sit under the coconut tree you'll get your head bashed in, get your head bashed in, get your head bashed in. No, don't sit under the coconut tree, unless you're suicidal!"

Oh – you've no idea how happy I was – a castaway with food! I was thinking then, "You know, I could actually survive this!" I'm still bewildered about where the owners of the yacht are and what happened to them, and how did the boat get so far away from the beach and up into the sand dunes, way, way above the high water line. I have a theory though. But I'll come to that a bit later on.

The wardrobe in the bedroom indicated a couple had been sailing the yacht – a man and a woman. As I only had the clothes I stood up in I, (very rudely, I suppose) "borrowed" some of the woman's clothes. This couple were obviously well-heeled. Her clothes are just beautiful – appropriate for sailing, tee shirt and shorts, but there are some gorgeous silk tops and black evening trousers, they were obviously going to go out on the town when they got to wherever it was that they were headed. The man's clothes too are really good quality, branded labels on his shirts – and even an evening suit, my goodness. I mean who goes sailing with an evening suit in the wardrobe? As you know I'm quite small and the woman was obviously a lot taller than I am (isn't everyone?) but we were basically the same size waist and I was able to get into her shorts and that was just fine. I'm always getting teased about how diminutive I am. I think it was the actress Estelle Getty who said in her book – "there are three (or was it four) sorts of people: those who accuse you of being short – they say, My God you're short. Or those who 'inform' you about being short, – Do you know, you're really quite small! And then there are those who 'forgive' you for being short. You know you're really short, but it's okay, good things come in little packages." I was at the railway station one day and as I came out a woman (a complete stranger) was on the platform obviously waiting for someone and she saw me coming towards her and she stepped forward and said to me, "Crumbs you are small, you know I once knew a girl I worked with and she was small too, but she could do her job alright!" I mean, what gives a perfect stranger the right to address, what could be termed a disadvantage in life, almost a disability: they have no idea if I'm sensitive about it or not. I mean if I was obesely fat, would they come up to me and say – "My God you are fat." No they wouldn't – it would be very rude. The same goes for people who are extremely tall – or very ugly – or very spotty – or very disfigured. What gives people the right to keep telling me how short I am – do they think I don't know – or that I can do anything about it? Anyway, that's my beef for the day, now, where was I? Oh yes, the wardrobe. Well it's quite hot here on the island so I don't need much. I just took a large tee shirt and a pair of shorts, and I have to tell you, one of the best things about being on your own (with little chance of meeting anyone) is that I can dispense with my bra.

Whoever invented brassieres should be shot. I don't need them now, they're torture, and the freedom of just wearing an oversized tee shirt is great.

The thing I really needed the most was shoes. I'm a size 5 in Australia and 3 in England (where I was brought up). This woman is a size 9 for goodness' sake. (Feet like flippers!) Everything is much too large for me but she does have some rubber thongs and some scuffs. I got the thongs and managed to cut them down somewhat with a Stanley knife. They look a bit rough, but hey, I'm not Cinderella going to the ball. On the right hand side of the cabin – just as you go in – is a sort of office space, well work space really, where obviously the navigation and planning was done. There are lots of maps in a drawer and I found "The Shop's Log". I discovered from the Log that the couple were Don and Sue Smythe from Brisbane, Australia. The yacht also is named 'Brissibabe" and was registered in Brisbane.

The last entry was dated 1st August 2002. It read:

"Position: 18 degrees. 20'N 149 degrees. 15' E

2,500 km NE of Manila

Fair sailing with 3 metre swell, wind to 15 knots

Spotted a small island with a nice looking bay, and as it's our Anniversary we are going to take the dinghy and have a picnic, along with the bottle of Moet we've been saving."

That was it – nothing further. As the log is a very large book, and there are pens and pencils aplenty here, I decided to continue the log – well just record really how I came to be here and what happened to me. Now my theory as to what happened to Don and Sue. Assuming they did what they said they were going to do and took the dinghy, they would have anchored the yacht in the bay and rowed the dinghy to the bay and pulled it up on to the beach and had their picnic. Now if there had been an earthquake in the area – out at sea – then the water on the beach (I think) would have receded very quickly – leaving the yacht stranded but anchored and the dinghy, maybe sucked out to sea. Then a short time later, what may have happened is a tsunami would have hit. A tsunami would roll in, and in, and in – easily overtaking the couple who may be running to higher ground. The tsunami would easily lift the yacht and crash it up and into the sand dunes – way higher than the high water mark, three or four metres higher, easily. I really don't know what happened, but that's my theory anyway. Now I have shoes (well sort of!) I have started exploring my island (from the log I now know it is an island). I have been looking to see if there are any remains of Don and Sue but I have not seen any clue as to their whereabouts. I explored further inland and at about 200 metres came to a marshy area. There's no standing water, as such, but the area (about the size of a tennis court) is very boggy and there is a sandy beach at one side and some samphire grass growing around the other edges. Now I know you can eat samphire grass and cook it like baby asparagus – so that's a brilliant find; a fresh green vegetable – wonderful. I collected an armful of the soft fleshy samphire and took it back to the yacht and boiled some of it. I ate it because it's a fresh vegetable, but I couldn't say that I enjoyed it – I think I need to add something to it, chilli powder, curry or something strong to make it more palatable. Nevertheless it was food, and food is my main priority right now. I've always been a bit of a health nut, as you know, Pete, and I read health magazines. I don't take them too seriously but you pick up a bit of knowledge here and there. Samphire grass is one of the bits and pieces – I've never tried to eat any, but I did recognise the plant – and it's growing on the edge of a marsh area – so I'm pretty sure that's what it is. I decided on my return to the boat, to go through the stores and record what there was and what I could use. There were jars of preserves, tins of vegetables, fish, sauces, meats etc. There was powdered milk, saccharine tablets, sugar and tea and coffee; Sue was obviously very methodical and had all her cupboards labelled and dated. One such label was "legumes". I was very excited at seeing this, as legumes, I know, are beans basically, and although her beans were dried, they had been boxed very carefully and were in good condition. There were borlotti beans, mung beans, haricot beans, dried peas, and one or two beans I didn't recognise. I realise all this food is a Godsend, but it can't last forever and, whilst I hope I will be rescued in the very near future, I must be sensible and understand it may be months before I am found – even years!

Now, Pete, I have to tell you that I seem to remember Robinson Crusoe, and other castaways always seem to be intent on counting off each day they are stranded. I have decided not to do this – and I'll tell you why. I'm not too unhappy – I've been incredibly lucky, so far, but I don't think I could stand knowing it was Christmas Day, or your birthday, or your dad's birthday, or our anniversary, or my birthday. It would make me so sad and depressed, especially Christmas Day. So I'm not going to record the days as they pass – but I will keep a basic check on the full moon as each month passes. That will tell me approximately how many months I have been here and I'll just get on with surviving as best I can. I've been thinking about these beans that are in storage here on the boat. I think I'm going to steep and cook some, but I'm going to experiment with a few and plant them – up the stream, next to, or just on the perimeter of the marsh. If I am here for months, or even years, the tinned food here will have run out and it would be my salvation if I could grow some fresh food. I took some of the beans and planted them in rows around the marsh. I also took the bag of vegetable rubbish from the fridge and planted that around also. There is ample water there and I've no idea how long it will take to grow some beans but I will watch the site for signs of life. Speaking of signs of life, up to this week I had seen hardly any signs of any animals at all. Well insects yes, and some birds, but no actual animals. There are seagulls overhead, and I think they are nesting on the cliffs around the headland, but other than them – no sign of proper animals at all. I saw sort of wiggly lines in the sand – and thought it could be lizard tracks, and really, really hoped it was not snake tracks. Anyway about four nights back it was a really clear night and the moon was so bright that it was almost daylight and I couldn't think why the birds were flying around at night and then it dawned on me – they weren't birds at all, they were bats. I was fascinated, they were flapping their wings so fast and flying so fast too, darting up and down, catching insects I suppose. Anyway they were the only animals I had seen, that's if they are actually, strictly speaking animals. I think they are mammals but I'm not sure. Maybe not. I've no idea where they are coming from – they must nest in some trees back towards the hills, or maybe there's a cave somewhere – I must go exploring one day. Well as I said, it was a very clear night and I now know what the wiggly lines in the sand are. I saw a little lizard running across my path – actually I think it was a gecko. It had funny eyes, sort of no eyelids and it was making a weird clicking sound. I'd heard that sound before but thought it must be crickets or something similar. Anyway my little gecko was cute and now that I know what makes that track in the sand I won't be so worried about it being a snake.

One scary thing I did see a while back was an enormous horrible centipede. It was a sort of rusty colour and when I lifted a rock it shot off away from me at the speed of light. I think centipedes can bite, so I shall have to watch myself when moving rocks etc.

The seagulls make an awful noise sometimes and I think I remember from my childhood holidays in Scarborough, Yorkshire that my parents used to buy seagull eggs, and eat them of course. I have been wondering if I could climb around the headland and raid a nest or two. I have no idea if seagulls lay their eggs on a seasonal basis but it might be worth a try. I wouldn't take all the eggs from one nest – I would only raid a nest that had more than one egg, and I would leave one egg for the parents to rear. Actually I know very little about seagulls, maybe they only lay one egg. I have to have a hunting expedition, see what I can find out.

CHAPTER 6

MAKING LIFE EASIER

I haven't written for ages, because I have been really busy. I decided to make the rock stairway up to the boat a bit easier to climb – by adding a few rocks, that was quite easy. Then I decided I'd had enough of living sideways, the boat is on an angle and it's getting on my nerves. So – big project: level off the floor! I can't move the boat of course, and I can't lift the floorboards – but over the top of the floorboards is a tough fitted carpet – throughout the bedroom, the galley and the living/cabin. I started on the bedroom and took out the bed, which was actually in three parts and the mattress arrangement was also in three parts. Oh, I forgot; under the bed were boxes of food which I have placed outside for the time being. I then laboriously carried some rocks up the beach and laid them on the floorboards on the down side of the boat only. The gaps I then filled in with sand, and levelled it all off as best I could. I had to make sure the legs of the bed didn't sink into the sand. It all worked reasonably well when I had replaced the carpet. Now I have a level bed (more or less!) This actually took three days to complete, but it was worth the effort – a good night's sleep is a precious thing. Then it was the turn of the kitchen – I mean galley. I just filled the sloping end with sand – no rocks. I can fetch the sand from the beach quite easily, (I have a bucket) but rocks are just too difficult – they're too heavy for me so I'll not be transporting rocks anymore. Although it's very time consuming I did the cabin and the office area, it's all a little lumpy, it will have to do. My next job was to mend the door handle. The screws had rusted through and I couldn't find any to fit so I have rigged up a rope arrangement on a hook and it works quite well – both inside and out. Now I've got the main jobs done I have time to relax a fair bit. I'm very grateful to Don and Sue for providing me with some good books. One or two I have read before but no doubt I will enjoy reading those again. There are about two dozen books I haven't read before, and a couple of cookbooks as well as a dictionary – so I won't be too bored – for a fair while anyway. There's also a bible, which I've never read completely through, so I may tackle that at some time.

I've decided to start collecting the bits of rope that are just debris on the beach: you never know when I might need a bit of rope. My father always said, you should never throw away good pieces of wood or rope. I've also started collecting my empty tin cans. I take the lid off and then wash the cans and I'm not sure what I shall use them for – but I just know there will be a time when I can use them. I was really needing a sun hat. I suppose Don and Sue may have taken their hats with them, I can't imagine they would have been sailing without hats. Anyway there is no hat on the boat and I thought I'd try and make one. I've been putting a tee shirt on my head but that's not very satisfactory.

Now I took a basket weaving class when I was at school – some hundred years or so ago – and I thought I would be able to remember how to do it and make a sun hat out of weaving some long grasses. Well it's not as easy as you might think. First of all I went looking for long grass and found rushes of some sort, with long leaves at the edge of the marsh. I brought an armful back to the boat and thought a long time about how I was going to tackle this. I first of all laid the longest lengths of grass on the ground, in a star configuration. That is each one crossing in the middle. Next I got a piece of rope (see – I knew I'd find a use for all this rope) and unfurled it – which gave me thin pieces, about 60 cm long. Starting on the middle of the star I wove up and down, around the centre. As I got the hang of it – the outer part became quite easy. However I realised what I was making was a flat circle. I needed a head shaped middle and then a brim. This was not very easy. So I started to tighten up the string – but still I couldn't get the shape of a head. I thought about it for a while and eventually decided to try weaving it over a rock. This worked really well, and once the rock was covered (approximately my head size) it was easier then to work on the brim. This I decided to do in grass weaving, not with stringy bits from the rope. It all worked quite well and I was able to tuck the ends of the grass back into the brim once I had it all to the size I wanted. When it was finished it was a bit big for me and a bit heavy, but now I know how to do it, I can make another one, much better than the first attempt. I was getting down the stock of food, tins and dry food stuff, and realise it will not last forever. I need to find a way to feed myself, and not from the boat's stock. Incidentally, there are dolphins just off the water's edge. They sometimes just swim up and down, sort of lazily, but one day they were dashing so fast across the waves – I think they were chasing smaller fish, but I couldn't be sure. Anyway they are very entertaining. The seagulls are entertaining too. There seems to be a hierarchy amongst them and the dominant male arches his back and make the most awful noise screeching at any other bird who gets to some food first. I used to feed the seagulls when I was a child – it was a necessity when you had fish and chips at the seaside. We always enjoyed throwing them a chip or two and watching the really clever ones catch it in mid-air, before the chip hit the ground. Of course, it's very much frowned upon today and apparently we made the seagulls dependant on us for food, and chips of course are not their natural food.

I heard a funny story one day, someone came up with a crazy theory: that, obeying the laws of "survival of the fittest" and "evolution" that eventually there will only be one legged seagulls – why you might ask, well in a flock at the seaside there was always a one legged seagull and we always felt sorry for it, so everyone threw a chip or two towards the disabled seagull – hence it was better fed than all the others – so evolution will give the world one legged seagulls. I know it's stupid but I like the theory.

Oh, I forgot to tell you I went exploring around the headland and climbed up one of the easier looking rock faces and there were some seagull nests there. No eggs, so it's obviously not the season, but every few months I'll return to that spot and check it out for eggs.

CHAPTER 7

LEARNING TO FEED MYSELF

I have managed to open a door leading from the bedroom. It was previously blocked by the bed and I think not really meant to be used from this end – rather from the front end of the yacht, and accessed, I think, from a forward hatch. Anyway, it turned out to be a storage area, with lots of gear for sailing the boat; spare sails, anchor chain, rope, and what I think is a sea anchor – a sort of funnel with a large opening at one end and ropes attached. Also I came across two fishing rods, two reels and two hand lines, and a box of fishing tackle. In the box of fishing tackle are hooks, weights, floats, metal lures, and some imitation little fish made out of jelly stuff.

So I decided to try my hand at fishing. Fresh fish would be just what the doctor ordered. I have fished before, with your dad, and I know how to handle a rod and reel. I used to enjoy going fishing with your dad – but he did all the messy stuff for me, you know getting a fish off the hook, gutting and scaling and all that sort of yucky thing. Anyway I got a rod all rigged up with a medium hook and a small weight on the bottom of the line. I didn't have any proper bait so put one of the jellyfish on the hook and took it out on to the rocks, where I had a clear patch, without any seaweed. On my first cast out I got a bite. Wow, I yanked it up fast but lost whatever it was, and it took all my tackle too. This was no good – I don't have so much tackle I can afford to lose it to some greedy monster. I need proper bait – so I thought I might go back to Windy Cove and collect some mussels. They should be alright for use as bait. (Incidentally, I have been collecting mussels some days and cooking them – they're great with a tin of tomatoes, coconut milk and some chilli powder.)

Collecting the mussels is easy, I have a big knife and I can cut them loose from the rocks. I put some in the bucket and brought them back to the boat and then selected the largest and carried them in a tee shirt for a bag, and took them out to the rocks. It's not so easy getting into live, fresh mussels I have found. It's alright once they are boiling, when you're going to eat them, but when fresh, for fishing, they won't open their shells. I tried with the knife but the shells are too slippy, so I resorted to bashing them with a rock and then scraping them out of the shell. It's an awful messy job, and I hate messy jobs, but it's just something I have to get used to nowadays. Well on my second cast, using mussels as bait, I got a bite and was careful not to yank it out of the water too fast. However it still took everything – broke my line and I lost more tackle. "Bugger!" – Back to the drawing board. What I need is stronger line and larger hooks. The second rod back at the boat had a heavier line so I took that and rigged it up with a larger hook and just a small weight. Back to the rock; baited up with a mussel, and after a few minutes, hey ho! A good bite. Now at this vital point your dad would take over – but he's not here. I pull in a good sized fish feeling very satisfied with myself. But now what do I do? I have a very wriggly fish firmly attached to the end of my line. I myself am squealing like a silly schoolgirl, and shouting – "For God's sake – get it off somebody – please!" It's jumping and jiggling and won't lie still. I'm a tad squeamish, so it was not going to be easy, and I knew I was just going to have to get on with it myself. Carefully climbing over the rocks, and crying, "Oh God – Oh God" every time it wriggled I carried the rod with the fish still attached, back to the boat – to deal with it there. Now again, as I said, this was your dad's job, not mine. I only ever dealt with the fish when it was caught, gutted, scaled, filleted and was ready for cooking. So first things first; stop it wriggling. I hit it on the head with the hammer – but I had my eyes closed so I missed it a few times – eventually I was brave enough to keep my eyes open – well sideways squinting really, and then I gave it a good hearty wallop. That stopped it in its tracks, probably gave it a really bad headache.

Next take the hook out of its mouth. Not as easy as you may think. It was right down its throat – but with a pair of pliers (from the toolbox) I was able to get the hook free. Now the worst part. I've seen your dad do this many times – but it was his job, not mine – gutting and scaling. Well the knife just skidded off the skin, but eventually I cut from the anal opening to the head and took out its guts. Oh God what a mess! Lesson learnt – do this on the rock, don't bring the fish, ungutted back to the boat. The head I couldn't bear to cut off and the scales were too hard to get off. So I cooked it over the fire and the skin and head just came away from the flesh quite easily. The cooked fish was then beautiful, soft, delicious. The best I've ever tasted. The pan was hard to clean afterwards though, so I set it aside with some water in it to steep. I've now set up a gutting table at the fishing rock. Actually it's just a piece of wood laid across the rocks at about waist height and held down with some biggish rocks. It's so much easier to gut the fish I catch and throw the waste into the water. The wooden board doesn't blunt my knife either. I've decided I quite like fishing – and the cooking – but not the gutting etc. Oh, Pete – how I miss your dad. I think I took him for granted – he was always there for me, we had our various roles to play and he never complained – he really was a good man.

Oh I forgot to tell you about the fire. Well I just don't know how long the gas bottle is going to keep going. There's actually a spare gas bottle in the store but I don't know if it's full or empty – or how to change the bottles. Anyway I've looked at the connection to the gas stove and I don't think it's all that complicated. As and when the current gas bottle runs out I'll certainly have a go at exchanging them – and hope the second bottle is a full one. Also hope I don't blow myself up.

Nevertheless I realise even two bottles will eventually run out so I have to have an alternative – and that means lighting a fire. There is no end of firewood. Lots and lots of driftwood on the beach and plenty of wood in the treed area around the marsh at the back of the sand dunes. There are some trees around the boat but no spare wood there, I've already used up what bit there was close by. Those trees do give me some shade too, but not a lot. So, first things first, collect some firewood. Easy job, but time consuming and heavy work. I have to learn to take things a little slower and make it easier for myself. I started out carrying huge quantities of firewood, which just exhausted me – so now I content myself with collecting a little each day and I have a wood pile at the back of the boat. My first attempt didn't go too well – I couldn't get the fire started – no matter how much I cursed and swore at the huge pile of wood. I then realised I would need some kindling and some very dry material at that, and only a bit of wood – not the mountain I had piled up high. I took the bucket to the trees and very soon had a bucketful of dry leaves and grass. Easy. With the battery operated gas kitchen lighter I had a small fire going in no time. After my first attempt I realised that cooking on a fire was going to be a bit difficult, and not ideal for putting a pan on. So, thinking cap on again. Just outside the boat, in the sand, I decided to dig a shallow hole and line it with rocks. The object was to make a stable base on which to put a pan, and also the rocks would stay hot longer than the ashes of the fire, and hopefully make cooking easier. Some rocks then around the fire would stop the wind blowing the fire (and any ashes) away. I found this method very efficient and the rocks do actually stay very hot and I can cook anything on the fire. I also found a long metal rod lodged in the top of the boat. I'm not sure what it was originally, maybe an aerial or antenna of some sort. Anyway I remembered seeing pictures of people putting meat and fish on a spit and I thought I'd see if I could rig up a spit of some sort and I could then skewer any fish I caught, or anything else for that matter, and cook it that way. It was easier than I thought it would be. I got two long branches from the trees and broke the ends off making a fork. I stuck them in the ground at opposite sides of the fire. Then I laid the rod, suspended across the fire and held up by the branches to make a spit – and it did, well, sort of. The only problem was that the fish sometimes spin around, slipping on the rod and so it's difficult to have all the sides evenly cooked, but it's not a major problem. I think I've been here about a month or so now. I do a fair bit of lounging around, and I always have an afternoon "nanny nap". I like to go fishing now and exploring the beaches further round the headland, looking into the rock pools and having a swim now and then.

Oh – I must tell you of one experience. I was getting my fishing line sorted out and when it was baited up (with mussels) I let the reel keep going, just for a moment. No problem, just wind it back up again, but it had dropped from my rock into a rock pool and guess what – I got a bite – in the rock pool for goodness' sake. Anyway I pulled it up and was really surprised to see a wriggling eel on the end of the line. I mean really, really, wriggling. It wrapped itself around the line and went all slimy. There was no way I could take the hook out of its mouth, it had a huge mouth full of very nasty looking teeth. At this point I was really "girly" and held it out from my body at arm's length shouting to anyone who would listen (I live in hope!) "Oh get it off, Ow! Ow! Just get it off – Yikes, what a bloody awful thing you are!" Anyway I took it to my gutting table, with it still wriggling and tying itself up into a knot on the end of the line. I left it there on the gutting block and went back to the boat to get the hammer and the gutting knife. When I got back the eel was in a real state – frothy and slimy and tied up tightly into a knot. Yuk! Well it was still attached very firmly to the line, so I held the line with one hand and hit the eel on the head with the hammer. This had no effect whatsoever – eels are tough creatures. Well I hammered it and hammered it and eventually it gave in (well his head was squashed in quite a bit). Once he was well and truly dead I could unravel him and give him a good wash. After that it was reasonably easy to cut his head off and then gut him and skin him. I skewered him with the antenna thing and barbecued him over the fire. He was delicious.

One day I decided to go further inland and explore a bit. There is a sort of mangrove on the right, which leads into the marshy area that feeds my little stream. The trees are growing right in the water there and all their roots are quite visible above the waterline. About 200 metres from the boat, inland, I saw an unusual bump in the reeds, stuck in the mud. It turned out to be a wooden and cane sort of donut shape, obviously man made. I couldn't tell what it was at first, but I decided to dig it out and see what it was. It was a fair bit battered and broken, but when I cleared it of all the mud, I discovered it was a crab pot, or craypot, I really don't know the difference.

Wow! What a find! It was far too heavy for me to lift though, and a long way from "home" (that's what I call the boat now). So I went back home to get some rope from my stock pile of beach rubbish. I tried putting some of the rope around and through the bars of the pot and pulling it along. That only broke more bars. I tried various ways of pushing and pulling – all to no avail. Then … Eureka! A thought…. The pot was heavy, but round on the bottom. So I lifted one end and managed to roll it – very wobbly and slowly – home. Once home I could take my time mending the pot; and that's what I did. With some flotsam rope, bits of wood, hammer and nails, I fixed it up a treat. (Well, not a pot that any self-respecting fisherman would agree to use – but hopefully good enough to fool a crab or two.) Next problem, how to get it into a suitable spot where there may be some crabs. I think I have been here on the island for about six months or so. I'm sorry I haven't written every day, or even every week, but I'm not normally the writing sort. I'd much rather telephone someone than write a letter. This keeping a written record of what I'm doing is a bit tiresome as well, I just wish I could pick up the phone and call you. Anyway, what I started to say was, I have been watching the tides go up and down each day and I have picked out a spot that might be good for crabs – if I can get the pot secured when it's low tide.

Now getting the pot, which was very heavy, over the rocks and into my selected rock pool was no easy task. It may sound like a simple job to you, but I'm not very strong at the best of times, so this operation took me two days to complete. Once I had the pot in place I had to secure it to make sure it wasn't washed out to sea with the tide. I have plenty of rope now and I was able to tie it down to a rock, just on one side.

The whole thing is quite a simple idea. The top part lifts up on a hinge affair, and the bottom part is very heavy and stays on the ground. The top has a peg/clasp that locks the top to the bottom. I'm pretty sure the idea is that one baits the pot with a dead fish and then locks the top to the bottom. There is a depression in the top part which is large enough for a crab to crawl through, and down to the bait. Then it's far too difficult for a crab to work out how to get out of the pot again. Well I went fishing the next day and got a few small fish (whiting I think) and used one for bait in the pot, when the tide was out.

It all sounds quite simple but the whole exercise took a lot out of me. Nevertheless, I was really looking forward to catching some crabs. I checked the pot the next day – and nothing. But there were no remains of the fish! Strange. I should have caught something! This happened four times and I was beginning to despair of ever catching a crab when, bingo! On the fifth day – there he was; a veritable monster (to my eyes).

I jumped into the rock pool and, without thinking, lifted the lid of the pot. The crab was very quick, and obviously far more intelligent than I was – in the blink of an eye, he was off – into the seaweed, never to be seen again. I screamed some blasphemy at him and then decided I had not thought this exercise through at all. Try again! I baited up the pot – locked it and retreated. Nothing happened and the tide started coming in again. "I'll get you tomorrow," I threatened! Well tomorrow came and this time I had given a lot of thought as to what would happen if a crab was actually in the pot. I have a bucket ready to scoop him up into. There was nothing in the pot for three more days, but on the fourth day, bingo again. Now, steady as she goes, lift the lid ever so slowly – and have the bucket at the ready for him to climb, obligingly into.

No – he didn't want to get into my bucket. He dug himself into the sand and shuffled under the bucket and – "bloody hell", escaped again. Now I'm really getting mad – and very determined. It really can't be this difficult, can it? I mean people catch crabs all the time. I am afraid of his claws though. One bite from his claws and I'll give up. Well, I thought this through again and after a bit of a rehearsal I worked out how to attack the crab (if I get one again) from the top of the pot. That is; take a thickish stick and pin him down in the pot, if I can, and then open the pot and grab him. It's two more days before I get a crab in the pot. In theory my last plan of action should have worked – but my arms aren't long enough to pin him down, and open the pot. So I have to be very brave and try and catch him when I open the pot. I know you have to grab a crab from the back, being very careful to avoid getting bitten. Well I decided to tilt the pot up, still keeping one end fastened to the rocks, so that the crab is at the back of the pot when I open it.

This was an extremely tricky manoeuvre but I had a further plan. I would taunt him with a little stick and see if he would catch a stick in his claws, then repeat that with the second claw. With both claws grabbing little sticks, instead of my fingers, I was able to make a quick attack and grabbed him firmly from the back and transferred him to my waiting bucket. I put a piece of wood over the top of the bucket to stop him climbing out and, feeling very pleased with myself, took the "spoils of war" home. Now to cook him. I took the largest saucepan I could find and filled it with water. I lit the fire and put the saucepan on the coals once the fire had died down. The crab was in the bucket and I had to be very quick to tip him into the saucepan. He was not a happy chappy and I told him he was just going for a nice hot bath – but that didn't calm him down, he struggled to get out of the saucepan, but I had a lid and a huge appetite for cooked crab – so, "settle down" I told him. As the water heated up he settled down nicely and turned a lovely shade of red. Once he had cooled down I knew I had to clean him up. Oh my goodness me, another yucky job. I have seen your dad do this job, so I knew you had to take the underside shell off and then take out the 'lites', the rest you can eat. WOW! He tasted so good. I had the hammer from the tool box and got into every claw, every nook and cranny – bliss.

CHAPTER 8

GETTING ORGANISED FOR MORE FOOD

I was now catching lots of fish and the occasional crab. More than I could eat at one go, so I decided to try and preserve some fish. I had a good read through the two cookbooks and they were no help at all. I decided to give it a go, even though I didn't really know what I was doing.

First of all I got four fish and gutted them, scaled them and took off the heads. (My goodness me those scales went all over the place, what a mess.) I left the skin on and washed them in seawater. I laid the four out on the rock closest to the boat and they did dry out in the sun, but two got blown off by the wind and were covered in sand. I decided to try another method. I got some rope strands and threaded the tails of the fish and then hung them up in the trees. This worked well and I now have lots of dried fish, which I bring in after they are thoroughly dried out. They are easily stored and will be a nice store for when I don't feel like fishing – or the weather is too bad to venture out. With the same idea in mind I collected about a dozen immature coconuts and put them into store in case I get some bad weather. So far the weather has been really good. It rains about once a week and the wind is fierce sometimes, but mostly quite calm and very pleasant. I think I've been on this island now for about seven or eight months and I'm sort of apprehensive about the seasons in this part of the world. Is this summer, and is it going to change for a winter season? I don't know. I'll just have to wait and see. I went across to the marsh yesterday and am very excited to report that there are some seedlings showing where I planted the beans and corn and stuff. I felt like I had given birth again – "I'm a mother" and these seedlings are my new babies. I shall be checking on them every day now and if the beans grow well I know I shall have to put in some support for them to grow up – beans are climbers I'm pretty sure.

I was reading the cookbooks to see if they have a section on identifying shell fish. Apart from the mussels there are various shells adhering to the rocks and I really don't know just what they are. I don't want to poison myself but I'd love to know if they are abalone or limpets. I couldn't get information from the cookbooks, so I didn't want to risk it and will content myself with what I know to be alright: that means I will only eat the mussels that are attached to the rocks. If I find any oysters or cockles in the water then I will recognise them – I've seen them in the fish market before – I will certainly harvest anything that I recognise. In the store room where the fishing tackle came from I found a couple of snorkels, flippers and masks. I'm a bit wary of going out of my depth into the ocean, and I'm terrified of the thought of sharks, but I thought it would be something different if I have a go at snorkelling and see what I can see. I took a snorkel, a pair of flippers and a mask down to the beach. With all the gear on I tried to walk down to the surf. I fell over three times, just walking. (Lots of blasphemy here – it would burn a nun's ears!) I tried walking backwards and still fell over. These flippers were just a nuisance and got in my way so I took them off and went into the ocean without them. Wow, what a beautiful sight – lots and lots of little fish, all colours – spectacular. A little bit further out than I was comfortable with, I could see anemones on the rocks and quite a few shells on the sand. I assumed they were some sort of clam, or cockles. I don't really know but I collected some and took them back home for cooking. I assumed that, like mussels, you have to put them into fresh water to clean them out and then you can boil them up. The cockles (if that's what they are) were closed up and I couldn't get them to open so I just popped them into the boiling water. After about two minutes I took them out and they had opened. I was surprised to see how small they were – a lot smaller than the shells, nevertheless I ate them and they were just fine. After that I decided to try my hand at a seafood chowder. I boiled some fish and then took all the flesh off the bones, next I put a bit of all the different kinds of seafood into a pot and with some coconut milk and powdered milk boiled up a great chowder. I'll do that meal many times more now, it's the best way to have seafood. The fish and crabs do take a lot of preparation, getting out the bones from the fish etc., but it's all worthwhile, and anyway, what else do I have to do? I have been doing quite a lot of reading actually. I've always enjoyed getting into a good book and now I have lots of time to indulge myself. I'm currently reading a very famous – old book, "Cold Comfort Farm" written by Stella Gibbons in 1932. It's about a young woman who goes to stay with relatives who live on a farm in Sussex. It's quite entertaining but one paragraph has me really perplexed. It states – and I quote:

"Claud twisted the television dial and amused himself."

Then further:

"She could not look at him, because public telephones were not fitted with television dials."

Now, I ask you, Pete, does that sound right to you? It doesn't to me. If the book was written in 1932, and the action of the book is set on a country farm – how come she refers to "television"? I just find it hard to believe that they had television, on a farm, in England in 1932. Oh I wish I could discuss that with someone.

I'm alone here, but as I've said before, I'm not lonely. However there are times when I could do with someone here to debate issues and argue beliefs etc. I am not a believer as you know, but I am quite interested in theology. There's a bible here with the other books and I decided to have another go at reading it. I tried years ago and read a bit, but not much, except the gospels. So I started this bible, which is a King James Version and would really love for someone to explain to me why God would make gold before he even made Eve. I mean what use was gold to Adam – who was supposed to be the only person on the earth at that time. I'll quote for you from Genesis 10:

"...and a river went out of Eden and became into four heads. The name of the first is Pison: that it is which compasseth the whole land of Havilah, where there is gold."

Now I ask you, Pete, what good was gold to Adam – was that a priority? Then I have another problem understanding Noah and the Ark. I mean God told Noah to take every living thing, two by two, and they were surrounded by water for forty days and forty nights. Right; now as far as I understand this all happened in the Middle East somewhere – so my question is, where did Noah get elephants from, and polar bears, and penguins, and kangaroos? If he took lions and tigers too, what did they eat – the other creatures? How much food would he have to take on board to feed just two elephants for forty days? Also what about the sea creatures, how do you take whales and their food? I just can't get my head around it all. My beans are doing really well and I have tiny corn shoots and

50

I'm pretty sure some broad leafed seedlings are actually pumpkin. I took some sort of hard stemmed rushes out of the marsh and cut the bottoms off and stuck them in the ground next to the beans for them to climb up. The beans, I found out, don't actually climb – I mean they have some climbing tendrils, but it's not enough, so I had to supplement their tendrils with staking them to the rushes, there's no end of rope on the beach and it's quite easy to unravel the coiling rope and use the thinner bits of string to help my beans.

There's an awful lot of work to be done with a vegetable garden, I'm finding out but I'm really enjoying doing it. I'm sort of sorry that I didn't do more at home when you were little – it would have been fun for you I think, learning how to grow things, especially fruit and vegetables. It gets quite hot here some days, and I realised I do need a new hat. Working in the middle of the day is quite tiring and it's easy to get burnt in the sun. The weaving thing was not really good enough. Back at the boat I had found a small sewing kit. Just a basic kit; needles and a couple of cotton reels, one black, one white. So I decided to do the Arab thing. Put a shirt over my head and hold it in place with a sort of band around my head. I raided Don's wardrobe and took a cotton shirt and cut out the arms. The rest I put on my head and secured it all with the band I sewed up. It really is a good solution. The large shirt keeps the sun off my head and off the back of my neck also. Whilst I'm on the subject of clothing I made a discovery going through Don's wardrobe. Don was smaller than Sue. At least his feet are smaller. The thongs I have been using broke and were not very good at the best of times. Anyway Don had various types of laced up running shoes. I managed to cut off the ends of a pair and poke in a few holes, closer to the heel to take the laces and make them tighter – and that way I can get around in Don's runners much better than the thongs.

I'm learning new things every day – especially from Sue's food stocks. She had rice – which I'm familiar with, but hers are "red rice" and "black rice". I've never heard of those before, but they are fine for eating. Actually they take longer to cook than ordinary white rice, but still they are fine. In the store was also some pearl barley, cous cous, and quinoa. I had no idea what they were and the cookbooks were no help either. Anyway I put a little barley into the fish chowders I make and it seems to thicken it all up a fair bit. The same with the cous cous and quinoa. I put them into stews and they are okay, not wonderful, but okay. There's still plenty of tinned fish, tuna, sardines etc. and I even found two little jars of caviar. I'll save them for a special occasion. I try not to break into the store of tinned food too much, I prefer eating fresh vegetables when I can, and I prefer to save the tinned stuff in case of emergency, maybe my vegetables could get blown away if we have a hurricane or cyclone, or whatever disaster can happen in this region.

CHAPTER 9

THOUGHTS ON THE FUTURE

Pete, I'm pretty sure I've been on this island now for over a year. I know I'm not writing as much as I intended to do, but writing was never my "thing" – but I'm doing it every so often. I'm not unhappy, I've resigned myself to this existence. I have plenty of food and everything I need to survive a very long time. I wish I could see you again and I miss your dad – terribly but I am content here. I do have my moments though. There are days when I just can't cope. It just takes a little setback and I give way to a fresh wave of self-pity and frustration. My mood can change from elation when I've accomplished some difficult task to downright anger and maudlin self-deprecation when I can't achieve what I want to do and when my thoughts of all that I've left behind get to me. However on the whole I am quite happy and the miserable days are getting fewer and further apart. My little garden keeps me busy collecting corn, pumpkins and beans etc. I'm always busy inventing dishes that go together with fish and mussels etc. I have planted more seeds to continue with the food, and with each collection I save seeds, and dry them, so that in a few months I'll have a continuous supply of seeds, and ultimately, food.

The pumpkins were a challenge as I don't have an oven and roasting them was the only way I was familiar with – but I've discovered I can boil them and even roast them in the coals of the fire. One of my problems is – I have no real strength in my hands and cutting into a pumpkin is really quite difficult. I found I can put them whole, keeping the skins on, and the embers of the fire cook and burn the outside skin, but leave the inside beautiful and soft. I don't do this too often though, as it cooks the seeds also and I don't think they will regenerate, once they have been cooked.

The gas bottle ran out the other day – no gas. I knew it was a finite resource and so have been using the gas as sparingly as I could but that bottle was definitely empty. Oh dear, I knew I would have to try and change the gas bottles, and hope the second bottle was full. I've no way of knowing if a gas bottle is full or not. Anyway the first bottle had a screw attachment from the leading pipe. After a bit of a struggle I did get the screw undone and then had a real struggle getting the old bottle out and the new (very heavy) one in. It wasn't too difficult once in, to screw into the cooker pipe. I didn't manage to blow myself up, thank goodness and now have a goodly supply of gas. I don't know what I can do with the old, empty gas bottle – it's just rubbish and will have to go on my rubbish tip. The boat is at an angle, so the cooker is at an angle and so to stop my pans from falling over I have rigged up a few small rocks at one end to stabilise my pans, it looks a little funny, but works. Anyway I do most of my cooking on the fire now – but I am getting worried about the pans, how long can they last being used over an open fire? Don't know! I don't actually have a lot of rubbish. I bury any kitchen waste – biodegradable stuff, over by the marsh to give the earth there more goodness once the vegetation has broken down.

I am saving tin cans for seedlings and use one for a watering can. I have a hammer and a biggish nail and I hammered holes in the bottom of tin cans – these I fill with soil and put in seeds until they are ready for replanting in my marshy garden. The largest of the tin cans I put in lots of holes in the bottom and use it as a watering can – and it works very well. I could just plant the seeds straight into the ground, but actually I quite enjoy seeing the seedlings pop up out of the soil. I have hung the cans around the boat, hanging from the guard rail – it makes me feel more at home – making the boat more "me" – more personal, I guess it's my way of decorating my new home. Anyway it gives me a great deal of satisfaction. Cardboard and packaging I use to light the fire – so you see I don't actually have much rubbish. As I mentioned to you ages ago, I planned to go exploring every few months or so to check on the seagull nests and this last week I found out that it's the "laying season". To my great delight there were two to three brown to greenish eggs in each nest. The seagulls were not happy to see me, I can tell you, but I ignored their squawking and just took one egg from a dozen nests. I brought them back to the galley and boiled three to see if they were actually edible. My opinion of seagull's eggs – wonderful – with plenty of salt and pepper it was a gourmet meal. I only ate one at first to see if there would be any adverse reaction from my stomach – just in case I got it wrong and that in actual fact humans can't eat seagull eggs, – but no, it went down a treat, as did the other two a few hours later. Now I will experiment with other ways of cooking the eggs and cooking with eggs. I just love experimenting – mixing different things together. The cookbook is not a great help – but I'm managing perfectly well on my own. I haven't stopped wondering if someone will ever find me, and I hope this record will eventually, somehow get to you, but I've been thinking what will happen if I do get rescued.

First of all you are the sole recipient of our wills, as you know, and I guess at some stage it would be acknowledged that the plane went down and that there are no survivors. The authorities would have to then assume we are deceased and will grant you probate (or whatever it's called) and you would be granted our whole estate. You should have received about ten thousand dollars from our account in the bank, then there's the car, the house and all its contents. Now I know you have been renting, and life hasn't been easy for you since your divorce, and that you have always stated you don't want to live way out of town, where the house is. I'm pretty sure you will cash in the car, the money and the house and contents, and buy a modern apartment for yourself in the middle of town, close to your work. I'm quite happy about that – it's the natural order of things. What I am more concerned with is, if, say I am found and rescued and return to Australia – well what then? My house and all its contents will have been sold, along with my car and my bank account emptied. Where will I go? What will I do? I want you to have everything; that's the right and proper thing to happen – but that was assuming I was dead – but if I return it makes it very difficult for you – and for me also. To start with I definitely do not want – and would refuse to go into, an old folk's home – that's for old, old, old people and I just don't feel that old. (In fact I'll never, never, be that old!) In homes they make the inmates have all meals together, the same people on each table – for every meal. They play childish games like passing a balloon to each other, or having quizzes that ask really insultingly simple, simple questions. They have visiting choirs, who couldn't possible get a gig anywhere else. NO and I mean really NO not for me. Also, I don't think I am particularly vain – but there's a mirror in the cabin and I'm sort of surprised whenever I glance into it. I'm seeing a little old lady, whom I hardly recognise, looking back at me. I used to dye my hair (as you probably know) and have always been dark brown with dark eyebrows. I have always kept my hair short too. Now that I don't have access to any hair dye, my hair is almost white, and is shoulder length. When I first found the boat there was a nice supply of face cream but that all got used up months and months ago. So I don't think you would recognise me – I hardly recognise myself. I'm just a wrinkled up, white haired old biddy. So, I think, even if someone comes and finds me, and wants to take me back to civilisation, whilst it would be wonderful to see you again, I might just refuse to leave my island. We'll see – am seriously thinking along those lines.

I was thinking the other day about the fact that you will have cleaned out my house and no doubt will have come across the second drawer down in my bedroom closet. I hope you got a bit of a laugh out of it. Yes I saved every drawing you did when you were a child. I was so proud of you; you were such a good artist. Do you remember I used to put all your drawings up on the fridge and after about a week or so your dad would take them down and want to throw them out, but I wouldn't let him, I wanted to keep them all – and did. I hope you had a bit of fun looking at them and kept at least some of them. For your age you were really good. I know we encouraged you to change from pure art to architecture, but there are times when I regret persuading you, I mean, wouldn't it have been wonderful if you had become a famous artist and had pictures hanging in famous galleries – we would have been so proud of you – Oh that sounds as if we weren't proud of you – we were – always – but I sometimes try and imagine what life would have been like for us, for you, if you had followed a different path, ignored us and followed your dreams of becoming a painter, or a sculpture. Anyway I hope your architecture has satisfied the artist in you, and that you are happy and by now making a decent living.

Oh dear I'm getting all upset now just thinking about it all. Maybe we shouldn't have talked you out of becoming a pure artist, we only did that because we thought it would be best for you to be able to make a career out of architecture and to make some good money, we always thought that it would be very difficult for you to make a good living from art. I still don't know if we did the right thing – I hope so.

Oh, I'd give anything just to sit down and talk it all over with you, I try and talk to your dad but he won't listen to me. I'll write more later, I'm getting emotional now, must go. I decided I needed an outside chair – so far I could only sit on the bed or on the bunk seats alongside the cabin table. Neither were very comfortable and I really thought I need a comfortable lounging about type chair. I've been looking for something I could turn into a lounge chair and it has been months that I have been looking. Every day I walk Peaceful Cove, in the shallows, sometimes going for a swim, and there's always stuff washed up on the beach. Mostly it's driftwood, or rope or empty plastic drink bottles, but one day the remains of what I think was a tea chest floated into the bay. It was very broken up but the base square was still intact and two sides joined together were very firmly attached to the base. This I thought might just be the thing.

I dragged it back to the boat and with the aid of a hacksaw, laboriously sawed through the base, end triangle, giving me the rough shape of a chair (no legs of course). I took a file also from the toolbox and smoothed off the rough edges and with three cushions from the bunk seats in the cabin was able to make a very good chair. I lodged it into the rocks just outside the boat and it's wonderful to be able to sit now, especially in the evenings and watch the sun go down.

I haven't mentioned this to you before, but I have some spectacular sunsets here. Reds, yellows, gold. The more clouds we have the more spectacular the sight. Sometimes the whole ocean turns red or gold too. I wish I had a camera to capture it for you. I sort of knew that the sun moves and sets in the far south west in summer (in Australia) and then slowly moves towards the north west each day until it starts setting a lot further north west in the middle of winter – after that it starts back again, towards the south west and in summer sets furthest southwest. I think it's called declination, but I'm not sure. Anyway what I'm trying to say is, that I have never actually noticed it before. Now that I have a panoramic view of the ocean – out to the west, I can clearly see and note this movement of the sun. It's quite fascinating, and will probably be the way I can tell if a whole year has passed. Birds here keep me amused too. One time a whole flock of geese flew in. They made a horrific noise honking and squawking to each other. They landed on the marsh and were obviously eating something in the shallows there – but I don't know what it was they were feasting on. Anyway they stayed about a week and flew off again, going south. I've had pelicans, a couple of sea eagles, gannets and lots of terns. They are all very interesting and I love watching them. I spotted a pair of rainbow bee-eaters a while back. They are the most beautiful of birds, tiny with multi-coloured bodies and wings. When you were a child a pair used to come each year and nest by the side of the road in the sand, just where we lived. I don't know if they ever reared a family as we, and our neighbours had a cat. They would have been easy prey for a cat. Anyway I have tried watching this pair to see where they are nesting and to carefully avoid walking near the nest, but so far I haven't been able to ascertain exactly where the nest is. I'll just avoid that area for a month or two.

CHAPTER 10

COLLECTING WATER

I haven't written for ages, months in fact, but I have been very busy. I don't find writing easy – I always intend to write a bit each day – but I procrastinate and put it off. However I'm in the mood again and want to tell you what I have been doing. I got to thinking about my water supply. I have to climb down the rocks to go and fetch water and it's beginning to irritate me. I have a sink and a tap, no running water of course, but if I did have running water it would be extremely convenient for me. So, how do I go about it? Your dad was an engineer, of course, and would have known this sort of thing and would have rigged up some sort of device. I had to think "What would Joe have done?" The answer quite simply is; I don't know. So Sally my girl, "Think for yourself!"

Now here on the island there's some, but not much standing water on the marsh, there's running water in the stream, and there's natural water when it rains. Which one can I harness? I ask myself. Well I looked under the sink and to one side there's a large water tank. There's no water in it, but it's got a pipe at the bottom, connected to a sort of pump, I guess. From the pump there's a pipe which comes up the back of the sink and is connected to the tap. On top of the tank is a small hole, for letting in air I suppose and there's a larger hole with a pipe which runs under the deck and to the back of the boat. This I think would be for refilling. I decided to try and get the tank out of its cupboard housing. First I had to hacksaw off the pipe from the pump and I decided to try and keep as much of the top (refilling) pipe as I could. It took me two days of struggling to get the tank out of its housing, but eventually it came free. With a lot more work I manoeuvred it up on deck and positioned it above where the sink and tap were. Just above the sink is a small window which does slide open. I decided to thread the lower (pump) pipe through the window. The top pipe I cut off flush to the tank top. Down to the sink and tap next – how to connect the pipe to the tap? I managed to get the tap out of its housing and then turned it up side down, and a bit sideways. It had a screw fitting which I needed to attach to the downward tank pipe. I went into the store and the tool box looking for something that would clamp the pipe to the tap. I found a hose clamp which wasn't actually the right size, but it was very close. I got some wire and twisted it around the pipe and it held. Next I needed some sticky tape (there was a roll of electrical tape in the tool box) and wrapped it around and around the connection. I reckoned that should hold and allow some water to flow through – but restricted by the tap. Back up on deck I now had a tank with a circular opening, about the circumference of a tea cup, and a little hole for airflow. So how do I get rainwater into the tea cup hole? "Think, Sally, think."

"What I need is a large funnel to catch the rainwater. Could I make one? I doubt it. Could I find one? Definitely not. No, think, girl, what can be used that would be funnel shaped?" I slept on the problem and worried about it all night.

Next morning it came to me clear and bright – the sea anchor I had found months ago in the storeroom. It was funnel shaped and had ropes attached which would be needed to keep it in place. There are some trees around the boat and I managed to rig up the sea anchor to stay in position and cut off the bottom of the plastic to fit into the hole. I decided a strong wind would probably blow the whole thing over, so how to stabilise it all and lock it down. Rocks and rope. I had plenty of both and although I really didn't want to start heaving rocks up to the boat again, I made a supreme effort and hauled up enough rocks to place around the tank and around the sea anchor. "Safe as houses," I reckon. I wanted to test it out and as there was no rain on the horizon I went and got the bucket and hauled up a couple of bucketsful. Bingo! It worked. The water came out of the tap (a bit sideways, but that didn't matter). The water was not very clean, but that didn't matter either. The drain in the sink went out to the side of the boat, above the waterline and just out. It all worked beautifully. All I needed then was a good thunderstorm and lots of rain. Whilst I was in the storeroom I took note of what I presume was a couple of spare sails, all rolled up. Now it's quite hot here in the boat and stuffy sometimes so I'm wondering if I could rig up a sail, to act as a shade sail. Shouldn't be too difficult I thought.

I hauled out the largest of the rolls of sail and dragged it on to open space to see just how big it was. It was really much larger than I had thought, but it had reinforced holes at each of the three corners and I thought if I could drape the sail over the boat and then pull it up into the air with ropes, it could act as a shade cloth for me. So, with great difficulty I took the thinnest top (top end I suppose) of the sail and with much huffing and puffing dragged it over the boat, and over the water tank and over the funnel. (I should have thought of this before I rigged up the water supply.) Once it was in place I got some rope – from the boat's supply (not rubbish from the beach) and attached three lines to the three holes in the sail. There were enough trees around the boat to be choosey about which one to use to secure the sail. So I attached each rope to a tree (temporarily) and decided I should, little by little, haul up the sail. A bit up at one end, then a bit up at another corner, and a bit up at the last corner. Repeating the exercise little by little until it was almost in place, it still had some way to go, but I could do that the next day.

Uh, Uh! – I forgot the water supply. I'm about to cover over where the funnel is supposed to collect water. Big problem! Sleep on it – maybe I could come up with a solution.

Next morning I have it……..I pulled up the sail a little more, oh so slowly, end by end – about 20 cm at a time, over the boat giving it great shade. I needed a hole in the sail just over where the water tank was and so lit the fire and put in a long stick to burn through. When the stick was red hot I took it to the boat and directly over the funnel, burnt a hole with the stick in the sail. I couldn't test it out there and then, but there were dark clouds forming from the west – always a good sign of rain. After about four hours it rained. I stood out in the rain and watched as the sail caught the rain, and how it drained through the hole in the bottom, straight into the funnel, then into the tank, and down to the tap in the galley.

I don't know when I've been so happy. It worked and I now have running water in the boat, and a shade sail to keep me cool. At the moment the water is not too clean, but it will be soon, when more rain cleans it. After that first rain the shade sail started to flap quite annoyingly in the wind so I got a small rough rock and rolled it on to the shade sail, and it rolled down to the hole. It stabilised the sail quite a bit, it didn't block up the hole completely, and still allowed the water to run through the hole. I would never have made a plumber or an engineer – but I reckon for an amateur I had not done too bad a job. It might all look a bit funny, but at least it worked.

I talk to myself a lot and I talk to your dad too. He doesn't answer back, of course, but I feel he is near me, and that he's watching over me. I found a pair of binoculars in the navigation office (well that's what I call it) and have been taking it with me on my morning walks. It's not a lot of use as there isn't really anything to see – that I can't see with the naked eye (and I still have good eyesight). However one day I decided to go inland and try to climb the closest real hill (beyond the sand dunes). It took me all morning but it was exhilarating once I got really high. Yes this is an island and for the first time I could see there was only sea all around.

I used the binoculars, scanning the ocean for signs of a boat or something, but nothing at all. After scanning the ocean I started to scan the beach beyond Peaceful Cove. There was nothing interesting until I spotted a moving object – a largish object, must be a metre high and a metre long moving out of the water, very slowly. Wow, I knew immediately what it was – a giant sea turtle. I rushed down the hillside (much easier than going up!) and chased across Peaceful Cove and around the next headland. I could see the turtle had shuffled up into the low sand dunes and was busy digging a hole. I didn't want to get too close and disturb her, as I knew she would be laying eggs. It took ages for her to do this and I watched as she used her flippers, or feet, (I don't know what the correct term is) to cover up the eggs. I think the poor thing was exhausted, but she didn't stay around for too long. She slowly make her way back down the beach – and off into the sea.

Wow, I just knew I had to protect these eggs – I didn't want any greedy seagull taking them, or anything else. I haven't seen a snake or a lizard on the island, only some unknown slithery tracks, but you never know. I decided to go and collect a load of small branches from the trees and make a sort of covered runway for the baby turtles to toddle down to the beach in safety, once they are hatched. I've seen David Attenborough on the telly and I know baby turtles are extremely vulnerable to all sorts of predators once they start their march down into the surf. Every day I went to the nest to see if the babies were hatching. I kept note now of the days and weeks. It was eight weeks before anything happened – I was beginning to think the eggs might have cooked in the heat, or been eaten by crabs or something. I had to reinforce the covered runway each day as the high tide kept washing my archway away. In case the turtles didn't know the way to the surf, I also collected some rocks and put them around the nest, in a sort of horseshoe configuration, so that the open end of the horseshoe was facing the ocean and the babies could only go that way. So this particular evening 'there was movement at the station, for the word had got around!" (That's a quote from Man from Snowy River, in case you didn't know.) The nest had a bit of a movement, a sort of depression of the sand. I realised what was about to happen and quickly checked the covered runway to give the babies a clear run. The tide was up quite high, but still they had a run of about 20 metres. Now I don't know how they knew – but suddenly, as the baby turtles stared to emerge and toddle down the beach – there descended seagulls and gannets ready for a feast. I had a long branch of a tree and as the babies waddled down to the surf, I ran up and down with my branch waving, and shouting at the seagulls. Some took flight as I got near them, but most ignored me and grabbed a baby and retreated a fair way to have their supper. This whole procedure took ages – I don't know, maybe an hour – I only know my covered runway did save many, many babies and I was exhausted at the end of it all. I had screamed abuse at the seagulls and my throat was sore – but I was so happy I had managed to stop an awful lot of babies being eaten. I now have named that cove Turtle Bay. It's a quiet cove, like Peaceful Cove and not at all rough like Windy Cove. I don't go over to Windy Cove much now, unless I'm scavenging for something on the beach. I've become a bit of a beachcomber and I collect anything interesting that I may be able to use. You might think I'm complaining, well actually I'm not – I'm finding this Robinson Crusoe thing quite liberating and creative – having to think for myself and operate without relying on Joe. I think I've been married for so long I've forgotten how to think for myself. It's not easy being here alone, but it's actually quite satisfying, having a problem and then solving it. It's surprising me; I'm alone and yet not really feeling lonely, I know Joe is with me. Pete, I'm not complaining about my life so far – I've had a good marriage and you were the icing on my cake, but your dad and I had our gender roles to play and duties to perform, which we both did quite naturally. I did all the cooking, cleaning, washing and ironing and your dad did all the manly stuff, gardening, mending things that went wrong – fuses, the car, changing light bulbs, painting the house, cleaning the windows etc. Your dad was very handy with a hammer and nails, drills and other masculine stuff – and he could make things too. However, he's not here now with me so I have to do things for myself. I don't believe in God but I do think we have a soul, and that when we die our soul carries on; souls are sort of never-ending. I feel that your dad's soul is with me – around me – taking care of me. I feel his presence and it comforts and sustains me. I talk to myself a lot now and sometimes I talk to your dad too. He never answers but that's okay – I'm not going doolally or balmy but it helps to talk out loud. I say things like "For God's sake, Joe, why didn't you teach me how to knock a nail in straight or set up a pulley to lift things, or how to make things?" But after all that, I'm learning to use my initiative and do things for myself. I feel a bit like a four-year-old learning to tie my shoelaces for the first time, and stating proudly "I can do it myself!"

The wind got up the day after the turtle run, and after having a long walk on the beach I was able to collect some coconuts that had fallen off the trees and carried them home in the fold of my shirt. You don't want to be hit on the head with a coconut – they weigh a ton and would probably kill you if they got a direct hit. I still enjoy eating them and save the outer shell and fibre inside. Once it's all dried out it makes excellent firewood.

CHAPTER 11

JOE

I love fishing now, and collecting mussels etc. and I have my vegetable garden to keep me busy. The beans grow so quickly and always need staking up. They do have tendrils but they still need my help. I have lots of bits of rope which I unfurl and use the stringy bits to tie up the climbing beans. The stakes I make from rushes and branches from the trees. It all keeps me quite occupied.

I do go snorkelling now and then but I'm not overly keen on it – I am always worried about sharks, I never go out any further than my mid-thigh level. I have seen sharks further out, I can see them clearly once I'm on top of the rocks. They don't swim very fast – just quite lazily really. I don't know what kind of shark they are, certainly not white pointers, they would be huge. No, these might be bronze whalers, or reef sharks, I don't know. A funny thing happened the other day – I looked up to the top of the sand dune and there I could swear I saw your dad. I was surprised and waved to him – but he just turned and disappeared over the top of the dune. I ran after him, calling his name but I can't run very fast up the sand dune, it's two steps forward and one step back almost. I got to the top of the dune and yelled and yelled. There was no sign of him and I just sat and had a good cry. Now I ask you, Pete – is it possible that your dad survived as I did? I don't know, it looked like your dad. Am I hallucinating? Am I losing my marbles?

I've been thinking about hallucinations a fair bit. I mean if I am hallucinating – well so what? When people go a bit crazy it really is unacceptable – why? Is it because they can't function in normal society or is it that normal society can't function with them around? Who does it hurt? If I am hallucinating I'm not hurting anyone. I don't feel crazy, in fact I feel great about seeing your dad every so often around me. It gives me great comfort to know, or to think that he is here with me. If that is crazy, well so be it. I'm not hurting anyone and it's allowing me to live here, happy and contented. It rained for days and days a few weeks back. I couldn't get out much so I had a good spring clean of the boat and found, of all things a box of chess pieces and a board. Now as you probably remember, Pete, your dad and I used to play a bit, usually when we were on holiday. I know it's not much fun playing on your own but I decided to set the board up and play a "day by day" game. I made up the rules which were: each player makes one move only on alternate days. So player A makes the first move on day one. Player B makes his first move on day two. Player A makes his second move on day three and so on. I thought at first it would be too awkward and I wouldn't be able to play – being two people, but after a few days I got the hang of it and am now enjoying it. And no matter what happens I am sure to win! Ha ha!

I talk to your dad all the time – sometimes he appears, but mostly he doesn't and he doesn't talk to me – it's all a bit weird, but it's nice to know he's around – watching over me.

There are things I really miss here – toothpaste being one. I used up the supply on the boat quite quickly. I usually take the brush (the second one I have "borrowed" and which is getting quite worn now) and clean my teeth in the shallows at the beach. I think the salt water makes a better toothpaste than the fresh water at the stream. Anyway I'd really love to have some proper toothpaste. I also miss having some face cream – my face feels tight and I know it's wrinkled, like an old prune. I thought I might be able to get some oil from the coconuts but that wasn't very successful. I did have a good idea though. When I opened a can of sardines, there in the tin was a whole lot of fish oil. I put some on my face, which felt really good, but golly gee, it smelled awful. The same with tinned mussels – I used the oil from that too, good job there's no one else here to tell me how smelly I am. I don't know what else to try – so I guess I'll just have to stay wrinkled. I'm not missing newspapers, except I would like a cryptic crossword or two to work on. I used to enjoy doing those. I never cared much for ordinary crosswords or even Sudoku. I liked doing code words too and those in the newspaper were always a good challenge to me and I thought, kept my brain working. I'm not missing hearing the evening news either – it seems to me that the media always reported the really bad things and told us hardly anything about the good things that went on in the world. I really don't like hearing about cruelty, and terrorism and such. I can't do anything about it, so like an ostrich putting its head in the sand, I'd rather not hear about it. Actually I don't think an ostrich ever did put its head in the sand – I don't know where that came from originally.

Oh, Pete I wish I could show you this island – it really is beautiful. You know when I was growing up in England we used to go to the coast each summer and we'd swim in the water and think it was great – which it was – but the water was always a muddy grey colour – and we didn't know anything different. When we came to Australia we were amazed at the colour of the water and the clear, clean beaches and golden sand. That's wonderful too, but I have to tell you, Pete, it's nothing compared to the amazingly crystal clear, pristine water here. It positively sparkles and you can see the fish down below quite clearly. I go fishing from my favourite rock which is about two metres above the sand level, and I can pick out the fish and watch them try and take my bait – it makes it a lot easier for me to quickly pull in the line and – bingo – dinner!

The weather here is quite balmy most of the time, but we do get high winds and it can really rain hard when it wants to. My water catcher works fine and I always have a good supply of fresh rain water. I only use this water for drinking and cooking – when I want a wash I go into the ocean and have a swim. Not out of my depth, and not when the surf is rough. I don't have the strength these days to battle the waves – I prefer a nice gentle bathe. Joe likes to go further in than I do though. I tell him it's dangerous but he just laughs at me for being a "worry wart" – that's what he calls me, or sometimes "Mrs Doom and Gloom".

CHAPTER 12

DISASTER

Haven't written for ages; was getting lazy I think.

An aeroplane went over a few months back – and I did have the urge to go out and wave and scream at it – but I've seen people in movies do that, and it's stupid – people in the aeroplane can't see you or hear you – so it's a waste of energy. I did try once to put an S.O.S. sign on the beach but I couldn't collect enough rocks to do that large enough for someone in a plane to see – so I abandoned that idea. I do have something to relate though which gave me much grief, pain and problems. Where to start? Well since finding the snorkel and mask I have been going into the surf and enjoying seeing the fish and sea creatures – it's a wonderful world under the water, there is some coral and sea anemones and lots and lots of little fishes, shoals of them sometimes. I thought I might make a harpoon or lance of some kind to spear a fish, but I gave that idea up – I just don't think I could do it, it seems to be too cruel, and I wouldn't be quick enough anyway. I'm also still crabbing with the pot when I feel like it, in one of the rock pools. So about a week ago I had been snorkelling and decided to go to my rock pool to see if there was a crab in the pot.

Surprise – there was a whopper. I put down my snorkel and mask and tilted the pot as usual and opened it up and was going to grab the back of the crab, even though I didn't have the bucket with me to put it in. On reflection it was a stupid thing to do, but I wasn't thinking straight. Anyway the crab made a grab for my fingers and I pulled back with a squeal. I dropped the pot and the crab came for my bare toes. I jumped in fright and backed up to the rocks behind me, trying to climb up to escape the crab. I got one foot on the bottom rock and then with the second foot I was trying to go higher – and that's when disaster struck. My foot slipped and instead of coming down on to the sand it went down in between two rocks. I screamed at the crab who retreated to the seaweed side of the rock pool, thank goodness (incidentally I really don't know if crabs have ears or can hear!) It wouldn't have been so bad but I had dislodged a large boulder which came down and trapped my foot. I couldn't move and was well and truly wedged in between two boulders. The angle of entrapment meant I couldn't stand up and was only comfortable laid down on my stomach. Of course I pulled and pulled at my foot and tried to push the offending, very heavy boulder up and off my foot, but I didn't have the strength – or the leverage to get it off me. I didn't know what I was going to do I just laid there and realised this is what a fish caught on the end of my line must feel like. – Stranded – caught – trapped. As the hours went by the tide started to come in. Now usually this rock pool fills to a waist high level at high tide. I was so scared – I knew I wouldn't be able to hold my head and body up that high for more than a few minutes. The water started to come in, there was no use screaming for help – there's no one out there to help me. My snorkel and mask were out of my reach but I realised I might be able to survive if I could put on my mask and use the snorkel to breathe whilst my head was underwater. As the water came in, the mask didn't move but the rubber strap was uppermost and waving in the movement of the water. The snorkel was further away from me but eventually the swirling of the water moved the snorkel, which was floating and soon it drifted towards me. I made a grab for it and with the curved end of the snorkel was able to hook the mask and drag it over to where I was.

The water was now going over my head and I was terrified – I was thinking how awful it will be to drown slowly, slowly. I put the mask on and adjusted the snorkel so that it tucked under the rubber strap of the mask. I now could breathe alright and provided the water didn't get any deeper may just hold out until morning. Oh yes, forgot to tell you – it was getting late and dark.

That night was the worst night of my life – even worse than the plane going down. Of course I didn't sleep; I just had to really concentrate on breathing slowly, not panicking or struggling too much. My foot had gone numb so wasn't hurting, which was a good thing, but I couldn't relax for a moment. The hours dragged on, I was cold, frightened and really angry at myself for being so stupid. To pass the hours I started singing in my head and blowing bubbles, which I couldn't see. I talked to your dad but he said he couldn't help me. I got so mad at him but I was more mad at myself. I needed to keep awake. I decided to play a game with myself, I would think of a song and sing as much of it as I could – and each song would be in alphabetical order, starting with A. I started with "After the ball was over, after the break of day, la la la something" … don't know any more. Move on… B. "Because you're mine the brightest star I see looks down my love and envies me, because you're mine. I only know, da, da, da," don't know any more of that either. C next – can't think of one, oh, yes, "California here I come, right back where I started from, those flowers" … don't know any more of that. D – "Dinah is there anyone finer…la la la," that's all I know. That went on through the alphabet missing out Q and X and Z but it helped to pass the time. Eventually dawn came up, gradually, and whilst still in semidarkness something hit me – a real hard hit. The two big rocks that I had slipped between formed a sort of V shape and the surf was breaking over the cleft in them. As I've told you before, there's always debris floating in from the open sea and I had been hit by a piece of it. As we used to joke – we would hit someone by a piece of two by four. (Never did of course.) But I had now just been hit, by the proverbial two by four – to the back of the head. I made a grab for the piece of wood. It was about a metre and a half long and had a large rusty nail sticking at right angles from one end. I don't know what kind of wood it was, but it was strong and about two inches by two inches wide. I didn't know at first what I was going to do with it but after a lot of thought I realised I couldn't move the offending rock with my own strength but if I could use the wood as a lever I might just be able to shift it.

I needed a fulcrum. There were no rocks within my reach – but there was a rock just beyond my reach. I've still got my mask on and breathing through the snorkel but I was able to use the piece of wood, and with the large nail at the end pull the rock towards me. Once I had the rock close to me I was able to move it down by my body and place it just before the boulder that was holding me fast. I turned the piece of wood so that I was now holding the end with the nail – and by an incredible effort put the wood over the loose rock and under the boulder imprisoning me. I tried so many times to press down on the wood and it just kept slipping off the first rock. I wriggled as best I could and after much effort managed to turn the rock over which exposed a more uneven surface that was easier for the wood to have a grip. I had to keep trying to push the piece of wood under the boulder but each time I did it was slamming into my foot and that was agony and I knew I was probably breaking some bones, but I was desperate.

After so many failed attempts I decided to try the nail end of the wood, I thought maybe the nail could give some grip and help with the leverage. Each time I tried to get the wood and nail to fit under the boulder it was jabbing into my foot – and now there was blood in the water and all I could think of now was sharks. However I'm in a rock pool so maybe they can't get to me here. The thought of sharks gave me that extra impetus (fear will do that) and I managed to lodge the wood under the boulder at long last. I now pressed down on the wood with all my strength and probably because the deeper water was now taking a little of the weight off the boulder and also because I tried to time my efforts with the wave surges I could feel, after what seemed an age the boulder gave way, just a fraction, but just enough for me to pull my foot out of the crevice. I crawled out of the rock pool absolutely exhausted, frozen to the bone, hardly able to move, I realised that the water couldn't actually be that cold, or I would have died, simply of hypothermia. I left the snorkel and mask high on the beach and as I couldn't walk or even pull myself up I just crawled on my hands and knees back to the boat. It took me a long time to get back "home". My foot was bleeding and I was in absolute agony, but I got into the boat and managed to get a drink and then collapsed on the bed and just cried and cried. I stayed in bed for two days, in shock I think. Cold and shivering. There was a very small first aid kit and I managed to get it down. I wanted the Panadol Osteo I had seen there months before. I took two pills every three or four hours and I think that helped to keep the pain down a bit. There were a couple of bandages and some Dettol. I watered down the Dettol and kept a bowl of it by my side. I had a teacloth soaking in it and kept washing my torn flesh to keep away infection. I was sure I had broken some bones in my foot, but couldn't see any obvious misaligned bones sticking out or looking out of place. I bandaged my foot up and basically stayed in bed for days.

Joe was a great comfort to me, I talked to him incessantly, I rambled on and on I know telling him how I missed our beautiful house, back in Australia. How I missed Peter and all our friends. I told him how sorry I was that I couldn't save him from the plane crash. I was so low physically and mentally at this time that there were days when I just didn't want to survive – it was all too much. Eventually I pulled myself together and found the will to live was still a strong emotional inspiration to endure and carry on. I had plenty of food in the boat and could crawl around a bit on my hands and knees, but basically stayed in bed for about ten days. The pain was abating somewhat and slowly, slowly it more or less went away – unless I knocked it or tried to stand on it. I had used up all the painkillers from the first aid box, so I just had to get on with life.

I thought, whilst I was incapacitated I would make a list of some of the things I miss and some of the things I don't miss. Just to keep me occupied and my mind off the pain.

Well first and foremost of course I miss you and all the family. I miss Joe too, but I feel he is here with me so that's a comfort. I miss my house, and the telly and my friends – but it's no use being miserable about what can't be helped. I miss music, good music, old fashioned music. My favourite CDs are (or were) Freddie Mercury and his duets with Montserrat Caballe – their Barcelona CD was terrific. I know most people will remember The Three Tenors, but I really liked The Three Irish Tenors – gosh they were good. I used to play their CD over and over. Other things I miss are the cryptic crosswords, code word puzzles and playing bowls each Wednesday morning at the club. What I don't miss are the TV ads that tell such blatant lies: "It cleans the mouldy bathroom tiles with a single wipe!" – Rubbish! "Put this cream on your face and you'll look just like the model on the screen" – rubbish – she's only sixteen so what would she know about wrinkles? "Take these pills and in seven days you'll lose ten pounds" – rubbish – unless of course you're having your leg amputated. I don't miss seeing all the garbage strewn around our Australian countryside and by the side of the road. Your dad and I went up to Payne's Find once with a metal detector to see if we could find some gold. I was disgusted – all we found were broken bottles, old tin cans, tons of papers strewn around and even some discarded filthy babies' nappies. There are so many abandoned cars in the "bush" and household litter – it's a disgrace. We have a fabulous countryside – it's just criminal abusing it so. Anyway I don't miss all that. I don't miss hearing the news – it's always about war, terrorism, violence, cruelty – they hardly ever report on good things happening – well sometimes, but not too often. I do go on a bit, I know, but it helps to pass the time, and I've had plenty of spare time whilst my foot was healing. Crawling around is very painful for your knees I found, so I managed to get some of Sue's thicker trousers, and on top of them, I also put on a pair of Don's trousers. Just getting into trousers was a real problem – very painful putting my injured foot into the legs of the trousers, but once on, it was easier to crawl around.

After about three weeks I felt I needed to get out and see my garden and collect some food. This was an incredible challenge but I took a shirt of Don's to act as a bag and crawled, oh so slowly and painfully to my garden. There were beans to collect and corn. Just getting the corn was a terrible job. It had grown so tall and so strong, but I managed to knock over the corn stalks and then, whilst laying on my stomach was able to twist off some corn cobs. After about six or seven weeks I started putting a bit of weight on my injured foot, just around the boat. I tried using a piece of wood as a crutch but that was more painful than the injured foot. It took a few more weeks before I was fully functional, but I had healed and was no worse for my ordeal. Since getting back on my feet I have had plenty of work to do so I haven't written for months. The garden keeps me busy and my dried fish stocks were depleted. I've been over to Windy Cove and collected some mussels. I cooked some and had them for supper, then I had an idea. I had found a piece of fishing netting – about three metres by two metres, all tangled up. I untangled it all and then made a sort of parcel of mussels in the netting, tied up with some rope. I took the pile over to my closest rock pool and put them in there to see if they would attach to the rocks and grow there. Your dad thinks it may take at least a year to get them to attach to the rocks and proliferate. We'll see. Oh, dear. There are people – I see people.

I was up on the headland this morning and I saw across Turtle Bay a large yacht anchoring. They were getting a little boat out and it looks as if they have a fair bit of equipment that they are bringing ashore. I knew this would happen sooner or later. I am found – if I want to be. But to be quite honest I don't want to be found and taken back to civilisation. If ever you get to read this, Pete, please don't be angry. You know I love you, that will never change, but I am happy here and don't want the hassle and trouble that my return will cause. Think of the press, I know what reporters are and they'll be all over me. I mean, I'm not important in the system of things but I realise an elderly woman spending years on an island will probably be of some intense interest for about three days, and then they'll forget me and get on with other news – but I don't want that three, or so days, of media scrutiny. You too, would be hounded by them – "What do you think of your mother's return?" and other stupid questions. No, I don't want it for me and for you too. If I go into an old folk's home – I'll be the one the others would keep talking about – "Oh look, Mavis – she's the one who was rescued from an island." No – I don't want fame – I don't want anything. I'd be begging for you to make them leave me alone. I've been alone now for so long – I just don't need people around me. I can do what I want here, and I have everything I need. Your dad says I should let myself be rescued but he says he couldn't come with me. I want to stay with your dad. We're happy here. Can they make me go back, can they force me? Maybe… maybe… Well your dad has challenged me to a swim in the sea – he thinks he can swim out further than I can. He knows I am scared of sharks and he thinks I won't take up the challenge – but I've a surprise for him – I'm going to do it. I know I'm a better swimmer than he is. Well I'm off now for a good long swim – if your dad's with me I won't be scared.

Maybe I'll write more later, Maybe…

CHAPTER 13

HOPE SPRINGS ETERNAL

Peter moved out of his apartment and into a hotel, taking a small overnight bag with him. He needed time to be alone. He certainly did not want reporters pestering him – he needed space, and time to think, time to absorb what he had been told.

Peter was creative, he had started to train as an artist and was quite a good painter, however it became obvious to him and his parents when he first left art school that it was going to be very difficult to make a decent living out of art. His parents persuaded him in his early twenties to change direction slightly and go to university and study architecture. This work was not so different to art and they felt it would be an outlet for his creativity. When he finished his degree with distinction he had the choice of working for a Perth company doing project homes, or taking a chance on a new company that had been given a contract in Dubai. The company that he chose was Jamison's Architectural Designers and he just loved the work. Although the contract was for designing buildings in Dubai the company was able to stay in Perth and the work was extremely creative and the buildings that the company wanted Jamison's to design were to be state of the art and very different from anything being built in Australia, there was also no limit as to cost, they were given a free hand to be as distinctive and creative as possible. That was ten years ago and he still loved the work, and working for Jamison's.

Two days after his meeting with Fiona Campbell he rang and asked if she would meet him for lunch. He was desperate to talk to her and find out more about the island and his mother. He picked a quiet restaurant, just off St. George's Terrace and they both arrived promptly at 12.30 p.m. Peter couldn't help noticing the sheen on Fiona's dark hair as the sunlight coming in through the window lit up the highlights of different subtle shades of light to dark brown – well auburn really. He was really quite nervous; firstly just because she was a very attractive woman, and secondly because he had so much to ask her, and had a problem with how and when he had been informed of his mother's survival. His kneejerk reaction was to get mad with someone, but she looked so calm, and gentle he held back his anger and frustration and calmed himself down. They both ordered the same lunch and Peter ordered a bottle of wine, which he thought would help them both to relax, as the tension in the air was quite palpable. Fiona was a little nervous too as she didn't know Peter at all and didn't know just how he was going to react to the news and information he had been given. Peter started out by thanking her for coming and hoping it hadn't interrupted whatever it was she was doing. Then he started in on the questions. He had meant to take it slowly but his mouth galloped ahead of his brain and he just blurted out the questions, staccato style.

"So, is my mother alive or not? Why did it take you four months to let me know what had happened? And just who are you anyway? And what were the conditions like for my mother on the island? Where is this island exactly? How can I get there?" He paused for breath and took a long drink of the wine. His heart was pounding and he was getting emotional, a thing he had sworn (to himself) he would not do. Fiona also took a drink and sat back in her chair and realised how careful she had to be with this emotional stranger. He looked like a respectable sort, well dressed in a casual sort of way. She had taken a covert look at his shoes – quite often, she'd been told once, a give-away as to the decency and respectability of a man. He was wearing soft leather loafers with black socks under a pair of well-cut jeans. She decided he was quite well-heeled, decent, and had already seen his up-market apartment and she approved of his style. Fiona started her side of the story. "Well, if you'll let me I'll tell you everything I know – but remember please, I'm only acting under instructions from the company I work for. So, as I told you when we first met, I'm a surveyor and I work for a company called Global Geosurveys and we do work for certain governments, mining companies, property developers, that sort of thing. Now once we found the wrecked, ocean going yacht the 'Brissibabe' and read your mother's report about the plane crashing, we knew we had to inform the authorities, but we were working for a very large company (can't tell you which) and we were doing confidential work which the company did not want generally known. Once decisions had been made about the suitability of the island for potential development, or mining, then we could let the information out to the authorities; and of course let you know also what happened to your parents. We only work under contract conditions and it's up to the people employing us as to what they do with the information we give them, and they are obliged, of course, to let the authorities know about crashes and wrecks and things, but it's their call, not ours, especially as to the timing of the notification."

"All right, all right!" said Peter, frustrated by the slow telling of the story. "I understand all that, but tell me is my mother alive or not?"

Lunch came and Fiona pushed it to one side, took a sip of wine and answered, slowly, deliberately. "As I told you before, I really don't know. No one knows. I take it you have read the whole of your mother's report?"

"Yes, yes of course," said Peter.

Fiona moved her plate back in front of her and started to eat her lunch as she went on. "Well her last report wasn't: shall we say: conclusive. She obviously didn't want to meet us, or anyone, or for us to bring her back to civilisation. In fact I think she was worried we might force her to come with us. So whether she just hid from us, or whether she went for the long swim, I, we, just don't know. We inspected the boat and her store of food, mainly beans, coconuts, corn, dried fish etc. She seems to have been a very resilient, resourceful lady. The water storage she had rigged up was working well and her garden over by the marsh was in full production. We did look quite extensively to see if we could find your mum, or even a clue as to whether she was still alive or not, however we didn't find any evidence of her actually still being alive, but just in case she was evading us we decided to leave some things that might make her life there more manageable. We left her some toothpaste and face cream (which she had mentioned in her report that she missed). We left some tomatoes with a note attached which told her she could save the seeds and plant them for a crop next year (although I'm sure she would have known that). Also some potatoes with the same note. We left two loaves of bread and some butter, slices of ham, tins of meat, a pair of my runners (which hopefully will fit her better than what she has there). We also left some more matches and a battery kitchen gas lighter. We left your mum a note telling her we would take the ship's log and her notebooks and deliver them to you when we could. We left a couple of notebooks and pens that we'd had on our boat, in our stock, so if she is still there she can still continue her report. We had a few out of date newspapers which we left, and we were happy to note that they contained cryptic crosswords, and code word puzzles, which we know your mum missed. That's about it really. Oh and I forgot, we left some chocolates and chocolate biscuits as well."

Peter couldn't help the tears unmanfully flowing now. Neither of them said anything for quite a while. Peter wasn't eating, but had some wine now and then. Eventually he ate his lunch and after blowing his nose discreetly he called for the bill. He asked Fiona, "Will you walk a little way with me? I still have some questions to ask you and I need a little time to think."

They walked down to the Esplanade and along Riverside Drive. Perth is a beautiful city resting on the Swan River and the local council had really gone to town redesigning the waterfront from a simple jetty to an upmarket marina with a unique Bell Tower and many restaurants. It was the terminal for river cruises and a ferry over to the Perth Zoo on the other side of the river. It is a very popular spot and the two of them walked quietly past the marina not speaking much. Peter was thinking hard and trying to form his questions.

At length, when he had composed himself he was able to ask Fiona, "So where is this island, and does it have a name? Can I go there? Oh, and thank you for all the things you left for my mum, that was very thoughtful of you."

"No problem," said Fiona. "To answer your second question, the island is called Du Pont Island and is 149.15 degrees east and 18.20 degrees north, that puts it about 2,500 km or so north east of Manila. There are thousands of islands in that part of the world. Some owned by the Philippines, some by Japan and some privately, or not owned at all. I can't tell you anything about its current ownership or what my company recommended or what is being proposed. That's all strictly confidential. As for you going there, that is absolutely impossible even if you have a small boat or yacht and go there privately. There is no commercial traffic that visits the island, and it is strictly prohibited for anyone, other than the company that I work for to land, or inhabit, or trespass in any way on the island."

Peter's face and shoulders drooped and his steps got slow and heavy. She felt sorry for him, he looked so forlorn and lost. They turned to go back towards town and she had an idea. She asked if he would excuse her for a moment as she wished to make an urgent call on her mobile. They sat on a bench seat at the edge of Langley Park and Fiona got up once the phone was answered and she talked quite softly to someone, whilst looking first at the ground and then back at Peter, slumped, dejectedly on the bench. When the call was over she went back to the bench and said to him, "What work do you do?"

"What's that got to do with anything?" he asked rather sharply.

"Well," she replied, "could you get a reasonable time off if you wanted? Say four months, maybe shorter – depending…"

Peter sat up straight now, if he had been a dog his ears would have pricked up. "What are you getting at?"

"Well, I was just talking to my boss and I have an idea. We have to go back to Du Pont in a week's time and do more thorough work. We only surveyed half the island last time and we have to do the other half next. We cannot take passengers, and no private individual is actually allowed on the island, as I said, but our company has to do work there and only employees are allowed on the island. We actually have a vacancy on the boat and that's for a steward/kitchen hand. The last one left; he was not happy with the job or the people (actually person) he worked with. It's not a fancy job, and it won't pay well, but it's available and if you can get time off from where you are working now, you could come with us, take the job as a casual, and have a bit of time to see if you can find your mother. You won't have much time off, you will have to wait on the two tables for all meals, and help in the kitchen cleaning up and preparing vegetables etc. There are four of us company employees on the boat, plus the skipper and his mate, plus the cook and kitchen hand, that's eight in all. We need feeding and generally looking after. Bathrooms cleaned, lounge and dining area cleaned, that sort of thing too. Oh, and you'd have to share your cabin with the cook (he's a horrible little man, but a good cook) – you'd have a bunk bed, and a very small cupboard for your stuff. We have a men's communal bathroom and a ladies' too – but as I'm the only lady – that's not a problem for me." She shrugged her shoulders and smiled at that last admission.

"Oh, my God," he cried, "when can I let you know? I'll have to clear it with my boss – get Luke to look after my apartment, get the mail, pay the bills. Oh, can I really go? I don't mind the work if it means I might find my mother." He was like an excited child just before Christmas now. He jumped up, his face flushed, tears in his eyes and said again, "When can I let you know? So much to do."

Fiona laughed and told him, "You'll have to let me know by lunch time tomorrow, as we need someone to fill the job and if you can't come they need time to get someone else. We only have a week anyway before I have to take the flight to Brisbane in order to catch the Global Geosurvey's boat."

Peter took her arm and almost marched her up the hill back into the city, on the way asking Fiona, "Did you come all this way just to deliver the log. It's an awful long way – but it was good of you to bring it personally."

She shook her head and explained, "No – I didn't come specifically for that reason, I'm from Perth originally and my family still live in City Beach. I'd been given a week off to visit my sick grandfather and as I was coming over, was asked to bring the log with me, and deliver it, if possible."

Peter was curious now, and wanted to know her personal circumstances and so, sort of conversationally asked, "So do you have much family apart from your grandfather here in Perth, or are all your family, you know, sisters, brothers etc. in Brisbane?"

She looked at him sideways and laughed and said, "I'm not married or anything if that's what you really want to know."

Peter smiled, bit his lip and got a bit red in the face. (Not just from the exertion of the hill.) Just to know she wasn't married, or anything, gave him a warm feeling inside – "Life," he thought to himself, "was always full of surprises." He was a man on a mission now, and was in a hurry. They walked back to town, and Peter said his goodbye quickly and promised to call her before noon the next day.

Peter had a friendly relationship with his boss Harry who was the owner of Jamison's as well as Chief Executive Officer. Harry was amazed that Peter's mother had survived and wanted to know all about it. He was very sympathetic and supportive of Peter's opportunity once it was explained to him, but laughed when he heard that Peter was to be a kitchen hand and cleaner – he just couldn't picture Peter doing it. He and Peter had a long discussion about the current project Peter was working on and after making notes Harry agreed to put it on the back shelf in order to let Peter take a leave of absence. He remembered only too well the heartache that Peter suffered a few years back when the plane went missing, and prior to that, the terrible tragedy with Timmy. Peter said he would take his computer with him and was sure he would be able to do a fair amount of design work whilst he was on the boat, so the time wouldn't be completely wasted. Peter started clearing his files, desk and packing his computer into his bag, the others in the office all wanted to know what it was all about. Over coffee he explained to the dozen other architects and office staff about the finding of the log that showed his mother had survived the crash. Everyone had questions and were shocked when he told them he was going out there to try and find her. They all wished him the best of luck and he left for the day, and for four months. He didn't want to hang around as he worried that he had so much to do and so little time to do it.

He called Luke his best friend and invited him round that night for a Chinese takeaway dinner, as he explained, he had a lot to talk about and to organise. When Luke arrived he was surprised to see Peter all flushed and animated. The takeaway had arrived and Peter was opening a couple of bottles of beer. "Come in, come in, I've got so much to tell you".

Luke could tell Peter was really excited and exclaimed, "Good God, Pete, what the hell is it? You're all of a twitter, whatever's happened – and why did you cancel breakfast last Saturday?"

"Sit down; sit down; here have a beer – you won't believe this."

"Spit it out, man – have you won the lotto or something?"

"No," said Peter as he took a swig of beer and started dishing out the food, "better than that."

"Hmmm, I don't think anything would be better than that – so – spit it out – what is it then?"

"Well, you remember four years ago my parents were killed in a plane crash?"

"Yeah, sorry about that – I know it was a tough time for you."

Peter nearly choked on his honey chicken as he blurted out, "My mother survived!"

"What?" ejaculated Luke, "You're joshing me – that's not possible – are you for real? Is this a scam, is someone having you on?"

"No, it's for real. There's an island in the Pacific called Du Pont Island and they found a diary that has been kept for four years and written by my mother."

Luke looked unbelievingly at Peter and, shaking his head he said, "No, man, someone's pulling your leg – that's got to be a scam – how much do they want from you to go get her?"

"No, I'm telling you, up to four months ago she was alive and well – whether she still is alive, no one actually knows, but I've been offered the opportunity to go and find out."

"It's a scam, I tell you. Don't fall for it." Luke was on his feet now with a beer in his hand, squarely facing Peter, quoted to him, "Listen, man, you know what they say, if it sounds too good to be true, it generally is. Don't fall for it. How much do they want from you to go look for your mum?"

Exasperated Peter finished the bottle of beer and got up to fetch another. "No, you don't understand, it's a legitimate company – doing a survey or something on this island. They found a boat and a ship's log, and my mother has been writing in it a report on what happened. The plane went down and my father was killed, but my mother survived. They brought the log home from sea and it's her handwriting, and it's for real."

Luke went and got another beer out of the fridge and leaving the meal almost untouched, flopped himself down on the couch and said slowly, "Alright then, matey, where is this supposedly authentic, Mum's handwritten log then? I don't suppose they actually showed you this log – and how much do they want before they get it for you? I still say it's a scam."

Peter quietly went into the bedroom and came back with a sly smile on his face and put it into Luke's lap. "There, what do you make of that then – and there's two more books that follow on from that."

Luke looked first up at Peter, unbelieving and then down at the large log book on his lap. He opened the cover and flipped through the pages until he came to the different handwriting and read the first bit, before looking up again at Peter. "Oh my God, is this for real? Oh, man is your mum really still alive after all this time?"

"Well she was, but now no one knows. I want to go to the island and see if I can find her. Actually no one is allowed on the island – it's privately owned or something, I don't know what. Anyway apparently no one can go there, except this surveying company, and they've offered me a job for four months, working in the kitchen, but it means I get a bit of time off, when they're on the island and I can have a look around to see what's what."

"Are you mad? Are you completely off your rocker? How can you think of working in a kitchen? You're a good cook I know but you'd be giving up a perfectly good job – and there's no guarantee that you'd find your mum."

"I know," said Peter excitedly, "but there's a chance. I've spoken to Harry and he's agreed to give me four months leave of absence – as of today. The flight is in one week and the boat leaves from Brisbane. I have to go; I have to see if my mum is still alive, I have to. Working in the kitchen doesn't mean I do any cooking either. The job is acting as a steward – well waiter really, and helping out in the kitchen, cleaning up and stuff. I can do it – it's an opportunity – if I can see my mum again it will be worth it – and of course if I find her I'll try and bring her home. I want badly to do this – will you help me? I need you to look after the apartment for me, you don't have to live here (although you can if you want to) but could you collect the mail for me and if I leave you some cash can you pay my bills please? I'll empty the fridge and the garbage, but I can't think of anything else – will you do it for me please, please?"

"Yes, of course I'll do it for you, but, Pete – for God's sake think about what you're doing. If, and I mean, if, you find your mum, what then? Can you bring her back on the boat? Where will she live? If I remember right you sold the family house and car to pay for this fancy place. There's only one bedroom here – where will you put her? She's an old lady now, how will you look after her? Think it out, man."

"I have thought it out, and I want to find my mum, I'll sort the details out later, if I find her."

"Ah well, good luck, if you're determined to go. I think you're mad, but I'll help if I can. That's what mates are for, even if they think you're wrong. So when are you off on this little jaunt – is your passport up to date? Do you need shots or anything?"

"No, I don't think so to the shots, and yes, my passport's up to date – it's got three more years to go."

They both sat back and reflected quietly on what they had just been talking about. Neither said anything for a long time. Luke kept heaving a large sigh and then sinking back into the settee thinking better about what he was going to say. He realised Peter was resigned and he didn't want to particularly rain on his parade. Eventually, after thinking for quite a while Luke asked, "Anyhow... how do you know all this and how did you get hold of the log?"

Peter sank back into the soft settee and had a silly dreamy sort of smile on his lips.

Luke looked at him and threw his head back and laughed. "My God, there's a girl in it, isn't there? I can tell, you've got a stupid look on your face. Come on spill the beans, who is she, what's she like, how come she's involved in all this, is she married, is she blonde and 19, are you sharing a cabin with her? Oh, you devil, I should have known this wasn't all about your mum – it's you – getting it off with a chic on board a nice pleasure cruiser."

"Get your mind out of the gutter," retorted Peter. "Yes there's a girl, well woman really. Her name is Fiona and she's a surveyor on this boat. She brought me the log from Brisbane. Before you ask, she's not married, she's very nice, brunette, nice figure, dresses well, no tattoos that I could see, lovely hair that shines in the sun, and alright, I think she's gorgeous. So there you have it, I want to find my mum, but I really like this girl and – well – if we're on a boat for four months, who knows what may happen."

"Be careful, man," warned Luke, "don't go and get your heart broken – you've had enough problems this last five years – what with your parents and Timmy."

That put a damper on the mood of the evening. They were quietly reflective now; had a few more beers and then Luke wished him good luck, and left promising to look after everything and to collect the keys and cash in three days' time.

CHAPTER 14

PETER'S FIRST TRAGEDY

So much to do, what to do first? Peter's head was swimming. On the one hand he was getting excited but since Luke left he had started thinking about Timmy again. Peter and his wife Lucy had divorced three years ago. Every time Peter thought about it he got so emotional and usually put his head in his hands and wept with guilt. He would say to himself over and over, "It's all my fault, why didn't I hold on to him – oh God, it's all my fault."

Timmy was Peter and Lucy's only child. Four years old, blond, blue eyed, intelligent little boy who adored his father. Sally and Joe Elliott were doting grandparents who looked after him three days a week and he attended the local preschool two days a week. Both Peter and Lucy worked full time but Lucy had Mondays off and worked Saturdays, Peter worked a conventional Monday to Friday, 9.00 a.m. to 5.00 p.m. Peter's favourite day of the week was Saturday when he had Timmy all to himself. He would take Timmy shopping in the morning and in the afternoons they would go down to the beach or to the playground, or even sometimes to the cinema if there was a children's film showing. Life was sweet for this little family and all was going well until the Saturday before Christmas. The shops were full of last minute shoppers and Peter had a full shopping trolley. Timmy was "helping" Daddy, getting things off the shelves and putting them in the trolley. A large man jostled Peter and as they both steadied themselves somehow a display of tins got knocked over. The tins were rolling around and both the man and Peter were picking up the tins and apologising for knocking into each other. It was a good natured exchange and when the stack was halfway rebuilt Peter turned to look for Timmy. Timmy was nowhere to be seen. Panicking Peter called out, "Timmy, Timmy!" Getting louder. "Timmy, Timmy!" Shoppers were looking at him now, and he started walking quickly up the aisle still calling his son. At the end of the aisle he looked across the bottom of the other aisles and then started running up and down all the aisles looking for him. The large supermarket was very busy and a child could easily be missed amongst all the adults and other children, and all with full trolleys. "Don't panic, don't panic, he's got to be here somewhere," he kept telling himself. After a futile search he approached the Service Desk and asked if the girl would broadcast a message, which came over the loudspeaker once they had stopped the Christmas Carol they were playing.

"Would Timmy Elliott please come to the Service Counter where your father is waiting for you."

The girl wandered off to serve other customers returning faulty goods. Peter waited a while and knew instinctively that his four-year-old would not be able to respond to any message – he certainly wouldn't know where the Service Counter was. He called the girl over, but she ignored him for five minutes whilst she was serving someone else. Eventually she wandered over to him and asked, "Yes, what's wrong now?"

Peter was exasperated and explained to her, "Look, my son Timmy is only four years old, he wouldn't know how to get to a Service Counter, or even what one is."

The girl was more concerned now, and asked Peter what was Timmy wearing, and what he looked like. The second message stopped the Christmas Carol and went out,

"We have a little lost boy in the shop. Timmy Elliott is four years old, blond curly hair and is wearing a red tee shirt and white shorts. Would anyone who sees him please bring him to the Service Counter."

Peter relaxed a little for five minutes, expecting someone to bring Timmy to the counter. Panic again. No one was coming forward with him. Peter pleaded with the girl. "Please can you put that call out again – I'm really getting worried." Now he was not so much worried as really scared. The girl could see he was in a state and suggested he go into the mall and look for Timmy there, and failing that call in to the Manager's office which was at the end of the shopping mall. With his trolley abandoned in the shop and forgotten, Peter half ran, half walked up and down the mall, getting in everyone's way. He was sweating and his throat was dry. Peter was not a religious man, but he started to pray now. "Please God, please God, don't let anything have happened to him." Bargaining now. "Please God, I'll do anything, just don't let anything have happened to him".

He found his way to the Manager's office and the bored secretary there told Peter that Timmy was the fifth child today who had misplaced his parents. Peter implored her to make an announcement over the intercom. The same message was relayed once again after the currently playing Christmas Carol was finished. Five minutes, ten minutes – nothing. The secretary didn't seem unduly concerned but Peter was beside himself with worry. "Oh God, where could he be?"

After 15 minutes Peter decided it was time to call in the police. Again, delays on the phone, it was a busy time, but eventually a security guard and two policemen came into the office. Peter wasn't in the office at the time, he was walking the length and breadth of the mall, looking into all the shops and calling out Timmy's name. Eventually he went back to the office and was told the CCTV film was being taken out for examination. An hour had passed, and the police and security officer were doing their best to scan the film for any little boy with blond curls and a red tee shirt with white shorts. There were five entrances to the mall and the film showing the end entrance eventually showed a couple of men holding the hand of a little boy fitting the description, leaving the shopping centre. They both had hats on and really couldn't be recognised, except for their normal looking clothing – summer in Australia, thongs, tee shirts and shorts. Peter felt sick, he didn't know what to do. The police asked him to meet them at the Police Station once he had collected his car. He knew he should ring Lucy, but he just couldn't do it. What could he say? "I've lost our child!" He couldn't even imagine how Lucy would react. The next few days were absolute hell for both the parents and the family, Sally and Joe included. The child was so loved and well... no one really knew what to say to the parents – nothing seemed appropriate. The newspapers and television got hold of the story and copies of the CCTV images were spread across the papers and on all the news channels. Lucy and Peter were basically not talking, except for screaming accusations from Lucy. Peter had no defence. His guilt was driving him crazy. A tragedy like this should basically bind two people together, holding on to each other for support, but Lucy wasn't like that. She was a mother tiger whose cub had been snatched from her. She was relentless in her fury at Peter. The police could see what was happening to the couple and had discussions with Sally and Joe, the grandparents, who were also distraught, but more objective and calm in their agony. When the child's body was eventually found, some seven days later, dumped on the edge of the beach, it was Sally and Joe the police went to first – hoping they would break the terrible news to the parents. The child had been sexually molested to the point of death and details were too horrific to give to the parents, the family or to the media. Lucy was taken to hospital with a nervous breakdown and Peter was left to try and come to terms with his feelings of utter grief and guilt. Sally and Joe were there for him, as was Luke his best friend. Harry at work gave Peter as much time off as Peter felt he needed. Everyone was sympathetic and the funeral was held a month later, after the coroner and pathologists has finished with their examinations. When Lucy came out of hospital the accusations and blame were relentless. Peter was an empty man, a shell, no life or interest in anything. Grief is a dark place, guilt is also a dark place, but grief and guilt combined was an abyss of misery that Peter found very difficult to climb out of.

Months went by and Lucy told Peter she couldn't live with a man who couldn't be trusted to even watch his own child. The divorce application went through quickly and both tried to put the terrible tragedy behind them, and start a new life – separately. Peter rented an apartment and leaned heavily on Luke for support and comfort. Joe and Sally, the grandparents had been through the mill too, it was a terrible time and after a few months, Joe suggested he and Sally take a holiday to get away from it all. The trip to Japan was taken at a sad time, but it was what they needed to "refresh their souls" as he put it. They invited Peter to come along too, but he was too guilt-ridden to consider any holiday. He got drunk most nights with Luke putting him to bed and steering him through that awful time. Peter got a postcard from Japan and was glad that his parents were able to come to terms with their grief and start to put it behind them. Constant misery would not bring Timmy back and it looked like the police had no clues as to the murderers of his son. Peter went to the airport on that fateful night in August to pick up Joe and Sally, and waited to meet his parents along with many other waiting relatives. He kept watching the "Arrivals" board and couldn't understand what was taking so long for their flight number to be shown. Other waiting relatives were starting to look worried – whatever was keeping them? There was no initial announcement of the non-arrival of the plane, but eventually people starting asking the ground staff for information. Nothing was given out for hours. Had the plane been delayed? Had it turned back for some reason? Relatives started talking to one another now, all looking fraught and worried. It wasn't until the next morning that the airport officials announced, *"Anyone meeting Asia Pacific Alliance Airlines Flight No. APA 300 from Narita, Japan, please meet airport officials in the first class lounge located at the rear of the terminal."*

Now they knew something was definitely wrong and as the second tragedy for Peter unfolded he didn't think he would be able to breathe and collapsed on the spot. Maybe other waiting relatives thought he was weak, but they didn't know what tragedy Peter had already, recently experienced. Women were screaming and crying and the staff were trying to calm them down by telling them that "where there's life, there's hope" and other stupid platitudes. A doctor and ambulances were called and those traumatised, along with Peter, were taken to hospital.

The media were very good and left those in hospital alone. No one picked up on the double tragedy for Peter and no one told them. His misery couldn't be measured. Luke was his saviour and took him home and stayed with him for a week. Harry was wonderful and, again gave Peter all the time he needed and didn't push him to return to work. The plane was never found and it was assumed there were no survivors. After weeks, living in a drunken fog, Peter picked himself up and started back on the road to recovery. "Life must go on," everyone told him. He always felt like saying "Bugger off!" but he knew they were only trying to be kind, so he didn't. He never heard from Lucy, and he didn't want to either. If time doesn't actually "heal" – it does dull the pain, and Peter started to join the "living" world once more. He threw himself into his work and slowly life settled down. Until now.

CHAPTER 15

PETER'S PILGRIMAGE

Peter called Fiona Campbell and arranged to meet her in town again for lunch. He still had some questions to ask, but he also just wanted to see her again. She arrived promptly and asked straight away, smiling, "Well are you coming?"

He thought her enthusiasm might just be for the sake of his project, i.e. finding his mother, but he hoped it was for basically just seeing him again, and the thought of four months of, what...? Well anything really!

"Yes, I can come, and everything is organised for my apartment to be looked after and my boss is holding my job for a four month leave of absence, so yes, can I come?"

Fiona put her hand over his arm now and smiled. "Great – I just want to make a quick phone call confirming that and then we can have lunch and I'll answer any questions you may still have."

The lunch went well and Peter fired so many questions at her. How big is the boat, how big will be his shared cabin, and with whom, how much space will he have for his own stuff, and how much can he take for his mother? Will his computer work on board, will he have Internet access? What kind of clothes will he need? Does he need to have a vaccination or a shot of any kind?

On and on the questions came. Fiona was laughing and answered all his questions as best she could. He noted her perfect teeth and beautiful tan. It was a warm day and she had on only a tank top and had thrown a wrap across the back of her chair. Nice figure too he noted, and was letting his imagination run away with him, whilst still trying to concentrate on the questions he had to ask, and the answers she was giving him. Halfway through the meal Fiona stopped and put down her fork and asked if she too, could ask a few questions. She wanted to know about the work he did and how come his boss was being so cooperative at such short notice.

"Oh, he's just a decent chap," lied Peter looking down at his salad.

"No," answered Fiona, "I sense it's more than that – were you working for the same company when you first heard about the plane crash?"

It took Peter a while to finish his salad before he answered her. He knew he wanted her to know the whole story, and in the telling, letting her know he was no longer married, and also that he had a past of misery and grief that he was still trying to overcome. It all came out slowly and Peter was careful this time to keep a hold of his emotions.

He was surprised though when he looked up to see Fiona was the one who was upset and as she dabbed at her eyes with her napkin with one hand, she put her other hand over his hand on the table. No one spoke for a long time, then she apologised slowly. "I'm truly sorry, how awful for you."

Peter changed the subject and went back to the questions about the boat and the trip. He particularly wanted to take some things for his mother. He had thought about her collecting heavy things, like pumpkins and rocks and stuff and he decided he would like to take her a personal shopping trolley – not the metal ones that the supermarkets have, but the fold-up ones on wheels very similar to a pull-along suitcase. He explained all that to Fiona and then asked her, "Just how much room do you think I would have, and can I fit all that I want to take into the cabin?"

Fiona assured him there wasn't enough room in his shared cabin, and went on to explain, "Unfortunately for you the kitchen hand shares a cabin with the cook and theirs is the smallest space on the boat. You will have only a small area to walk around in and a very small cupboard for your personal stuff. Professional staff, I'm glad to say fare much better, however as a special favour I could let you store such a large item in my cabin, I'm the only woman on board, so there's more room for me than anyone else aboard. Not only that but don't expect any favours or cooperation from the cook – he's a horrible little man – I don't know why – he just is, however he is a brilliant cook, so we have to forgive him for being the surly individual that he usually is."

All was organised and it was agreed that Fiona would get the tickets and would meet Peter at the airport in two days' time. Perth Domestic Airport is never very busy, except for the mining "fly in fly outers" section, so checking in, electronically was a breeze. Luggage was not a problem and Fiona and Peter passed a pleasant two hours in the waiting area having coffee and cakes. It was a chance to chat about this and that, getting to know each other. Peter asked Fiona about her work, but she was not allowed to tell him too much as the work was quite confidential and no one outside the company she worked for was supposed to know exactly what they were doing, and where they were doing it. She explained though, "Well the actual work that I do, surveying is not really much different, wherever I, or the company I work for do it – in the city, in the country – or on uninhabited islands."

She was interested in Peter's work and they discussed some of the projects he had been involved in over the last few years. Peter was a good architect, creative and technically proficient. The challenges he had faced, designing way out buildings in Dubai, were fully satisfying his artistic temperament. He explained to Fiona, "I feel especially lucky that Harry, my boss, has been able to maintain his contracts, working from Perth. This is unusual, but with modern, up to date electronic communications and Internet facilities, most of the design and technical work can be done in Perth, whilst the actual interpretation and construction work, of course, has to be done in Dubai. It does mean travelling to Dubai every now and then, but that's no hardship, Dubai is a very interesting place to visit."

Fiona confessed, "I've never been to Dubai, but it's on my list of things to do – sometime in the future."

The two were interested in each other's professions and career choices. They talked easily, frankly and were beginning to become friends, rather than just acquaintances, thrown together by circumstances. The flight was passed pleasantly, especially after five hours when Fiona's sleepy head drooped on to Peter's waiting shoulder. The shopping trolley had been packed with all the things Peter could think of to help his mother if she decided to stay on the island, assuming of course he found his mother alive and well. He rehearsed his speech to her over and over, appealing for her to return to civilisation, assuming he found her at all. Getting to the port in Brisbane was no problem and the taxi driver helped Peter put their luggage on to the dock. There were some formalities to go through but within half an hour they were on the launch going out to meet a large ocean going yacht, with the company name emblazoned on the side. Fiona introduced Peter to Blake

Hooker, who was the skipper of the yacht. Blake was a grey-haired stocky man of 60 years, ex-navy and extremely experienced, exuding confidence and reliability. He said to Peter and Fiona, "Just call me Skipper, everyone does and it's what I prefer – I hate the name 'Blake' – it's so … well, flaky!" Fiona laughed and Peter liked him straight away. Skipper drove the launch and chatted to Peter on the way across. He seemed a very pleasant fellow, and explained that he and his mate drove and navigated the launch as well as the yacht itself. Fiona went up the gangplank first, and at the top stopped to wait for Peter who was struggling with the luggage for both of them. Two pleasant fellows came down the gangplank and helped him bring the gear on board. Once at the top Peter was introduced to the guys. Firstly to Alan Bennett, Head of Operations, then to the other two guys. Alan was 52 short and stocky but not fat, and had intense blue eyes; intelligent without being intellectual. Skipper asked one of the guys to help Peter stow his gear and then for Peter to report back to him. The two willing hands were Robert and Richard.

Robert had been to university with Fiona and so the two were good friends, happy to be working for the same company, on the same project. Richard was the quiet one of the party – a family man with three young children at home. They all made a good team and had been on field trips like this one many times before. The next few hours went by in a blur, getting instructions, getting to know the other guys, learning where one could go and where one couldn't. Skipper explained that he, whilst not one of the surveyors, was in actual fact the captain of the ship and everyone was under his orders when at sea, or when it was anything to do with the sailing of the ship. The launch was his responsibility too and no one except Chip, and he stressed that again, no one was allowed to use the launch except under his authority. Peter was introduced at this time to Chip, who was the Skipper's mate and helped with the sailing of the yacht. Chip, (real name Charlie Gordan), was aged 26, no great academic but good natured and a willing worker. He had been given the job of First Mate because his father had been in the navy with Skipper many years earlier and had saved Skipper's life. Skipper felt he owed Chip's father a favour and so agreed to take Chip on. He was not sorry for the indulgence because Chip was actually a good worker and a pleasant young man, not given to excesses of the flesh – i.e. drinking, womanising, gambling etc.

Fiona was kind enough to assume ownership of Peter's excess luggage and no one questioned her about that. Apparently they were to set sail later on the evening tide, and they had about five hours to get themselves organised and for Peter to meet the cook and get started.

CHAPTER 16

THE COOK

The cabin was even smaller than Peter had imagined. There was a bunk bed, and the bottom bunk had clothes and a computer on it, so he assumed the top bunk would be his. There was a small cupboard and two drawers, hardly room to swing the proverbial cat. He noticed however, that the cabin was air-conditioned and he had a small shelf above his bunk. He would have to remember to sleep with his head away from the shelf, otherwise he would be in danger of banging his head each time he sat up. There was an overhead central light and individual reading lights for each bunk. He was so grateful to Fiona for taking his mother's pull-along to her cabin – wherever that may be. A change of clothes and a shower were called for and he stripped off and then realised there was no shower in the cabin, and remembered that Fiona had told him, back in Perth that it was a communal men's bathroom. "Ah well, no matter." He just put his trousers back on and went looking for the bathroom. He hadn't met the cook yet and assumed he would, all in good time.

Halfway through his shower he heard the bathroom door open and a rough loud voice shout out, "Where the hell is the lackey?"

He didn't answer as he didn't know who or what a lackey was. The shower screen was rudely thrust aside and a little terror of a man threw a towel at him and demanded, "Get your gear on and get to work – what do you think this is, a bloody pleasure cruise?"

Somewhat stunned, Peter dried himself and returned to the cabin where he met up with Jock MacDonald, the cook. They didn't shake hands or pass any pleasantries at all, Jock just bellowed at him to get dressed and report to the galley immediately – and look sharp about it.

"My God," thought Peter, "am I in the army or something? This guy can't be for real."

Although Peter got dressed quite quickly, into what he assumed would be work clothes, he hadn't been shown around the yacht completely, and only by following his nose did he find the galley. There was a smell of roast lamb and rosemary, which made him realise he was really quite hungry. Jock stopped doing something to a pan of sauce and looked up at Peter as he entered over a large step.

"Where the hell have you been? I can't do all this work myself – you can get started on the potatoes over there, and after that carrots, we don't do frozen or tinned stuff here for days yet."

Peter walked over to the stack of vegetables and took up a peeler and started in on the job. In an effort to get acquainted Peter asked, "And what do I call you then?"

"You call me Cook, and I'm in charge of everything in the kitchen and in the dining room. Now get on with the job and stop your lallygagging!" Peter had no idea what lallygagging was, but assumed it was idle chitter chatter.

He braced his shoulders to the job and got on with the vegetables. The evening meal was a very busy affair. There were two small tables with bunk seating around each. Everyone was very friendly and Alan told Peter that everyone had been told why Peter was on board, they had all been told of Peter's mother and were keen to help him. Peter asked if Skipper and Chip would be joining them. Alan explained that Skipper and Chip usually took their meals in the kitchen, or in the wheel house, and not usually with the surveyors. Peter had worked hard preparing all the vegetables, and then served the meal. He had to acknowledge that Cook knew what he was doing, the roast lamb smelt delicious and everyone hungrily tucked into it. He had never worked as a waiter before, but had eaten in so many restaurants he knew the basic routine and all went well. Peter and Cook ate their meal later, after Peter had done all the washing and cleaning up, and clearing away. Peter decided to go for a walk on deck before turning in for the night. The surveyors, Robert and Richard, as well as Fiona were on deck, and they all chatted amiably as they watched the lights of Brisbane disappear over the horizon. Fiona was anxious to know if Peter was settling in and asked him, "How's things down in the kitchen – how are you getting on with Cook? Are you finding your way around alright?"

Peter answered brightly. "Yes thanks, everything is just fine. It won't be too difficult in the kitchen once I've learned where everything is and how to do things. You know," he said, "it's not exactly brain surgery but Cook seems to be an efficient and competent chef, even though he's quite a stern task-master. I think we'll get on just fine."

Cook had retired to bed and the other surveyors also turned in, leaving Peter and Fiona alone. They walked, a little unsteadily on the swaying deck of the yacht and talked about everything from the stars above to the political situation of the world. They talked easily and Peter discovered they had many similar opinions about sport, books, and music. However it was getting late and Peter had to get up very early in order to prepare for breakfast. He said, "Goodnight," as they parted and Fiona joked as she left, saying, "Yes goodnight, sleep tight, don't let the bed bugs bite!" He laughed and they went down below in different directions. Peter didn't know if Cook would be asleep, so was very careful opening their cabin door and closing it behind him. The overhead light wasn't on, but there was sufficient light coming from Cook's computer screen which was on his bed, by his feet. Cook was fast asleep and snoring gently. Peter starting getting undressed, quietly, when he looked at what Cook had been watching on the computer screen. He was shocked and disgusted by the scenes he was seeing. There were naked children – boys, being abused and molested. He watched in horror as he saw two men abusing two little boys, who couldn't have been more than seven or eight years old. He didn't dare breathe, he didn't want to wake Cook and was even more astounded, as he watched to see the men, one he recognised and couldn't believe it – the man was Cook himself, doing terrible things to the distraught child. Sickened, Peter stood there not knowing quite what to do at first. Then he made a decision. He would get into bed and talk to Cook about it tomorrow. As Peter climbed up into the top bunk he made a noise on the bed and Cook woke with a start. He turned off the computer and went back to sleep. As he lay in bed Peter thought over what he had seen and the situation he was in. Rage, fury, and pure hatred raced across Peter's brain. When Timmy disappeared and his body eventually found, Peter swore to himself that if ever he found, or met a paedophile he would do something drastic – he didn't know what, he wasn't a violent man, but the thought of that kind of evil just boiled his blood. He then had an idea. He thought the best way of stopping this evil, was not kill, maim or damage one individual, but to get information about the group of people who organised and carried out such a terrible trade. That information, given to the police might just be the way to get some of the trade stopped and the people involved prosecuted, and put away, for long stretches. Apparently paedophiles were not treated well in prison. Peter started work early the next morning and worked hard all through the day. He kept thinking about what might be the best way to get information out of Cook – and to get him prosecuted and locked up. He realised he couldn't do anything whilst on the yacht – so maybe he would have to bide his time – but how to get the information he needed. He wondered if he should talk to someone, Alan, or Fiona, but decided to keep it all to himself for the time being. He needed time to think. After a good night's sleep Peter worked hard in the kitchen and formed a plan as he peeled potatoes and cut the kidney beans. He would try and befriend Cook and somehow let him think that Peter was interested in little boys. This was not the case, of course, but Peter thought it might be one way of getting some information.

Over the next few days Peter ingratiated himself carefully with Cook, trying to get him to be a little more friendly, hoping somehow the conversation might turn to the subject of boys. An opportunity arose when Cook started to tell Peter that they would be calling in to Manila before going to the island. Peter asked, casually, if there might be time to walk the back streets of Manila – he'd heard they have places there that would be willing to indulge a man's "needs". "If you get my drift," he said whilst tapping the side of his nose, sort of conspiratorially.

Cook took the bait. "Well they have everything a man might need – but what precisely are you looking for?"

"Well…" said Peter slowly, as if not wanting to explain in too much detail, "I do like young flesh, you know, nice and smooth, not too soft."

Cook was slow to respond, but after a moment asked cautiously, "Well, do you prefer girls or boys? I prefer boys myself."

Keeping a straight face, and trying not to let the anger and hatred show, Peter replied that he also preferred boys and it would be interesting to visit Manila if that kind of business was possible. Cook assured Peter everything was possible in Manila. If they got the chance Cook might even accompany Peter and show him some "places of interest", as he'd been there quite a few times and knew the ropes.

Days went by and just as Cook had predicted the Skipper decided to call in to Manila before going on to the island. Peter was worried. He and Cook were getting on quite well now and Cook had mentioned once or twice that he was looking forward to a good night out on the town. Peter didn't want to be involved in any back street sex trade, he just wanted information from Cook that would, on return to Australia, be evidence of illegal production of pornography, and evil practise of using children in this way. On the morning of the scheduled docking in Manila, Cook and Peter had been given the day off by Skipper as there were boat maintenance problems that may take hours to fix. Alan, who was Head of Operations, invited the surveying team to accompany him to the Granger Hotel for lunch; this left Cook and Peter time to explore Manila unaccompanied, and unfettered by others who were not looking to fill their time, the same way that Cook intended to fill his. Peter was scared and worried. How was he going to get out of this predicament? He decided the only way was to fake being ill.

Peter served breakfast to the staff and cleared the tables and then cleaned up the kitchen. He decided he had to start to be ill there and then. Whilst Cook was sharpening a carving knife Peter gave a groan and clutched at his stomach. "OWWW... I think I've got Delhi Belly or something."

"Bloody hell – you can't be sick, we've all eaten the same things," remonstrated Cook. "Jesus, man, pull yourself together – we're going ashore in ten minutes' time."

Peter groaned again and took off for the bathroom. He was in the bathroom and tried making noises that sounded like he was heaving his guts out. Cook banged on the bathroom door. "Are you alright, man?"

"No, go away," shouted Peter.

He stayed in the bathroom until he heard Cook again. "Listen man, I'm sorry you're not feeling well, but the launch is waiting and I'm going, alright?"

"Yes, just go, I'll be fine." Then Peter made another very loud imitation of someone being violently sick. Late in the afternoon the launch returned with the staff and Cook.

Fiona was the first to go to Peter's cabin and after knocking timidly on his door asked, "Peter, it's me Fiona, are you okay?"

"Come in," called Peter. He was sitting on his bed working on his laptop.

"I heard you were ill, what's wrong?"

Peter didn't want to go into any details of his problem with Fiona so he simply told her, "I had an upset stomach, but I'm fine now."

"I was worried when I didn't see you in the launch," she said, looking very sympathetic.

"Well, thanks for looking in on me but I'm just fine now. In fact I must get into the kitchen and start preparing for dinner."

"Well before you go I have a little gift for you. I cleared it with Alan and whilst in Manila got you a little something, well a little four things really. Well, for your mother, if you find her, really." Fiona pulled a box from behind her back and carried it carefully over to where he was sitting. The box had holes in the top and was making some funny noises. He looked up at Fiona quizzically and held out his hands to receive the box.

Gingerly he opened the box and a big grin spread across his face when he saw four of the cutest little chicks. "Oh my, oh my. Aren't they just gorgeous? Oh thank you so much – but how can I look after them here until we get to the island? There's no room here and baby chicks need special food, you can't give them steak and chips."

"It's alright, don't fuss, I've cleared it with Alan and Skipper and I'll have them in my cabin, until we get to the island, and I bought some chick food from the market where I got the chicks. It's something I've been thinking about for days now and we all agreed it would be a great thing for your mum, if ever you find her, and if she intends to stay on the island."

Peter thanked her over and over and then he had to leave as work was calling. He promised he would talk to her later – after dinner if she was free. They talked on deck for a couple of hours, about this and that. Peter didn't want to jeopardise his intentions at all by divulging his plan to Fiona, about Cook. Fiona might inadvertently spoil the plan by some action of her own, like involving Alan or Skipper. Peter needed information and didn't want to compromise that opportunity. "Get the information first and then let all the authorities know," he told himself. He was so glad his work didn't involve much thinking, the boring monotony of the job gave him time to consider exactly what information he wanted and how was he going to get it. He was sure that paedophiles, like the people who took Timmy were organised and fraternised with each other on the Internet. Cook was obviously involved, and the pictures on Cook's computer were evidence enough for Peter. After they left Manila, Peter asked Cook how was his trip ashore. Cook's eyes lit up and he looked straight into Peter's eyes and asked, "Do you really want to know, man – I mean do you really want all the gory details?"

"Yes," said Peter, "it was pretty miserable here – being ill but thinking what a good time you'd be having. Did you get…? Well you know what I mean, what was available? Were there any boys, and how much did it cost?"

"My God, man – you've no idea how easy it is. If you've got money, and I don't mean lots of money – anything is possible."

Cook then went into raptures describing in detail what he had enjoyed in Manila. Peter was disgusted and appalled, but kept his thoughts to himself and encouraged Cook to talk on and on. Peter surprised himself with his acting ability, he kept saying to himself, "I should go on stage, be in films – I would never have thought I could do this sort of thing – keeping a passive face whilst lying to this man, it's difficult, but I can do it, and if I can get this man and any others involved, prosecuted then my hard work will not be in vain and I will have achieved something worthwhile."

As Cook got more confidence in Peter's – supposed interest, he started to elaborate on past experiences. Peter encouraged him to talk and asked questions about how he could satisfy his "needs". Peter explained that although he was very keen to participate in this kind of thing… he, Peter, had never actually done anything about this interest before. He thought a lot about it but did nothing as he didn't know how to go about it, especially in Australia where that kind of market just wasn't available. Cook laughed and said, "Oh, man, it's available all right – you've just got to know where to look, and who to talk to."

Peter was then asked if he was interested in seeing some images on the computer. Peter pretended to hesitate, but then agreed to have a look at some images later that night when all the work in the kitchen was done. What

Peter saw sickened him, disgusted him but he had to show a keen interest in the images and the possibility of getting some images available for his own pleasure. Cook told him that he could transfer some images onto Pete's computer. Peter assured him he shouldn't do that as the laptop Peter had on board was not his own personal one. It belonged to the company he worked for and was subject to much scrutiny by his boss. He explained that he was expected to work on some designs whilst he was on this trip. However he had a computer at home that was new and he hadn't put any code words in yet, or booted it up.

A few days passed and the night before they were due to arrive at the island Peter and Cook had a drink after work in their cabin. Peter thought if he could get Cook drunk he may be able to get more information out of him. In a fairly intoxicated state, Cook decided he could trust Peter and told him, conspiratorially that he would let him in on how to get involved in the group, if Peter was interested in the group's activities too. Peter jumped at the chance to gain all this information. His acting ability was impressive. His face a picture of keen anticipation. Cook started drunkenly showing off now, encouraged by Peter who kept topping up Cook's whiskey. "Oh brother – you've no idea what we get up to – it's a breeze. Sylvester's a chemist in South Perth and he gets us really organised. We can pick up a 'toy' as we call them whenever we like. Sylvester rings us when things are right and two or three of us go out and collect our toy. We can all then enjoy our toy at his place. It's a hoot. You'd love it!"

Peter was absolutely disgusted but pushed on pleading Cook for more information about how he could get involved. Cook was flattered, and was enjoying being an instructor to a novice. He had thrown caution to the wind in his inebriated state, and without hesitation gave Peter names, contacts, email addresses, mobile phones and details of online sites that could be downloaded. Shortly after, Cook fell into a deep drunken sleep and woke up without even a headache and without any real memory of what had transpired the night before. Peter wrote down all the information he remembered, stored it away safely and then wandered up on deck and met up with Alan. They exchanged a few pleasantries and then had a quiet chat about the day ahead and what would be happening. Alan explained that the group had already surveyed half the island, the one Peter's mother had been living on, and now they had the other side to do. It was a more difficult side as there were hills and cliffs but they expected to have the work done in two to three days. Alan had drawn up a rough map of the island and showed it to Peter, explaining how he would be able to find the 'Brissibabe' which was situated over the headland, away from where they would be landing. Alan also explained that they were on the island to work, and would have absolutely no time for helping Peter. He would have to fend for himself getting to find his mother and getting back to the launch in time. Alan also explained that, different to the Manila stop, this time, only one of the kitchen staff could be released from duties on the boat at a time – so he would allow Peter to have the day off first, and then Cook could have the second day off, and so on taking it in turns for however many days it took to complete the work.

Alan was sympathetic to Peter's pilgrimage and encouraged him by saying, "Well, Peter, I really hope you find your mum alive but have you thought out what you will do if you do find her? I assume you will try and persuade her to return to civilisation. I just want you to know that if she is alive and if she does agree to return it's no problem for us on the boat, there's ample room and I've already spoken to Fiona who is quite willing to share her cabin."

"Thanks, Alan, it really is good of you to be so concerned, and so willing to help me. I've thought about this a lot and if I do actually find my mum alive I will of course try and persuade her to return to Australia with us, but if she really, truly, doesn't want to return, then I'll respect her wishes. I know life can't be that easy for her on the island, alone, but I've brought some things with me that I hope might make her stay on the island a little more interesting and easier."

Alan slowly drank his evening coffee and looking up at Peter said, "None of us should ever force anyone to do something they don't want to do – it's a very tricky situation – I don't know how I would feel if it was my mother."

Peter stared out over the heaving ocean, deep in thought and after a few minutes' reflection said to Alan, "Can I ask you something, Alan?"

"Of course."

"Well," went on Peter, "did you personally get to read my mum's writing in the log?"

"Yes," answered Alan, "I did, why?"

"Well," went on Peter, "What did you make of my mother's mental state? I mean she talks of conversing with my father, who is of course not there. Do you think this whole experience has turned her brain? I mean, do you think she is capable of making rational decisions about her future?"

Alan took in a deep breath and carefully answered Peter. "Well, I think whether this experience has badly affected her brain or not you should still respect her wishes. If she is alive and is finding consolation and comfort in the imagined companionship of your father, then I guess she is happy in her own little world – maybe you shouldn't shatter that, why not leave her to her fantasies, if that's making her happy. She obviously loved your father very much and maybe she just can't accept that he is gone. I don't know, I'm not a psychologist."

"I guess you're right, thanks," answered Peter.

Peter was quiet for a while and then asked Alan, "So, can you tell me anything about this island, what kind of place is it?"

Alan explained, "Well the island is actually private property and the work we're doing will be the precursor to large developments. I can't be precise about that as it's all in the confidential stage of negotiations. I can tell you though that anyone found living on the island would be considered a trespasser and I can't say what would happen then, with the proposed development – but I'm sure nothing concrete will happen for at least two years, as negotiations are still underway, and developments, such as are being proposed, generally take years to come to fruition."

Peter nodded understanding the situation. Alan then remembered something and said to Peter, "Just wait a minute – I've got something for you – I'll be back in a minute."

With that he left Peter alone on deck and returned a few minutes later lugging a spare gas bottle behind him. He dumped it at Peter's feet and declared, "Here, a goodwill gift from the crew on board for your mum. If she is still alive and if she intends to stay it will see her through a few months of cooking. You can take it to the wreck and install it for her. Well, we've got an early start tomorrow, so I'll wish you a goodnight – I'll see you by the launch in the morning. Good luck, I hope everything turns out alright for you."

Peter hardly slept that night, imagining, wondering, dreaming, hoping; planning what he would say, if he found his mother, planning his argument if she insisted on staying. He tossed and turned whilst Cook quietly snored his way through the night.

CHAPTER 17

FINDING MUM

Peter could scarcely breathe as they approached the island, he scoured the headland with the ship's binoculars, hoping to catch a glimpse of his mother and yet at the same time knowing that if she was still alive, and in the same frame of mind as when she wrote the log, that she wouldn't want to be seen, and of course she had no way of knowing that he, her only son was on board the yacht and was desperate to see her.

The island looked interesting enough to him, lots of sand dunes, coconut palms and hills in the distance. It seemed green and fertile and there were hundreds of seagulls weaving overhead making an awful racket with their screeching. He was impatient with the anchoring of the yacht and the procedure for getting the launch into the water but eventually all was ready and he had his parcels, trolley and gas bottle all stowed in the bottom of the boat. Only Skipper and Cook stayed on board the yacht, everyone else was packed into the launch. As soon as the launch was safely anchored in the shallows the surveyors collected their equipment and took off over the headland, leaving Peter and Chip with the launch. Peter took the gas bottle first and dragged it up from the waterline and left it on top of the closest sand dune. He then collected the rest of his gear and presents and slowly made his way through the sand going in the direction of the "Brissibabe" which Alan had pointed out to him. It was hard going and the trolley had difficulty being pulled through the sand but eventually all the equipment was taken over the headland, away from the launch and away from Chip – who settled himself down with a book and had strict instructions from Skipper to not leave the launch. Sally watched the yacht approaching the island and was scared and nervous. She hadn't thought the yacht would return and she was still firm in her mind that she didn't want to return to the real world. She realised she had compromised her position if they were the same people as before, and, she supposed they may well come to the "Brissibabe" again, looking for her. They had been kind enough to leave supplies for her last time and she had used them – planted the tomatoes and potatoes, used the cream etc. They would see all that and realise she was still alive. Of course, word of her survival must have got through to the papers, the media, and to Peter. "Oh," she thought to herself. "What if Peter has sent a message to me – or even come to find me himself? Oh, too good to even think about." She watched from the headland as the team unpacked their gear from the small boat. The large yacht was anchored way out in the bay. There were two people left in the launch and from that distance she couldn't tell who they were. The four surveyors headed off across Turtle Bay and disappeared over that headland. The small boat was obviously left in the care of the driver, and the one remaining passenger was struggling with a pull-along case/trolley and a box of something in the other hand. He also had a gas bottle which he took to the high water mark and left there. He had a sunhat on and was ploughing through the sand with some difficulty, but even so she could tell who it was. Her heart just about stopped beating. She wanted to run and help him, but she didn't want the one man, remaining in the dinghy to see her, so she bit her lip, and impatiently watched him struggle across the beach and then over the headland, heading towards the wrecked "Brissibabe". As soon as he was over the headland he put his parcels down and turned around and went back down the beach and picked up the gas bottle and came back over the headland with it. When he was safely over the headland and she was sure he was out of sight of the launch she started towards him. He heard her, before he saw her. He knew she would have changed but he was startled to see this almost strange little lady approach him through the undergrowth. Her hair was pure white and she was more bent than he remembered – but it was his beloved mum, and he put down his encumbrances and ran towards her giving her a bear hug and crying her name over and over. She released herself from his hugs and held him at arm's length to survey her only son, with tears running freely down both of their faces.

"Oh, Mum I can't believe it… you're really alive, after all this time. It's been four years and we thought you were dead, that you'd gone down in the plane with Dad. You look so healthy, how have you managed here on your own? – Oh, Mum I've so many questions to ask you."

"And you too, son – how are you and how have you been, and how did you manage to get here? Tell me everything."

It was 10.30 in the morning and the day just flew by. Peter had to be at the launch for 4.30 in the afternoon so as the afternoon wore on he kept glancing at his watch, wary of not overstaying his time. They had not stopped talking, catching up on family news and gossip and Sally showing Peter all her resourceful efforts at sustaining life. She was thrilled with the chicks and Peter set to with hammer and nails and put up a pretty rudimentary hen shed. The chick food was welcome and Sally said the chicks would be ready to eat greens and some of her ground up sweetcorn in no time at all. There was enough fishing net (that had been washed up on the shore) to go around a frame making a hen run, not that there were any predators, as far as Sally knew, except the greedy sea gulls, who would probably take a baby chick if they had a chance.

Sally was delighted with all the packets of seeds, especially those for fruits like Cape Gooseberries, and strawberries, and seeds for asparagus too, her all-time favourite vegetable. She was particularly pleased with his gift of books, and a small CD player, with plenty of spare batteries. He had brought about 50 CDs which he said, laughing, "Well they should keep you going for five minutes or so!"

Sally then asked, "So how come you're on a surveying boat and did it cost you an arm and a leg to be allowed on board as a passenger?"

Peter explained, "Actually I'm not strictly speaking a passenger, guess what? I'm a kitchen hand, working my passage."

She laughed at the thought of him in the kitchen, labouring for a living. "You've got to be kidding!" she joked, "you a kitchen hand, I don't believe you!"

He explained, "Well it's true. Actually I'm just on a four month leave of absence and no, I haven't taken to kitchen work as a new career, but that was the only way that I was allowed on the boat and so, on to the island. You see, Mum, this island is going to be developed and in a few years you may be asked to leave, if anyone ever found out that you were still living here. The island is actually called Du Pont Island – did you know that?"

"No I didn't."

"Well," continued Peter, "it's apparently off limits to any unauthorised visitors – so strictly speaking you are trespassing – and I don't know what would happen if the authorities find out that you are living here."

Sally wasn't particularly upset with this news as nothing was imminent. She was very philosophical and stated, "Well until anything happens, I just have to forget it. I'm not going to worry about what I can't change, that's always been my motto."

Peter then got on to the main topic of conversation he wanted to have with his mum. Taking her home. They talked calmly at first, Peter trying to convince her of the disadvantages of being on one's own. "What if you get sick, or hurt? There's no one here to help you. What if you run out of food, water? What if there's a hurricane or worse, a tsunami?"

Sally listened and then started to get agitated telling him she had thought a lot about it all and was willing to take her chances. She wanted to stay and that was that. They argued a bit but Peter realised her resolve and gave in. He told her, "Look, Mum I have to get back pretty soon, is there anything else you need? The surveying team expect to be on the island for about three days and I may or may not be able to get back myself but I could send one or two things for you with one of the other guys, maybe."

Sally got very agitated again and stressed vehemently that she not only didn't want to return to civilisation but that she definitely didn't want anyone – not anyone, other than Peter to know that she was still alive. She knew there would be reporters, and any developers who came would want to see how the "crazy old lady" was getting on. She made Peter promise he would not tell anyone on the boat or even once home, that she was alive. She would try as best she could to hide so no one would find her. She stated so strongly, she wouldn't ever – ever leave the island and leave Joe. Peter quietly placed his arm around his Mom and spoke gently, "Mum, you know Dad is gone – he's not here – you're on your own, please reconsider."

Sally looked puzzled at first and then looking straight into Peter's eyes said slowly, "Yes, I know he's gone, but he's sometimes with me – that's all I know. I love him and I'll never leave him."

Peter gave a big resigned sigh and kissed his mum. "Okay, okay, Mum – have it your own way."

Sally then went on, "You know my only regret will be not seeing you get married and having children – that I would have loved."

Peter thought that would be a good time to start talking about Fiona. He told Sally he thought he had at long last, found the one, and after this trip would try and find out more about her and start seeing her, if she would have him. Sally was delighted at this news and wanted to know all about Fiona.

"There's not much to tell really, Mum, I hardly know her, but from what I do know she is everything you would want in a daughter-in-law: beautiful, intelligent; likes the sort of things I like, thinks like I do – she's just right for me, Mum."

Sally put her arms around him and hugged him to her saying, "I'm so glad, son, I really am."

Peter didn't want to stir up old, sad memories but before he left, he felt he had to tell his mother about Cook. Sally had suffered the loss of Timmy as much as Peter had, and shared his grief, and Peter wanted to tell his mum of his plan to avenge Timmy in some way. Sally was appalled at what Peter now started telling her. She had been so angry and grief stricken at the time of Timmy's murder, but what was most frustrating was the inability to do anything about it. The perpetrators were never caught. Peter made sure she understood, Cook had nothing to do with Timmy, as far as he knew, but it was men like Cook who had committed the murder. Sally asked him if he looked like a murderer. Peter gave a hollow laugh, and said, "Who looks like a murderer? They could be anybody, the man next door, the postman, the plumber, anyone – they don't have 'murderer' tattooed on their forehead. He looks like a little weasel actually; thin, (which is unusual for a cook), spotty, weedy, and bright red greasy hair."

"Yuk! Do you think this Cook is really as bad as you say, Peter, or is he having you on?"

"Honest, Mum, he's worse, I haven't told you the gory details of what he told me they do to kids. It's plain evil and I'm going to do my best to get them stopped. I've got enough information now to put some of them at least out of the way. When I get back to Australia I'm going straight to the police."

Sally had a strange look on her face now – she was thinking hard and although was sad to be saying goodbye to Peter she was forming a plan in her mind – and was preoccupied. She made Peter again, and again, promise not to tell anyone of her current survival – not even Fiona. She said she would stay hidden, unless she was sure it was Peter, if he could get away, and even then, only if he was alone. He made a solemn promise not to reveal her survival and they said some very tearful goodbyes, but Peter said if he could come back in two days' time he would. He had already told her that tomorrow would be Cook's turn to visit the island. He had also warned her that Cook knew of the original log and would more than likely come looking for Sally, as he wasn't part of the surveying crew and therefore had all day to look for her.

When Peter arrived back at the launch Fiona was the first to ask, "Well how was it? Did you find your mum, is she still alive?"

Peter really didn't want to lie to Fiona and at first just shook his head. Fiona continued her questioning. "Well did you see any sign of her at all?"

He was sorry to be lying to her, but had to deny seeing his mother. He said he had found the wreck and had spent all day cleaning it up and tidying her garden, which was still producing food. He was sure she wasn't around, but just in case he had left all the gifts they had sent for her in the boat and had put everything away – nice and tidy the way she would have wanted it. He said he had left the chicks to fend for themselves but had put a sort of open box up for them to shelter in. He told her there was plenty of food around and the chick food they had brought with them he had put into a sort of hopper arrangement which would allow them to eat just a little at a time, and hopefully last until they could fend for themselves, eating grubs and greenery.

Back on the yacht once more it was work, work, work. Lots to be done, Cook only had the cooking to do, but Peter was responsible for the bathrooms, cleaning the cabins, changing sheets, as well as preparing vegetables and cleaning all the pots and pans and clearing away after each meal. Cook asked Peter in passing did he find his mum. Peter replied, "negative" and didn't talk much as they cleaned up at the end of the day. Cook assumed Peter was upset at not finding his mother and respected Peter's reticence to speak about it.

CHAPTER 18

TIMMY'S REVENGE

The next day Chip took the surveying party and Cook from the yacht to the beach in the launch. As the surveyors took off up the beach and over the headland Chip set up the awning, to keep out of the sun. He was under instructions from Skipper not to leave the launch, no matter what. He, like everyone had a packed individual lunch and stowed it away out of the sun. Cook had boiled a silverside the previous day and then carved it for sandwiches that morning. Each person in the party was also given two small bottles of water and a piece of fruit. Chip settled himself down with his book and thought he might take a swim a bit later on; he meant to enjoy his day off. Peter was left with a list of work which needed to be done but even so he knew he wouldn't be too busy. He had been able to do a little work on the computer, adjusting some designs and correcting some inadequacies in structural measurements. Lunch was a breeze for just himself and Skipper, the silverside was all gone but there was prosciutto ham, pickled olives and a nice gooey Camembert cheese. He decided dinner would be made easier if he could prepare simple food in advance as he was, for once responsible for the evening meal as Cook would have been on the island all day. Peter was a reasonable cook himself at home, but had never cooked for so many people before – but, he told himself, eight is not out of the way at all, just multiply everything you ordinarily would do by four and bingo, how hard can it be? He knew how to cook lasagne and decided that would be a decent meal with a nice green salad. The fresh vegetables bought in Manila had just lasted and would not last another day. As of tomorrow it would be frozen or tinned vegetables.

Cook was grateful for a day off and decided he would go exploring. He was curious to see where Peter's mother had been living and knew it would be on the opposite side to where the surveyors had gone. They were over the headland and Cook, leaving Chip reading a book in the launch, took off in the opposite direction – heading towards Sally, who was hiding way up on the hill, watching everything.

Once around the headland Cook became very hot with the unaccustomed climbing and decided he could do with a swim before going inland to look for the wreck. Sally watched as he took off all his clothes and laid them on the beach at high water mark. She knew it was him alright, he had flaming red hair, and he wasn't part of the surveying team. He was small, thin, and as Peter had observed, spotty – especially down his back. No one else was around and she had come prepared. She had passed a sleepless night planning her revenge for Timmy. It wasn't that she was a murderer by inclination, just that she had been so upset, so incredibly angry and so impotent to do anything about Timmy's murder, that at long last here was her chance to avenge the child and any other child who might have been a victim of this man and his cohorts – also it would be one paedophile off the planet and unable to bring misery and suffering to any other family. She knew murder was not the answer to these kinds of problems, but in her case she felt vindicated and satisfied that at long last she would be able to do something concrete to stop at least one person from carrying out any more abuse. "No," she said to herself, "I'm not a murderer – this is no different to a crime of passion. I don't care if it's right or wrong I'm going to do it, and, if by any chance I get caught and prosecuted,… well … I'm an old woman, … I've had a good life, so if I can rid the world of a pest, an evil like this man – well I wouldn't object to going to jail for my crime. I'm doing the world a favour really." So she was settled in her mind and determined to carry out her own version of justice. When he was in the water, splashing around, having a good swim, she ran down the beach, picked up his clothes and ran to the rocks. When she got there she started to yell at him and wave his shirt and shorts in the air for him to see. There was a gap in the rocks, and it was really the only one gap that was wide enough for him to run through. He looked up at the yelling and realised someone had taken his clothes. He splashed around trying to get out of the waves and eventually, after falling over twice, ran up the beach and towards the gap in the rocks. He was modestly holding his hands in front of his "bits" trying to hide his genitalia, but that made running properly, comical and almost impossible. Sally was waiting for him as he ran through the gap. He couldn't see her, but she was still yelling, he couldn't tell what it was she was yelling, he only knew she had his clothes and he had to get them. As he came through the gap she was behind a big rock and she let him have it, right between the eyes, as they say. She hit him full in the face with the hammer, with all the force she could muster. Sally was not very big, but her fury, hatred, and anger gave her strength she didn't know she possessed. Cook went down, probably dead straight away, but just to make sure she hit him again, this time on the back of the head. The hole that the hammer made assured her he was well and truly dead. He bled into the sand and she sat down and cried – for

Timmy. She kept saying quietly to him, "That's for Timmy, that's for Timmy." There was no remorse, only sadness.

"Okay," Sally said to herself after quite a while, "keep calm – what to do next?"

She went back to the boat and got the small fold-up spade that was in the storeroom. Once armed with the spade she went back to Cook and started to dig a hole next to the body. She knew she had hours and hours before anyone would come looking for him so there was no rush. He was not very much bigger than she was herself, so it was quite easy, once the hole was about three feet deep and five foot long, she started to roll him into it. The blood stained sand was also turfed into the hole and before she covered it all up she piled large rocks on top of the body. When she had covered the lot with sand and a bit of seaweed nothing unusual could be seen. She decided that once the yacht had left the island she would dig him up again and send him out to sea for the sharks to deal with. After all her exertions she calmly took all his clothing except his shoes and socks, and put them about 500 metres, much further up the beach, well away from the rocks, and above the high water line. She had obliterated his footprints from his bathing spot by means of a large branch of a tree and obliterated all her own footprints as she retreated back to where he had come down from the grassy headland and on to the beach. She had taken also her hammer and spade up on to the grass so that she could retrieve them later without leaving footprints. She knew he had walked across the beach in his sandshoes, and so she stuffed his socks into his shoes and put them on herself. She then walked across the beach to where his clothes were. She took off his shoes, pulled the socks out, and walked barefoot down to the water. With each step she moved her feet slightly forward so that anyone smart enough to check the footprints wouldn't be able to say if the prints were his or not. Checking that there were no telltale strange footprints, and that all was in order and nothing missed, she entered the water and swam across to the end of that beach to where she could get out of the water and on to the smooth rocks there, and with a bit of an effort, jump on to seaweed and then on to the grassy high water mark, pick up the hammer and spade, and back home to the wreck. The idea was sound but unfortunately the seaweed was wet and very slippery, and she was not as nimble as she used to be. Sally misjudged the jump and her foot slipped from under her. She let out an involuntary scream as her ankle buckled under her weight and she went down in a heap of soggy seaweed gasping for breath. She grabbed at her ankle and cursed at her own stupidity. She realised at once that she hadn't actually broken any bones, only sprained her ankle, still it was extremely painful. Now she crawled out of the seaweed mess and gradually proceeded to hobble back to the boat. Once back home she got out the first aid box and managed to strap up her ankle with two rolls of bandage, which she then soaked in cold water. This was something of a relief but it was still quite painful. She was worried now that she may have left some footprints or evidence of her presence and so forced herself to go back a little way and check out her approach to the boat. She had a good look around the boat and eliminated, as best she could the few traces of her footprints. She knew they would come looking for Cook, even though it was evident that he had entered the water and not come out. Provided Peter kept his promise and didn't tell anyone that she was alive – well it was a perfect murder. She told Joe… "Just what the bastard deserved – and yes I know I'm a lady and I shouldn't swear… but I'm Australian so it's alright."

Sally's worry now was that if Peter managed to return to her boat he would see her strapped ankle and would, she knew start to berate her about the sensibility of her being on the island alone, without any help, and again try and persuade her to return to civilisation. She didn't want him to see her with a bandaged ankle and worried about it as she lay on her bed with her ankle elevated on a pillow. After about an hour she was too curious to know how Cook's disappearance was being taken and so, in some pain, she forced herself to hobble away from her "home" and placed herself up on the headland, hidden is some low scrub to watch the drama unfold.

CHAPTER 19

COOK'S DISAPPEARANCE

Cook had been due to return to the launch at 4.30 p.m. but by 5.00 hadn't showed. Alan was getting a little angry and kept looking at his watch. By five past the hour there was still no sign of Cook. The guys were talking amongst themselves, unconcerned, whilst Alan and Fiona went looking for Cook.

Chip told them the direction Cook had taken and the two went across the beach and over headland looking for Cook and calling his name. Alan was getting angry and complaining to Fiona. "Where the bloody hell is the little swine? He was told to be back by 4.30 we have to get back and get our reports written up, and I'm getting hungry."

Sally was hidden up on the headland, away from the beach but high enough to see everything that was going on. Her ankle was throbbing but she was too interested in seeing everything and didn't want to miss the opportunity of getting a good look at Fiona. "If this is the woman who has captured my son's heart I want to have a good look at her," she said quietly to herself. She saw that Fiona was of medium build with striking dark brown hair pulled back into a pony tail. She had a good figure, without being too skinny. From the look of concern on her face, she was obviously a caring person who was worried about a fellow passenger. She had a nice face too, quite beautiful with big brown eyes. "Yes, I quite like the look of you, young lady. I think you'll do very nicely for my Peter."

The two walked over the headland and on to Peaceful Cove. They walked within five metres of where Cook's body was buried, but they saw nothing. A silly notion crossed Sally's mind, she wanted to shout out, "Don't bother calling him, he can't hear you!" She didn't of course but had a little giggle to herself. She wasn't feeling at all sorry about killing Cook – it was revenge for Timmy and that felt quite good; cathartic actually. Alan and Fiona walked across the beach calling Cook's name, until they came to his clothes at the high water mark. Both were shocked and looked out to sea and running into the shallows calling his name again and again. They decided to go back to the launch where they relayed the news that they couldn't find Cook, only his clothes. Everyone was in shock and Sally saw the two return to the beach whilst the launch came around the cove and trolled across Peaceful Bay over and over again. Everyone was shouting now Cook's name and Sally just lay hidden on a grassy knoll and watched the drama. Eventually the group gave up the search and motored back to the yacht, where Skipper and Peter were waiting impatiently.

"What the hell have you all been doing?" demanded Skipper. "I expected you back over an hour ago."

Alan picked up Cook's clothes to show Skipper, and then without explaining climbed on to the yacht. Skipper quickly realised the implications of the clothes without the man. "What the hell happened over there?" demanded Skipper.

"We don't know, Cook was on his own all day, on the next cove," explained Alan. "When we went looking for him all we found were his clothes."

"Oh Jesus Christ! What are we supposed to do now?" exclaimed Skipper.

Alan shrugged his shoulders, Fiona burst into tears and Robert, one of the surveyors put his arm around her to comfort her. At that point Peter came up from the galley to find out why the party was so late. He had lasagne in the oven and it was drying out. He was pretty pleased with himself, as lasagne was his favourite meal and he knew how to make it well. With Cook being off all day Peter had been assigned temporary chef and he had enjoyed the time alone in the galley. He first noticed Robert with his arm around Fiona, and Fiona in tears.

Jealousy raged through his blood – but then he realised something must be really, really wrong – everyone was looking drawn and stressed. "What the hell's happened?" he asked.

Skipper was the first to speak. "They've lost Cook!"

Peter turned to stare at Alan. "What does he mean, lost him? Did you leave him on a bus or something?"

Alan, looking shocked, tried to explain. "It's not funny. Cook went to the next bay on his own and when he didn't turn up on the beach to come back here – well, we went looking for him of course, and all we found were his clothes, and that's it – there's nothing more to tell."

Peter sat down on one of the hatch heads and put his head down. All he could say was, "Oh my God!"

Robert released Fiona and went over to Skipper and asked simply, "Well what do we do now? Do we keep looking for him? It's nearly dark now – but shouldn't we look anyway?"

Alan took over the conversation and declared, "No it's too dark now but we'll hang around for a couple of days and try and see if we can find his body. It's obvious he went into the water – and he must have got into difficulties. If we can recover his body we shall have to take it back for his family and whoever you have to deal with in these sorts of cases."

With that declaration they all went below deck and into the dining area for a very sombre meal. Peter wanted admiration for his lasagne, but no one took any real notice of it, which disappointed him, but it was a bit overcooked. They did eat it though, so he was satisfied in his own mind that it must have been alright. After the meal Skipper and Alan had a good talk and then called in Peter from the galley to talk to him. They explained that with Cook gone Peter would have to take over the duties of chef and still do the kitchen-hand work. They wanted to know if Peter could handle all that. Peter thought about it for a moment and then declared that he could do the work but he would change things a little, if he could, and was it alright if he requested the team help out on the journey home with housekeeping and looking after themselves more. They agreed that the team should be asked and Alan called all the team together in the dining area for a meeting.

Peter stood in the centre of the small room and addressed the group. "Look, guys, this is a terrible situation and I will do my best to cook decent meals for you all, but I'd like to change things a bit to make it easier. If it's alright with you all I'd like to put the food on the second small table and that way you could have your meals, 'buffet style' – just helping yourselves to what is put out. You could also bring your dirty dishes into the galley for me and clear the table. That will cut down the work for me in the kitchen. Secondly, you could all help by keeping your cabins clean yourselves and your bathrooms too. The towels can be taken back to your cabin, hung up and reused, you really don't need a fresh towel every time you shower." They all agreed and after the meeting, everyone retired to their cabins, quiet and subdued.

Peter sat on the bottom bunk and thought seriously now about what had transpired. He wondered if his mother had anything to do with Cook's disappearance. "No," he told himself, "Mum is just a little old lady, she couldn't have done anything to Cook – or could she?" He smiled to himself. "Well, what if she did? It would only be what he deserved," he reasoned, – but the disappearance might now change his objectives – how to bring the other paedophiles to justice.

CHAPTER 20

BACK ON DU PONT ISLAND

After limping around gingerly Sally brought the chicks to the wreck and settled them in the sink for the night, before going to bed. She had no conscience about the murder she had committed; she talked it over with Joe and then tried to get some sleep, but the throbbing from her ankle and her worry about Peter's reaction to her bandaged foot meant sleep evaded her for the most part of the night. The chicks were doing well and the sink seemed a good place for their overnight safety. Any mess they made could be flushed down the drain, to the outside.

The next day Sally's ankle was not quite so painful, and she managed to hobble up on to the headland to see what would eventuate following the disappearance of Cook. She limped slowly to her observation post and watched the yacht and the launch with some interest. No one seemed to bother about looking on land for Cook, they were concentrating on searching in the water for his body. Up and down they trolled, but to no avail. It was useless, they all knew, but realised they would have to report to Police and Water Authorities and they would have to show and report that they had made a good effort to find the missing man. For two days the launch trolled up and down, it went around the headland to the next cove and then around the other headland, never finding anything of course. After the two days Sally was in two minds about the situation, firstly she was sad and disappointed that she hadn't seen Peter again, but on the other hand was sort of glad that Peter hadn't returned to see her bandaged foot and try and persuade her to return to the real world. She was however happy to see the launch stowed away and the yacht start to move out of the bay. She needed to deal with Cook's body and wanted to get on with the grisly job as soon as she could. She sat on the headland and watched the yacht slowly move towards the horizon. She was reflective on the fact that she hadn't been able to see Peter again, but she had seen him the once and that was sufficient. She waited until the yacht was over the horizon and eventually she hobbled down over the rocks to the beach. She didn't want to run the risk of anyone on the yacht having a powerful telescope and being able to see what she was about to do.

The tide was in and it was an easy job to remove the stones that covered the body. The water was knee deep and after digging for five minutes only, Sally uncovered the body. Cook was naked and a pathetic sight, skinny, white, every bit of his body flaccid and repulsive. Sally rolled him out of the shallow grave and floated him across the water to the clear beach. She remembered once reading a murder mystery where the pathologist declared that the victim had been killed before being put into a bath. He knew this because there was no water in his lungs. So, with this in mind Sally made sure Cook's head was underwater and then pressed down hard on his puny chest. Bubbles came out of his mouth and nose and she was satisfied that if the body should happen to be found then there would be water in his lungs and he would be declared, dead by drowning – the wounds on his head could have been made by him crashing into rocks. That was her reasoning – just in case the body might be washed up on some other island, or if some boat picked it up. She was hoping the sharks would deal with him but realised that there was a very slight chance that the body might drift somewhere and not get eaten by sharks at all. A silly thought crossed her mind, that any self –respecting, decent shark would not want to eat a disgusting, distasteful evil human like Cook. She rolled the body through the shallows and out to as far as she could stand. The tide was on the turn but still it kept bringing the body back to the beach. Each time Sally pushed it back into the surf, cursing and swearing, until eventually it stayed in the deeper water. She watched, fascinated as the body drifted deeper and deeper – the water was crystal clear so it was quite a while before she could see it no more.

Sometime later she was up on the headland and could see distinctly through the clear waters three large sharks, just lazing along, as sharks usually do. She smiled to herself. It felt like Christmas to Sally. She hadn't unpacked all the things Peter had brought for her and now she had time to herself and she could enjoy looking through the gifts, just like opening her Christmas stocking when she was a child. The shoes Peter had brought fitted very well and the books she arranged in the bedroom, on a sloping shelf, but where she could get them quite easily. The kitchen lighter and matches were stowed in a drawer in the galley and the packets of seeds put carefully in another drawer to keep them dry. There were two spare toothbrushes and three tubes of toothpaste along with two jars of really good face cream. The three packets of painkillers were a timely good idea, she thought, as she remembered the pain when she hurt her foot before, and now needed some pain relief once again. She took two pills with some water and was grateful for Peter's forward thinking and kind consideration. The reading glasses were wonderful; she could now dispense with the magnifying glass and enjoy her reading in comfort. The family photographs were put up on the walls around the interior of the cabin and bedroom. She managed to tuck them under

141

various bits of wall cladding that had come adrift. She was happy and content and limped out to tend her garden and bring in some vegetables for dinner that evening. She also brought some outer leaves of the vegetables for the chicks to scratch into. There was also half a coconut with the soft flesh still intact. She gave this to the chicks who had a good peck at the flesh but didn't eat much, still they were healthy and thriving.

Sally told Joe all was well, her ankle was not so painful now and she fancied some mussels for dinner. She took a bowl to collect the mussels and saw through the crystal clear waters the three large sharks she'd seen before, and she smiled again to herself.

CHAPTER 21

THE RETURN TRIP

Skipper and Alan decided not to call in to Manila on the way home, as they would rather face the police and authorities in Australia to report the missing man. They were not sure of the laws in the Philippines but felt much more comfortable about reporting it to the authorities in Brisbane. After two days wasted looking for Cook, Alan was eager to get back to his company and sign off on this particular job. Fiona was working on a contract with the company, and her contract expired on her return to Australia. She didn't think her contract would be renewed either as the company had been winding back operations for a few months previous to this trip. She wasn't particularly worried as there was a company back in Perth whom she knew would be looking for a replacement for an old friend of Fiona's, Beth Downing, whom Fiona knew was pregnant and not wanting to continue working after the baby was born. The girls had been friends since university and had kept in touch ever since. Beth wanted to be a "stay at home" mum, so Fiona was pretty sure that opening would be available in a month or so. Peter was coping quite well with the cooperation of all the crew and Skipper had come in to Peter's cabin to collect Cook's meagre belongings, ready to parcel them up to send to the family.

After dinner on the third night out Peter had finished clearing all the dishes away and was free to go on deck to enjoy a very pleasant full moon and reasonably calm sea. Fiona and Robert were in the middle of a discussion as Peter approached them. Fiona addressed him and invited his opinion on the subject of frozen fruit and vegetables as opposed to fresh ones. Robert was convinced that frozen food was better as it was snap frozen as soon as it was picked. Fiona on the other hand maintained that nothing could be better than fresh vegetables and fruit. Peter jumped into the argument with the thought that; whilst he thought fresh fruit and vegetables were better, when one buys them from the market or supermarket you very rarely get actual, real fresh goods. Apples and pears can be a year old, having been in cold storage and vegetables can be days old by the time they get to market and then sit on the shelves of shops for days before they are sold. They all agreed on that point and eventually after some good banter Robert excused himself as he said he was heading off to bed. Peter's closing call to him was, "Cheerio, Robert – and don't forget frozen strawberries just go to mush!"

They all laughed and Fiona and Peter were alone, at last. There was no hiding the mutual attraction and for a while they both just leant on the guard rail and gazed out to sea and to the moon. Peter broke the silence first and pointed to the low sitting moon and remembered seeing a similar sight in Broome. "Look at that," he said as he pointed to the reflection of the moon on the water, "it looks a bit like a staircase with the moon's reflection on the waves; that happens up in Broome in WA."

"Yes, it's beautiful," said Fiona. "I've heard about that phenomena in WA but I've never been to Broome, it's on my bucket list."

"Well I'd like to take you there some time and show it to you," said Peter, taking a step closer to her.

"You're taking a bit for granted aren't you, young man?" she said smiling, but she didn't move away from him.

"Have you been up to the Kimberley's, or to Karijini or anywhere up north?" he asked. "It's a long way to go from Perth but it's worth it, the scenery is spectacular and the wide open spaces are mind blowing."

She laughed at his enthusiasm and told him she had never been further north in WA than Geraldton. As they chatted about Peter's home town he questioned her about her family in Perth. Fiona was an only child, her parents were quite elderly, having conceived her later in life than was normal. Her mother had been forty-one when Fiona was born. She then told him about the contract that she had with Global Geophysics and her expectation of being offered the job in Perth, to replace Beth, her good friend. This was unexpected good news for Peter and he suggested they might just meet up once this horrible business with Cook was completed and they were back home again. She laughed at him again gently, he was quite shy really and a gentleman, not pushy at all, but she knew what she wanted – and what she wanted was – him.

Chemistry is chemistry and fate cannot be denied. The two of them were feeling the same and words were not really necessary now. Feeling quite daring Peter put his arm around Fiona and was pleased to feel her warm body respond to the gentle caress. She moved closer to him and he leaned in to smell the intoxicating aroma of her hair. He was more or less behind her, but he leant in and softly nuzzled her neck, hardly touching her at all. She gave a slight shiver as her nerves were tingling and she turned round to meet him face to face. Both his hands came up then to tilt her face upwards to meet his waiting lips. Peter had kissed many girls before, but this time he wanted it to really mean something, she was what he had been waiting for and he didn't want to ruin it by rushing her, or being too brutish. He let his tongue slide across her lips, first the upper lip and then the lower lip, she responded by gently nibbling his lower lip and by this time they both knew where the situation was heading. Anticipation is part of the pleasure and Peter took his time. He held Fiona close and with one arm around her shoulder, the other arm started to explore her back with a short stroking motion, as one would with a kitten. She put her arms up and around his neck, leaning in to him and she knew he could feel the swell of her breasts. His free arm then came around her ribs and down to her hip, from there he travelled slowly, oh, so slowly up to caress the curve of her breast. She moaned and they kissed again, and again. After a while Fiona pulled away from him and laughingly said, "I need to come up for air – listen, Pete, you have a little cabin all to yourself and I have a much larger cabin all to myself as well. It's a pity to waste space."

He didn't give a reply, he just held her hand and guided her down the steps and towards the crew cabin quarters.

Once in the privacy of Fiona's cabin, clothes became an encumbrance and she started to unbutton her blouse. He stopped her and whispered, "No, let me do it." And so she stood at the foot of her bed and he slowly undressed her down to her underwear. At that point she stopped him and did the same for him. His urgent need was hidden from her view by his underwear, but it was evidence of his desire and she slowly peeled off his underpants. She coyly looked up to him and all she could say was, "Wow." He chuckled and took his attention back to her underwear. He ran his index finger under her bra strap on one side and then on the other, moving up and down and with each movement moved the strap further outwards and over her shoulder. He tormented her by kissing her breasts, through the thin material and when her nipples stood erect he nibbled them through the material. Her legs were trembling and she knew she was being tormented and she laughed and called him some rude names – "Oh, you swine, just get on with it, you're killing me."

Peter gently laid her down on the bed and let his hands do magical things to her nervous system, she was tingling all over and wanted him to go on exploring; further – to other places which were crying out for attention. He was in no rush and whilst his one hand ministered to her breasts his mouth and tongue started a journey of exploration. He was breathing close to her ear and the warmth of his breath made her wince with the tickling sensation. After each ear was dealt with he moved to her mouth and let his tongue do his talking. He was a master of eloquent oration. Oh, she was loving this. The gentle swaying motion of the boat and this gorgeous man doing wonderful things to her body – she was in heaven. "Please never let it stop," she said to herself. It didn't stop; Peter was in heaven too. He knew he had fallen in love with this woman and he meant to make her his own. He was intent on making this a night to remember and took his time, not wanting to rush and not wanting to spoil the ambience of their first night of making love. He let his mouth now taunt her beautiful breasts, first one, then the other, at the same time his hand reached across her tummy and started to move in soft undulations round and round. With each rotation his hand got firmer and firmer until he was pressing down on to the top of her vagina, still on the outside of her tummy, not too hard, but firm. With her breasts being massaged as well as her tummy Fiona was getting desperate, she wanted him inside her, but he wasn't going to give her that pleasure, not yet. Again his hand moved and now he pulled down her panties, one side at a time. She wriggled to allow him to get them below her knees and she did the rest herself. Then his hand travelled from her knees caressing her thighs.

Fiona was not thinking, not doing anything, her body was one whole sensation, she couldn't separate one part of her body from the other. Each tactile sensation coalesced into a whole. She was floating, she wasn't aware of what Peter was actually doing, she only drowned in the pleasure of it all. Eventually satiated, they both fell into a deep sleep, with arms and legs entangled around each other. Peter was up early, he had breakfast to prepare. When Fiona came into the dining area Robert looked up with a sly smile and asked, "Good morning, – and how are you this morning, and how are you two getting on then?"

"Wouldn't you like to know," she retorted. She and Robert were good friends and she ruffled his hair, knowing that he knew, and therefore, probably they would all know, just what was going on. For the rest of the trip home, after the evening meal, everyone left Peter and Fiona alone. They walked the deck and talked of everything, finding out about each other and making plans for the future. Peter wanted Fiona to return to Perth and live with him in his apartment. His job as an architect paid well and he could support Fiona until she took over from Beth, when she leaves her employment to have the baby. Or even if Fiona didn't get that job, his apartment was a good size, even though only one bedroom and it was right in the centre of town. Fiona was looking forward to seeing her parents and introducing them to Peter. She'd had boyfriends before, but she knew Peter was special and hoped her parents liked him, and why wouldn't they? she reasoned. He's everything a girl could want.

CHAPTER 22

THE INVESTIGATION

As they were approaching Brisbane Skipper called them all together and gave them a briefing. He wanted to be sure they were all confident with their reports to the police about Cook's disappearance. He was worried actually for Chip. On the day of the disappearance the surveyors had all been away from the beach and stayed together, but Chip was left in charge of the launch with strict instructions not to leave the launch. Skipper was absolutely sure Chip was telling the truth, he trusted him and believed him when he said that he had never left the launch, and did not go with Cook around the headland. Chip told him he had put up the small awning to keep out the sun and had settled himself down with a good book. He admitted that he'd actually paddled in the shallows by the side of the launch and in the afternoon had stripped off and gone in for a short swim, also by the side of the launch, but he swore he had never left the launch. Skipper believed him and just hoped the police would believe him too.

When they were within radio contact with the shore Skipper informed the Harbour Master of the tragedy. When the yacht berthed the next day there was a posse of Police,

Customs, Immigration, Passport and Border Control people waiting for them. They had to pass through Passport, Customs and Immigration officials first, but then the whole crew were escorted to the Police Officer's area within the Immigration Department.

Each person on board the yacht was extensively interviewed and statements were taken from them all. It took two days and the police were extremely cooperative and sympathetic to their loss. They were told they could go their separate ways but none were to leave Australia until the Coroner had brought down his findings, which could take a month or so. Alan and his team had to report back to their office and further reports had to be filed as well as their professional, surveying reports. Peter was told he could go home, but to stay in contact with the Brisbane Police, via the Perth Police as Cook was from Perth. Cook's belongings would be returned to his family in due course. Peter was not to be entrusted with Cook's belongings, but he very much wanted to get his hands on the computer and was not sure how to go about it without implicating himself. He wasn't feeling guilty at all, as, in truth, he'd had nothing to do with Cook's disappearance, nevertheless he didn't want any association with Cook's paedophilia and the history of Peter's loss of Timmy. In the end he decided it would be better if he came clean and told the police about his knowledge of Cook's paedophilia and Peter's efforts at getting information which he had hoped might lead to a conviction and prosecution of the whole group of paedophiles. Peter asked Chief Inspector Lloyd if he could have a few words with him as he had more to say on the matter, even though it seemed all the interviews were over. This worried the rest of the crew who had no idea as to what had been going on. Chief Inspector Lloyd sat back in his chair with an enigmatic smile on his face. Peter told him everything, how he had wheedled the information out of Cook, and why. "It's a good job you came to me of your own accord," admonished the inspector. "We already had all the information from Cook's computer, and you were mentioned in his emails to members of his group. You were going to be put under surveillance. As it is, you have a motive for murder; we were about to start an enquiry into your background and activities."

"Look, Inspector, I realise it seems as if I had a motive for vengeance, but I was on the yacht all day when Cook went missing. I was kept busy with my duties and Skipper was on the yacht too. I couldn't have murdered Cook, there was no opportunity."

The inspector leaned forward and said, "Well, it was very opportune for you if he just did a Harold Holt, went for a swim and didn't return."

Peter didn't want to leave it at that – he wanted an enquiry into the group's activities back home in Perth.

"You don't have to worry about that," exclaimed the inspector. "The police in Perth have already been notified and I believe the paedophiles are being rounded up as we speak. We had to move fast before any of them got wind of Cook's disappearance and realised we had access to his computer and prosecutions would follow."

Fiona was particularly alarmed and slightly angry that Peter had not confided in her. He apologised to Fiona and to the rest of the group about not letting them in on his motives for his apparent friendship with Cook. After relating the story of Timmy to them, they said they understood and hoped that the police in Perth would prosecute and jail all those involved.

Peter stayed in Brisbane only a few days, he wanted to get back to his apartment and relieve Luke of his housesitting duties. He also couldn't wait to tell Luke all about Cook – but he remembered he couldn't tell Luke about his mother, he couldn't and wouldn't break that promise.

After saying his goodbyes to Fiona he caught the Qantas flight home. As Fiona expected, her contract was not extended and she as well as Robert were paid off, and now unemployed. She stayed for a further month selling her house in Coorparoo on the outskirts of Brisbane, and then flew to Perth to be with her parents and Peter.

CHAPTER 23

GOING HOME

Luke met Peter's flight and already knew the story about Cook as it had been in all the papers, especially the local papers in Perth. There was a reporter there also to meet the plane and started firing questions at Peter as the two men made their way to the airport parking lot. Peter had no idea how they knew who he was or that he was on that particular flight, he just held up his hand and kept repeating "no comment, no comment." The reporter was extremely annoying and wouldn't take no for an answer and kept up a barrage of questions until the pair drove off in Luke's car.

"Wow," Luke breathed out loudly, "a reporter, just for you – fame at last."

"Knock it off," laughed Peter. They drove out of the domestic terminal and headed for town. Luke wanted to know everything and kept asking questions until Peter stopped him and said, "Look, Luke, I'm knackered, can it wait until tomorrow?"

"No," Luke insisted. "Tell me everything. What was this Cook fellow like? Was he a nice chap – are you going to see his parents, apparently he was from Perth?"

"Well to answer one question at a time, if you insist. Yes, I'll be going to see his parents tomorrow, although I believe they have been notified. No, he wasn't a nice person he was a bloody paedophile."

Luke almost went through a red light. He stopped just in time and turned to look at Peter. "Are you sure? How do you know? Did he tell you? Did you tell the police?"

Peter looked weary and simply answered, "Yes, yes and yes. Look, I need a beer and then we can sit down and I'll tell you everything. I don't trust your driving – you're going to get us killed if you don't concentrate!"

Luke was quiet for a while and then, as he turned into Adelaide Terrace he remembered the girl. "Oh, how did things turn out with the girl? Did you get on alright with her, is she married with six children?"

Peter laughed and said, "That part of the trip was brilliant. I think this is the one Luke, you know – really the one I've been looking for all my life."

"Wow!" was all Luke could say at first. Then after a moment's pause, "Well, come on, mate – tell me everything – did the moon and the water and the sun setting get to you – did you tell her how you felt? You are seeing her again aren't you? She didn't brush you off did she? Does she feel the same way you feel?" On and on the questions came. Luke wanted to know it all. Luke also remembered then the reason Peter had gone on the trip in the first place, and asked, "Well, did you find your mother, there was nothing in the newspaper reports about that?"

Peter hated telling lies but he had promised his mother that he wouldn't divulge her survival and so he simply said, "How I wish." Peter hung his head down and Luke took this to be a sign that Peter didn't want to talk further on that subject, so he parked the car and they went up to Peter's apartment and broke open their first beer on the small balcony overlooking Perth City. It was the weekend so they arranged to meet next day for a jog around Langley Park. Every hundred metres or so they stopped for a breather, Peter was out of condition having done no exercise at all on the boat. Luke teased him about this telling Peter he was getting old and fat. At each stop Peter related the story of what had happened on the yacht, except the personal details with Fiona. They had coffee and breakfast at Luke's apartment and Peter continued with his story.

Luke was suspicious of the disappearance of Cook and asked, "You know, given the circumstances, if everyone on the boat knew about the cook, well it seems to me that you probably all could have colluded to kill off the man. It would have been a reasonable thing to do. Did you?"

Peter chuckled. "It would have been a good idea, actually, but, no, no one else knew what he was, only me, and, no, I didn't kill him – I should have, but I didn't."

After breakfast Peter went home to shower and change and then set out to visit Cook's parents.

The parents were a middle-aged ordinary, decent couple, living in an ordinary house, in Morley, looking like everyone else. Peter had a silly notion that the parents of a paedophile might just be as bad as their son had been. The father was a robust sixty-year-old, balding, a bit overweight, but in his bedroom slippers, shorts and tee shirt, he was a working class man, proud of his plumbing profession and his life's achievement in paying off his mortgage and having a house he could call his own. The mother was a thin weedy woman with greasy long hair, pulled back into a bun at the back of her neck. Peter could see where Cook had got his DNA from. She had a high pitched voice and a nervous twitch to the left side of her face. They invited Peter in and gave him a cup of tea and asked him all about the disappearance of their son. Peter related the events of that day and didn't think it prudent to mention their son's predilections. He tried to say something nice about their son, and decided to focus on his cooking.

He told the parents about the delicious meals he had prepared and about how all the staff had enjoyed his roasts. They were obviously proud of their son and were obviously distraught at losing him. The mother asked if Peter thought the sharks had got to him. Peter answered truthfully that he had not seen a shark near or around the island. He tried to assure them that it was highly unlikely that sharks were in that area. The mother was grateful for this information. They seemed to be genuine grieving parents and were grateful to Peter for explaining what had happened that day. He left with a guilty conscience as he thought that sooner or later they were going to find out about what their son had been getting up to, but Peter didn't feel it was his job to tell them that sort of thing, so he left them with a handshake and a promise he would attend the memorial service the parents were organising. The memorial service was a debacle as far as Peter was concerned. The father and various relatives stood up to give glowing eulogies, which sickened Peter who knew what the dead man was really like. He didn't say anything of course but felt something of a hypocrite just being there. He looked around the other mourners wondering if any of the men were part of the paedophilic group, but as he had told his mother, paedophiles obviously look just like everyone else – they don't have it tattooed on their foreheads.

Peter returned to work on Monday morning and Harry was sympathetic to Peter's story about not finding his mother, but everyone in the office wanted to know about the disappearance of Cook. Again he related the story without going into details about the evil activities of Cook and others in the city. Cook's disappearance had been in the newspapers and on the television but nowhere had it been mentioned about the paedophilia or the group. Fiona and Peter exchanged emails each day and phoned each evening. He couldn't wait to see her again and was pleased when she was able to tell him that she had sold her house in Brisbane, got rid of all her furniture, and was coming to Perth; home to her parents. He begged her not to return to her parents; see them yes, but he pleaded with her to come and live with him. She wanted to, but was apprehensive as she said, "We really don't know each other – what if it doesn't work out?"

"Well," he explained, "if it doesn't then you can always go and live with your parents, but please, please give us a chance?"

She acceded and he met her at the airport and took her straight home to his apartment. It was two days later that they, as she put it, "Came up for air!" Their reunion was spectacular, they were in love and there was no denying it. Their lovemaking was different now. They knew each other (in the biblical sense) and there was no holding back – no need to keep quiet – no one in a cabin next door. They could walk around the apartment naked and unashamed and they showered together – delighted to be able to express their love, unfettered.

Fiona was keen to see her parents and it was agreed they would meet them that afternoon. Her parents lived in a beautiful old colonial style house at City Beach, just back from the main road overlooking the ocean. The furnishings were not new but were obviously of good quality and showed good taste and an ability to match walls and flooring with the appropriate colours for the furnishings. It was a very pleasant living room that the Campbell's invited Peter into. Fiona's parents had emigrated from Scotland many years earlier and spoke with a strong accent which Peter found hard to understand. Fiona laughed at his problem and translated for him when a particular word or phrase was lost on him. They were warm and welcoming to Peter whom they could tell was something special to Fiona. This wasn't just another boyfriend; he looked like a man of integrity, intelligence, caring. A man they felt they would like to become a permanent fixture in their daughter's life. Again there was a barrage of questions about Cook's disappearance, and Peter was glad for Fiona to relate what had happened, he was fed up with repeating the story. Howard and Gloria Campbell were saddened by the tragedy and were worried that the event had upset their daughter so much. They were interested in how the authorities had taken the news, and if there was to be a court case or an investigation into the disappearance. Peter and Fiona had to assure them that they didn't know what was to happen now, it was not their responsibility and it was out of their hands. They didn't discuss the paedophilia side of the story and Fiona was not too sure how much her parents knew about it, but the subject was avoided. Howard was an enthusiastic gardener who prided himself on his vegetable patch. He asked Peter if he would like to go outside and see the vegetables he was growing. Peter agreed and admired the crop of sweetcorn and asparagus and discussed pruning techniques. They collected some strawberries to take back into the house for afternoon tea and then Peter took the opportunity of asking an important question. He knew it was old-fashioned but he wanted to do things right and this was a good time to tell Fiona's father that he was serious about his daughter and could he have permission to marry her, if she would have him. Fiona's father was delighted and slapped Peter on the back saying, "Go for it, son, her mom and I can tell she's smitten with you – and we know you have a good job. Just look after her, won't you? She's very precious to us." Peter told him that of course he would look after her and that they were very much in love. However he hadn't proposed to her yet and so, would her father please not spoil things by mentioning this conversation? They returned to the house and once afternoon tea was over Peter and Fiona returned to the apartment in the city.

On the way home Fiona asked, "You were in the garden a long time with my dad, what were you two talking about for so long?"

"Oh, just this and that, you know; men's secret business!" answered Peter with a sly smile on his face. Fiona thought they may have been discussing the relationship that Peter and Fiona had and so decided to leave it at that, but Peter did finish the conversation with an acknowledgement that her parents were really interesting people who were obviously very fond of their daughter and that he liked them very much.

Alan and Robert both kept in touch with Fiona and after being in Perth one month Alan informed Fiona that the Coroner in Brisbane had brought down a verdict of Death by Misadventure following Cook's disappearance. This was a great relief to them all, especially as they all realised that Chip just might have been suspected of doing something, especially if he had known of the paedophilia – but of course he hadn't known and no one could say he had, not even the police.

It was a few weeks later that they heard on the news that a large paedophile group had been charged in Perth with various offences, from kidnapping, deprivation of liberty, immoral dealings with children and murder. Ten men were prosecuted and all of them given a jail sentence from ten years to thirty years. Peter was so glad and wished he could tell his mother, whom he thought about every day. He also wanted very much to tell Fiona that his mother was still alive, but he had promised and meant to keep the promise. Beth's baby was due any day and as she had expected, Fiona was offered Beth's job. She welcomed the new job which kept her in WA and as it was basically the same sort of work, that which they both had been trained to do, it was no hardship and life settled down to a familiar routine. Peter and Fiona visited her parents each Sunday for lunch and the occasional celebratory dinner if it was a special occasion. Life was good and Peter was desperately trying to think of a really good way and place to propose to Fiona. He had been to a good jeweller in the centre of Perth and bought a pink Argyle solitaire diamond ring which he hoped she would like. It had cost him over three month's pay but she was worth it and he was sure she would appreciate the delicate hue of the perfect stone. But where to do it, and how?

He remembered that when they were on the yacht she had told him that she had never been to Broome and had never seen the "moonlight staircase" on the water. He decided that would be the place and as the Easter holidays were coming up he told her, "Fiona, don't book any social obligations over Easter, I'm thinking we might get away for a few days – you know, a sort of mini holiday."

She was curious and wanted to know details, "Great, where are we going, for how long?"

Peter smiled an enigmatic smile and wouldn't tell her anything except, "I'm not saying, it's a surprise, but we'll be away for seven days. You should pack for sunny daytime wear, including bathers, and also some warm evening wear."

Intrigued she complied and on Good Friday he took her to the airport, from where they flew to Broome. When she realised where there were going she threw her arms around him and thanked him for the surprise mini holiday. It was just what she needed as work was getting monotonous and a break was very welcome. It was just a two and a half hour flight from Perth and they touched down to a tropical oasis of striking contrasts in culture and colour. The hotel at Cable Beach, Broome, was pure luxury and they were enjoying the food, the swimming, and all the facilities of the resort. The friendly barman at the pool explained to Fiona that Broome is affectionately known as the "pearl of the north" and that it's the home of the South Sea Pearls which are some of the largest and most coveted commercially harvested cultured pearls in the world.

"Broome" he explained, "is the most multicultural town due to the original discovery of the pearls in the eighteen hundreds when there was a mass migration from the Japanese, Filipino and Malay pearl divers. You can see that influence with the different restaurants we have here and all the different little shops and businesses."

Peter excused himself on the second afternoon and left Fiona by the pool whilst he went to discreetly organise the main event – his proposal. He asked the concierge about the famous "Moonlight Staircase" and when was the best time to see it. He had decided he wanted to do it on the beach, looking out at Roebuck Bay but he didn't want an audience, he wanted to do it quietly, privately, but still showing Fiona the spectacle. It's quite normal on Cable Beach to take the camel ride out at night to see the spectacle, and Peter told the hotel concierge that he wanted to take Fiona on a camel to see the staircase, but could they do it without any other guests in attendance? This was unusual because generally there would be a party of a dozen or so people taking the camel ride in procession, however he would see if he could arrange it. Of course they wouldn't be allowed out with a single camel unaccompanied. The next day the concierge took Peter aside and reported that he had managed to arrange for the camel operator to take them, and them alone, along the beach to Roebuck Bay the next night.

After dinner Peter took Fiona to the designated area and to her surprise there was a single camel, all saddled up and ready to go. She was somewhat surprised and Peter told her to, "Come on – get up there!" She laughed and obeyed; and was helped into the saddle in front of Peter who sat directly behind her. The camel keeper had a bridle on the head of the camel and he walked along, leading them off down the beach. It was a perfect night and Fiona was delighted to see the rising moon's reflection on the exposed mud flats, showing an illusion of the most perfect glistening white staircase, leading from the receding water to the moon. The camel driver had been primed and at the right spot stopped the little party and helped the two down. They stood at the water's edge whilst the camel driver took the camel further up the beach. At that point, when they were completely alone, Peter went down, as tradition dictates, on one knee and asked breathlessly, "Fiona Campbell, will you do me the greatest honour by agreeing to be my wife? I mean, will you marry me?"

"Yes to the first question, and yes to the second." She laughed. She then gasped with amazement as he presented her with the most beautiful ring she had ever seen. It was a simple setting, but the diamond sparkled in the strange moonlight and she was dazzled by its beauty and by the wonderful spectacle in front of her. He put the ring carefully on her finger and she threw her arms around him. They kissed and held each other tight for so long, and didn't break until they heard a polite cough behind them and realised the camel and its driver were waiting to bring them down to earth and return them to the resort.

The next day Peter took Fiona to see the ancient dinosaur footprints at Gantheaume Point and on the way back to the hotel stopped in to a small jeweller, where he allowed her to choose for herself a beautiful pearl as a moment of this trip. He told her again that Broome is the centre of the pearl industry and so he wanted her to have the best. She protested as the ring had taken her breath away and she didn't need any other souvenir. Peter insisted and eventually she gave in and chose a simple gold chain with a perfect single pearl dangling from the centre. Peter carefully placed it around her neck, and in front of the embarrassed Asian jeweller, kissed her neck and let the kiss travel up over her chin to her waiting lips. There was so much love, Peter just wanted to cry. They held each other so tight that night and swore to love each other for ever.

It was a holiday to remember and they did.

CHAPTER 24

THE WEDDING

Howard Campbell, Fiona's father, had always dreamed of walking his daughter down the aisle of St. George's Cathedral in Perth, with Scottish pipers heralding them in at the entrance, (he hailed from Shots, a small mining town between Glasgow and Edinburgh, and he loved the bagpipes), the choir singing and the enormous church organ playing Gounod's Ave Maria. Gloria Campbell wanted to see her daughter in a frothy meringue white crinoline dress with a crystal tiara and a long, long, tulle train carried by two little girls in lovely pink long dresses and a little boy in white satin bearing the ring on a white satin cushion and a little girl in front of it all scattering rose petals. They both wanted all the family and friends to be invited and for them to have the reception at the best hotel in Perth, with all the trimmings; champagne, cabaret, and a sumptuous meal, flowers everywhere and an orchestra playing throughout the meal. Howard fancied himself in a tuxedo and he thought he might even wear a top hat. When all this was proposed, Fiona and Peter had a good laugh. This was most definitely not what they wanted. They had discussed their plans endlessly with each other, and visited many parks and riverside picnic areas to see what would be the most suitable for their kind of simple wedding. Howard and Gloria were so disappointed, there was much argument but Fiona especially, was adamant, it was going to be "her" day and she would have it the way she wanted it – and that was that. What they planned eventually was for a simple ceremony in the Harold Boas Gardens with a celebrant officiating. The park was just on the edge of the city centre and was quiet and secluded with a tiny stream connecting two small lakes. There were three little waterfalls with many wild ducks leisurely swimming around and a few of the black swans that Perth is so famous for. It was an idyllic setting and Peter was all for a simple wedding too, so long as he could have Luke for his best man, and he didn't have to wear a formal suit (which he hated). Fiona was to wear a very simple pure silk white empire line dress which she reasoned, could be worn at some future date, if ever formal evening wear was necessary. There were to be two adult bridesmaids – friends of Fiona; Sharon and Marilyn. All three had been at school together and had stayed firm friends ever since, even though the last few years had been turbulent for one of them. Once they left school, Fiona went to the Institute of Technology to study Surveying, whilst Sharon went to Murdoch University to study Law. Marilyn wanted to be a nurse and so studied at the Devlon Institute for Technology. The three met up only occasionally during their Uni days, but once they had all graduated they had more time to catch up and see each other.

Sharon was the serious one of the three. She studied Law but wanted to go into politics, really to further women's rights. Mrs Pankhurst was her heroine and whilst at university she joined the Young Labour Movement. There were various rallies and meetings, about all sorts of socialist issues, but Sharon's interest was focussed on promoting women in the workplace, and equal rights and opportunities across the board. She knew "The Glass

Ceiling" was preventing so many women from advancing, and she wanted to change that; she wanted to change the world actually. When she heard of child brides, and women being forced into prostitution, it just made her blood boil.

Once she had graduated and been accepted to the Bar she then set out change the world. She didn't want to join a law firm to make her career in law, but she wanted to open a Women's Advocacy Retreat. She was lucky and was given a Government Grant which enabled her to get a property and set up her retreat but it wasn't enough to keep it running. She was almost on the brink of bankruptcy and having to close down when her parents were both killed in a car crash. Not only did she inherit their house, two cars and money in the bank, but her father had a generous life insurance policy which Sharon then inherited and altogether, this made her quite a wealthy woman. She used this money then to keep her retreat going and in doing so helped hundreds of women escape domestic violence. She had a staff of six women who ran the centre for her and she herself started on a political career, being a member of the local Labour Party and rose to a position of General Secretary. Fiona and Sharon had been worried for a few years about Marilyn. She always said she was fine, but they thought there was something wrong with Marilyn's marriage and her bully of a husband. He rarely came to the social get-togethers, and when he did he was nearly always, rude, abusive and put Marilyn down. They couldn't see why she stayed with him, but she always said she loved him and made excuses for him. Marilyn had worked in the geriatrics ward of the local hospital and loved looking after the old people there. Her favourite old lady, just before she had to leave, was Mrs Dobbs. When Marilyn asked her one day how she was, the old lady said that, as usual she was suffering from "The Mouse!" Marilyn laughed at that and asked her what she meant. Mrs Dobbs explained that it's an affliction that affects many old people. "You see," she explained, "you can wake up one morning with a pain in your ankle, nothing caused it, you were in bed all night, but there it is a pain. Now that pain may last a few seconds, a few minutes, a few hours or a few days. It is then always replaced with something else totally unrelated, say, a pain in your right thumb. Again, nothing has caused it, but there it is; a real pain. Again it might last one day, or a week, or more. When it goes it is always replaced with something else, maybe an ache in your knee, or your elbow – you see, dearie, it's the mouse running around – when he stops, where he stops, that's what hurts. There's no reason to it – it's just what happens." Marilyn sympathised and wondered if really, all the old folks suffered similarly.

Fiona and Peter's wedding was definitely not going to be a big affair, only close friends and family had been invited. There was to be a practise ceremony on the Friday before the main event and it was there that Luke met the bridesmaids.

Sharon was quite serious and talkative, she wore thick spectacles, was quite tall, "solid" not fat, but "solid heavy", and towered over the other girls. Luke recognised her from the television interviews he had seen and was a bit overawed by her domineering and quite famous presence. As General Secretary of the local Labour Party she was often on the news and being interviewed about one thing or another. She was set for a political career and was working towards that goal. Marilyn was quiet and subdued, almost shy. She had long blonde hair and freckles and dimples when she smiled. Luke was smitten – he fell for her from the moment he saw her, however his hopes were dashed when Fiona explained to him the Marilyn was married. His frustration showed and Peter asked him what was wrong. Luke just shrugged his shoulders and said, "Nothing… it's just that when I, at long last find the love of my life, I discover she's already married, it's not fair."

"Ah, yes," replied Peter, "that's a bummer, I take it, it's the lovely Marilyn you are referring to. Anyway put her out of your mind – she belongs to someone else, and he's big and mean!"

The wedding itself went off without a hitch. The day was warm and balmy without a cloud in the sky. The park was deserted apart from the wedding party and the garden smelled of freshly cut grass. Fiona and Peter had prepared their own wedding vows and Sarah, the Celebrant had told them that there were certain legal utterances that had to be made. Fiona's parents were a little miffed at the simple ceremony but put their objections behind them and were just glad to see their beloved daughter so happy. Instead of the choir and Ave Maria that Howard had wanted, Fiona had chosen The Hawaiian Wedding Song – sung by Elvis – to be played as they signed the official papers.

The reception was held at the Perth Yacht Club and a band had been hired to play for them after the meal had been served. Howard had prepared his speech and had done a photo presentation, on to a screen, showing Fiona as a baby and then pictures of her growing up. He was, as one might expect, a very proud father. As tradition directs, he requested everyone raise their glasses and drink a toast to the happy couple. Peter had prepared his speech thanking the bridesmaids, and toasts were given for them too. All went well until the dancing started. As is usual Peter and Fiona took their first dance together, alone on the dance floor. Everyone clapped and the newlyweds had a passionate embrace at the end of it. Everyone was having a lovely time and Luke, following tradition asked one of the bridesmaids to dance – he chose Marilyn of course. Most people got up to dance and Luke then noticed a very tall, stocky man approaching him. The man could have excused himself and danced with Marilyn, instead said quite loudly, "Get your filthy hands off my wife!"

"Wooooh, mate – no need for that – we're only dancing," replied Luke. With that Luke, quite sensibly retired back to the tables and sat down feeling very embarrassed. Everyone pretended not to hear anything as no one wanted to make a scene which would ruin Fiona's wedding.

The rest of the wedding went off as per normal and the couple were sent off on their honeymoon in a car festooned with balloons and shoes dangling from the back. After they had gone the party got underway and everyone had a great time dancing, and drinking. Marilyn and her husband, (Hans) had been dancing and after a while he left the dance floor and went to the bar to get them some drinks. He had been drinking the champagne that was provided but was also topping himself up with whiskeys between each champagne. Marilyn could see he'd had far too much to drink and was trying to persuade him to take her home. She pleaded with him and was up close whispering into his ear that they really must leave now. He pushed her away roughly, and she fell over backwards. He was shouting loudly ordering her to stop nagging him. One of the other guests stepped in and told him to be sensible, and just go home. Then Hans became even more aggressive and told the other guest to mind his own business. Two other guests now could see things were taking a nasty turn and stepped in. Hans was outnumbered but threw the first punch anyway. Three against one was never going to be in his favour, but he cursed and swore at everyone and threw wild punches at the three guests, making the most awful scene. Howard was so glad that Peter and Fiona had already left and that it wasn't ruining their day for them. The three bundled Hans out of the room and out to the car park. Marilyn wasn't hurt but was crying and the other bridesmaid, Sharon, was consoling her. Howard and Gloria tried to get everyone back into a party mood, but it was too late and the mood had left the wedding guests. Marilyn was taken home by Howard and Gloria and Hans was taken to the hospital with a broken jaw, lacerations and many bruises; he had been given a good beating but nothing too serious. Luke was drinking heavily too, and was in the men's room when all the fighting started. He came out and enquired what all the shouting was about. By this time the fight was out in the carpark and Luke had missed all the action. The party was over, people were leaving, he couldn't see Marilyn anywhere and sat at the bar until everyone had left. The barman was sympathetic as Luke poured out his drunken heart – how he was too late – the love of his life was already married and he didn't think he would ever, ever find anyone so beautiful as the lovely Marilyn. Eventually the bar staff called a taxi and bundled him into it. He wasn't so drunk he couldn't walk, but when he got into his apartment he just collapsed on to his bed, fully clothed and, being very inebriated, wept for his lost opportunity, and his lost chance at finding real love.

CHAPTER 25

FOUR YEARS LATER

Christopher Elliott was born just one year after Peter and Fiona were married. Peter had always had a shock of blond curls and Christopher had inherited this trait (just the same as Timmy had so many years earlier) and was born with blond hair, already starting to curl. Peter rented out the apartment in Perth and bought a large house in South Perth. There three-year-old Christopher could run wild around the large garden with a swing, and play set to keep him occupied. Fiona had gone back to work part time and Chris, as he was generally known, attended the local play school two days a week. Harry had made Peter a partner in the firm of architects and all was well in the Elliott household. Dubai was burgeoning at an incredible pace and there was so much work available that Harry was happy for Peter to take over some of the administrative and technical work as well as the design work. Peter and Fiona were happy and had hardly a care in the world. Luke was their best friend and was invited round for dinner at least once a week and he would drop in occasionally to discuss designs, or just generally to have a beer and relax with the couple. They all got on really well and occasionally Fiona would invite a girlfriend over for dinner making up a table of four. They tried many times to hook up Luke with a girl, or double date if they went out to a restaurant, but he could never quite get Marilyn out of his mind, and seemed to measure every girl by what he remembered of Marilyn. Fiona tried to get him interested in various friends of hers. There was Emily who was a nurse at the local Silver Chain Nursing Station, but she was very loud and over enthusiastic. Luke preferred his women to be a little quieter, not so aggressively "available". He tried to explain this to Fiona, but she just laughed. Then there was Brenda who was a dancer with a legitimate company by day, and a stripper by night. Not exactly Luke's style. Then there was Rachael who was a bible student at the Theological College. When Luke proclaimed he had a headache, she "laid hands" on him and then declared him "cured", which he wasn't. Luke wasn't into such mumbo jumbo and decided Rachael wasn't for him either. Fiona gave up then saying, "Luke, you're impossible, I'm washing my hands of you – you're just too fussy, if you don't accept people, women, for what they are you'll never find anyone suitable."

She turned then to Peter and admitted, "I give him up, Peter, and I'm giving up trying to be a matchmaker, he'll have to find a girl himself, I'm obviously no good at finding a girl for him." They all had a laugh and enjoyed the usual good banter.

Chris enjoyed attending play school. He made friends easily and his very best friend was a cheeky little redheaded boy called Morgan. The two played almost exclusively together and the four parents became friends as a result of the boys' friendship. Sometimes the mother would offer to pick up Chris and take him home at the end of the day, but Peter was never going to allow his son to be out of his trusted circle of family for pickups or anything else. He had suffered too much at the loss of Timmy to ever risk losing Chris. His guilt had never left him and many times he woke in the night suffering from a recurring nightmare of trying to find his son. Many times the vision of Timmy got mixed up with the vision of Chris. When he woke in a lather of sweat it always took him hours to calm down again. Fiona was very understanding and sympathised, but was powerless to help him get over his fears of losing his son.

At the end of one particularly long trying day, both carers at the play school that Chris attended were busy sorting out an argument with two little girls and took their eyes off the other children in the garden. Someone once said, "It only needs one freak positioning of participants to coincide, to create a hitherto unforeseen possibility, leading to freak interaction coupled with an unfettered opportunity which can create an accident." Such a freak positioning did on this day create an accident. In the garden of the playschool there was a climbing frame leading up to a platform, with a roof above to shade the children from the sun. It was regulation, and built to Australian Standards, not too high and with a reinforced rubber flooring which would absorb any fall and not seriously injure a child. However, children, especially boys do not always use equipment as it is intended. A creative and inventive child may see playground equipment differently. To Chris and Morgan, the climbing frame was not a piece of play equipment, it was a space ship and they were astronauts going to the moon. Chris wanted to get higher and so climbed up the pole supporting the roof on the left side, whilst Morgan, his little friend climbed the opposite pole and both children met on the roof which was never intended for children to climb upon. Both boys were strong for their age and played make-believe games each day. They were being silly as they sat precariously on the roof and started pushing each other as both wanted to be the leader and didn't want the other one on the roof with him. It was not a serious push, but Chris was unbalanced and when Morgan tried to remove him from the roof, Chris had nothing to hold on to to steady himself, and inevitably fell over the edge. The carers were busy with the squabbling girls and only at the last moment did one spot the two boys on the roof and could see an accident about to happen. She shouted out and ran blindly to the climbing frame. In her panic and haste she collided with a child riding a plastic pushbike. The child and the carer tumbled over each other on the rubber matting and the pushbike careered on, alone to crash into the climbing frame. As Chris fell, the bike broke his fall but the solid plastic handlebar did not give when it collided with the head of the child.

The carer shouted for help from the other staff as she ran to attend to Chris. One carer had done an advanced first aid course and took over the situation, checking his breathing and pulse. The child was breathing but had a nasty gash on his head, and he was unconscious, and not responding at all to her calling his name. The remaining staff collected all the other children, including Morgan who was crying from being pulled down and admonished for his "naughtiness" in pushing Chris off the roof, where they shouldn't have been in the first place. Everyone was taken to the day room where afternoon activities had been organised. Two carers stayed with Chris in the garden and called for an ambulance. Fiona and Peter were notified and both left work and hurried to the local children's hospital. Both distraught parents met in the Emergency Department and hurried to see their child who was being examined by two doctors in Triage. The gash in his head was deep and needed stitching but that was not what was worrying the doctors. They wanted scans and X-rays for the child, to see if there was any internal bleeding and had him hurried down to the MRI centre for tests and X-rays before cleaning him up and suturing his wound. Fiona and Peter clung to each other and Peter tried his best to reassure Fiona that Chris would be alright, but he was so choked up himself he could hardly get the words out. They called Fiona's parents who dropped everything they were doing and hurried over to the hospital. The four waited anxiously for the results from the X-rays and MRI scan. A young doctor came to them eventually and asked them to accompany him into the Parents' Waiting Room at the rear of the Emergency Ward. He explained that young Chris was having bleeding on the brain and needed to be admitted to the Intensive Care Unit immediately. There the doctors would monitor the bleeding and if it didn't stop spontaneously they would have to operate to alleviate any pressure to the brain.

That first night was a frightening vigil that all four kept, comforting each other and trying to be brave and keeping optimistic. Two days passed and still Chris was unconscious. The hospital gave the parents access to a small bedroom for their personal use and vouchers for meals in the upstairs cafeteria. Each day Howard and Gloria, the grandparents, came, stayed for a couple of hours and then left, fetching toiletries and clothes for the parents. They had a key to the house and generally looked after things whilst the two anxious parents kept watch over their child, day and night. Chris was never without someone at his side, waiting for a sign that he might recover consciousness. Peter was not religious but took himself off for an hour to the quiet little chapel at the back of the hospital. He went down on his knees and wept, and prayed. It was there on the third day that Luke came and found him. Peter was an emotional mess and Luke was worried for Peter's sanity. He remembered only too well the former tragedies that Peter had endured and Luke worried that this latest ordeal might just tip him over the edge. Peter openly cried to Luke, "Honestly, Luke I don't think I could take it if anything, final, happens to Chris. It's more than a man can take." Luke was wonderful and talked Peter through the events of the last few days, encouraging him and giving him strength to carry on, and support Fiona, who needed him to be strong. On the fourth day the doctors told Fiona and Peter that, although the bleeding into the brain had stopped, there was still fluid there and pressure building up that had to be released. An operation was organised and when the child returned to the ICU the parents were shocked to see tubes and pipes and various equipment leading from their child's head to so many machines. It was terrifying and Chris looked so frail and white. There was a large dressing round his head and a large lump covered by a bandage. The doctor explained that they had put a stent into the scull cavity and a drain was being used to relieve the pressure.

Fiona had a break and went home for a few hours each day, but Peter wouldn't leave the hospital at all. Howard, Gloria and Luke all came each day and gave what comfort they could whilst they all waited for Chris to regain consciousness, or not! The doctors were optimistic but warned the parents that Chris should recover with no ill effects, or could recover, but have some brain damage, or may not recover at all. Howard and Gloria spent many hours in the chapel, praying, appealing to God for the safety of Chris. Fiona drew her strength from Peter who never let her see the depths of his despair and disconsolation. He said all the right things to her, encouraging, soothing, calming – things he didn't actually believe himself. He held the hand of his son throughout his vigil, and pleaded with God for the recovery of his only child. Peter remembered only too well how the tragedy with Timmy, his first son, had come between the two parents and how it had demolished their marriage, and turned it into a battle ground between him and his wife. He loved Fiona so much and loved Chris too; he was desperate to keep both of them and made a supreme effort to comfort and encourage Fiona. They clung to each other for support and Peter thought that, – this time – a tragedy would hold them together, not separate and divide. There was too much love at stake here – he had to be sure to give Fiona absolutely every bit of his love, devotion, and support to get them through this terrible time. Chris's vital signs had been erratic and the doctors kept adjusting the medication which worried Peter and Fiona. They had a difficult time keeping up with their understanding of what medication and treatment Chris was receiving. There was a Clinical Psychologist who ran the Parents' Advocacy Support Unit who helped them understand what was going on, but Peter was too distraught to think clearly and admitted to Fiona that they had no choice but to trust in the doctors and medical staff.

On the fifth day of their vigil Peter felt a slight movement in Chris's hand and watched intently as the child slowly opened his eyes. He was conscious. The doctors came immediately and started checking on his vital signs and doing tests to see if Chris was responding. Both parents and grandparents were at his bedside and all in tears, watching the child, willing the child to come back to them.

Chris was doped from all the medication and just looked at his mother with a deadpan expression. No recognition and no reaction. He just stared straight through her as though she wasn't there. Both parents held his hands and talked incessantly to him, trying to get some sort of reaction from him. The doctors were encouraging and told them not to worry, this is normal, he is so doped up with drugs he is in a fog and won't respond for many more hours. The doctors were slowly reducing the strength and potency of the drugs they were giving Chris. They told the parents to be patient, it would be many hours before they would know if Chris would fully recover. Before this terrible accident Peter used to tuck Chris up in bed each night and read him stories from the many books they had for him. His favourite book and story was "The Three Little Pigs". He used to say, "Daddy, read it to me again," and Peter always obliged, he couldn't say no to the child. On the third day that Chris was in hospital Fiona had gone home to shower and collect some clothes, and as she was leaving the house she thought she might take a few of Chris's books with her. The "Three Little Pigs" was his favourite, so she packed it along with the other books in her overnight bag. Once Chris had regained consciousness the tension should have been relaxed for the parents and grandparents, but the doctors now were not so sure that Chris would regain his full faculties, in fact that his brain would be unimpaired. They were worried by the non-recognition and no verbal response of the child. They now warned the parents that it may be that Chris had received more internal damage than previously thought. Time would be the only way to tell. It was a nightmare and the waiting to see if there would be any on-going problems was a terrible strain and stressful for everyone. The doctors told the anxious family that it could go either way, there was no guarantee. They would just have to wait until Chris made some sort of response before they would know if there was to be permanent damage. Chris was awake, but was not responding to any stimulation at all. Fiona and the grandparents went to the cafeteria. They ordered coffees and just sat mute, miserable, staring into their cups, not knowing what to say to each other, nothing seemed appropriate. Peter was left alone with the child. Quietly, gently, he dropped from his chair on to his knees and with tears cursing down his cheeks prayed to God for his son's recovery. He didn't know any proper prayers, he just opened his heart and told God how much he loved his son and that he would do anything, anything, if Chris could just recover and be normal. He didn't know how to pray, he just kept bargaining with God. "Please let him recover, I'll do anything you want – please, if you love little children let him come back to us – he is so loved and I don't think I could survive if my child is lost to me again. Please, God, help us… please."

He eventually sat back on to his chair and picked up one of the books by the side of the bed and started to read, not really concentrating on the words, only on the child. The book was "The Three Little Pigs" and as he was reading, with the child only staring straight ahead, he made a mistake. Instead of reading "And the big bad wolf, huffed and he puffed and he blew the house down" he unwittingly read out, "And the big bad wolf, huffed and he puffed and he knocked the house down."

"No! That's not right," came a protesting little voice from the bed. Peter's mouth fell open, he gave a big drawing in of breath, and he sent a quick prayer heavenwards. "Oh thank you, God, thank you!" He dropped the book on to the bed and leant over him, turning the child's head toward himself. "Chris, Chris, it's me Daddy, can you see me?"

"Yes, Daddy, but you got my story wrong!" Peter covered the child with kisses and called the nursing staff over to check him out. Fiona and her parents returned to see the two deep in conversation. Everyone was weeping tears of joy and hugging each other and then hugging and kissing Chris. Chris wanted to know where he was and why he had all these wires and tubes and things stuck into his arm, and could he go home, he didn't want to stay here, and "Mummy where's my teddy?"

The doctors gave Chris a good going over, checking all his vital signs and monitoring his progress. They said if he kept up this level of recovery he should be able to go home in three or four days.

Everyone was so happy, Chris was a bit bewildered with all the fuss people were making over him but the nurse gave him some ice cream and promised to give him some more later on, if he was a good boy. The next day all the tubes and wires were removed from the child and he was free to sit up, and play with some toys. The doctors proclaimed him fit and well and a paediatrician gave him some tests to ascertain any level of brain damage, but it didn't appear that there would be any ongoing problems – in fact he had made an incredible full recovery. Peter and Fiona took their child home and held each other tight that night, grateful for each other's support and love. Peter knew he would have had another breakdown if Chris had not made a full recovery. He was strong, but not that strong.

CHAPTER 26

THE FUNERAL

Fiona had always kept in touch with Alan and Robert and one day there was an email from Alan letting Fiona know that all their hard work on Du Pont Island had come to fruition and there was to be a large Club Med style resort built by the Japanese in the very near future. Alan knew it had taken three years of negotiations and planning and, apparently it was all coming together now. Fiona was pleased and told Peter about the development at dinner that night. Peter was none too happy and Fiona couldn't understand why he looked troubled. He didn't, and couldn't tell her what was bothering him, but his mind was flying across the waters to his mother. If she is still alive, how will she cope with an intrusion of this magnitude? Her little world would be shattered. There was nothing he could do, and no one he could discuss it with, so he just had to put it behind him and get on with life, but his dreams were tormented with thoughts of his mother.

Chris was a darling child, talking endlessly and always asking questions, "Why is a tree so big? Why does it rain? Why do I have to go to bed? Why, Why, Why?" He had a mop of blond curls – just like his daddy – and the same as

Timmy had been blessed with so many years earlier, and he always laughed when Grandad Campbell ruffled his hair, saying he looked like a girl. Although Chris had his daddy's curls he had his mummy's fair skin, the bluest of blue eyes and a beautiful nature. He enjoyed learning and was interested in everything – a pleasure to be with. Fiona's parents doted on him and did a fair amount of babysitting when they could. Peter would look at them enjoying the child and wonder how it would have been if his parents had not gone down in that crash, and could be here having a full family life with this beloved child. His tragedies still haunted him. He still had nightmares about Timmy and the day he disappeared. Whenever he took Chris out he never let go of his hand, and when Morgan at play school invited Chris to have a sleep over, Chris pleaded with his daddy to let him go, but there was no way Peter was ever going to let Chris out of his sight, other than with people he knew and trusted. Fiona thought he was being over protective, but understood his reasons. However it was difficult saying no to the child. They had Morgan come to their house to stay overnight with Chris, and both boys had a great time, but Chris wanted to go to stay at Morgan's house. Peter was adamant, he wasn't going to take any chances and it was his job to protect his child, his family, and he took this job very seriously. Peter took Chris each weekend to the local swimming pool and was teaching him to swim. They had floating toys in the water and Peter used them to get Chris confident playing in the water first, and then moved on to showing him some strokes. Chris loved to jump into the water, into his daddy's arms, and then Peter would swing him round whilst they both laughed and had such fun. Chris was learning so fast, everything came easy to him and they decided to put him to some music. They had heard of a teacher in Como, not too far out of town who taught children the violin – by the Suzuki method. After talking it over with the teacher they enrolled Chris in the infant's class. The violin they had to buy for him was incredible. A modified, tiny, almost miniature facsimile of the real thing. Parents were allowed and encouraged to sit in on the lessons and it was fun to see the children, not actually playing the instrument, but playing around it. They walked and jumped around their violins and they played endless games just using the bow and then putting it on to one string only. Chris enjoyed his lessons and he was taught the rhythm they had to master first, which was called "rattle, rattle, dump truck". This they sang and played on one string only with the tiny bow. After a few weeks they were taught to finger on this one string and then week by week the children followed the simple tune of "twinkle, twinkle little star" using the "rattle, rattle dump truck" rhythm. It was so simple, but combined with the games they played the children thoroughly enjoyed it.

Father Christmas came that year with so many presents for Chris but all the child wanted was one special present. When questioned by Peter and Fiona he wouldn't tell what his "special present" was. He always said, "Santa will know what I want." They tried so many ways to get the information out of him, but he wouldn't divulge what he wanted most in the world. "It's a secret," he told his daddy. Fiona was really worried, she didn't want the child to be disappointed on Christmas morning, but didn't know what to do about it. Grandma and Grandad Campbell took him to the local shopping mall the week before Christmas, where he sat on Santa's knee and whispered to the whiskered old man what he wanted for Christmas. Grandma Campbell excused herself two minutes later, leaving Howard in a café with Chris devouring a huge ice cream. She went back to have a little chat with Santa about what Chris had whispered. Prior to that Chris wouldn't tell anyone what he wanted for Christmas – as he said, he would only tell Father Christmas, no one else. The store Santa was very good and let Gloria in on the secret – Chris wanted a puppy.

"Heaven's above," she exclaimed. She thanked Santa and moved to quiet spot in the Shopping Centre and rang Peter to let him in on the secret. Peter and Fiona were surprised and agitated. They had to find a puppy – their child had been through so much only a little while ago, – but where at such short notice? It was a weekend and so both parents were at home and had their own computers. They both stopped what they were doing and went on the Internet to try and find a puppy.

There are always puppies for sale, but at this time of the year they were all taken. There just were none to be had.

All that weekend the frustrated parents scanned the newspapers, eBay and all the online sites they could think of, to no avail. Peter called Luke and asked desperately if he knew or had heard of anyone having a puppy to dispose of. Luke didn't know any more than the parents but did make one suggestion. "How about trying the local dog pound – or the dog shelter?"

"Brilliant idea – thanks," said Peter. He rang the local pound and the dog shelter to no avail, but one of the carers there told him that there was a serious charge of neglect that had just occurred and that the RSPCA had been called to a property where there were many dogs being kept in terrible conditions, including puppies.

Peter rang the RSPCA and was advised that, yes, there were some puppies and if Peter could go round there immediately there would be one that could be suitable. Peter and Fiona went immediately and fell in love with the tiniest black and white fluffy puppy they had ever seen. They accepted the puppy gratefully, signed some papers and then had a problem, they couldn't take it home as Chris would see it and there were still three days to go to Christmas Day. Fiona rang Luke and they pleaded with him to look after the puppy for them until Christmas morning.

"This is stretching the friendship," Luke chided. "Do you know how much trouble a little puppy can be?"

"Yes, but I'm begging you – please, please?"

Luke took the puppy, telling them, "You guys sure do owe me one!" It was arranged that Luke would bring the puppy round to Peter's house at 6.00 a.m. on Christmas morning. He was to stay with them for Christmas day anyway.

All was quiet and Luke had put the puppy in a cardboard box with a red ribbon around its neck. The box had air holes in the top and they were pleased to note that the puppy was asleep. The two carefully carried the box and laid it by the side of Chris's stocking, and then retreated quietly. Luke and Peter had a very quiet breakfast and just one hour later there was a yelping from the puppy, which woke Chris and then it was mayhem. The child and the puppy rolled around the bedroom playing and laughing. All the other presents were ignored and Chris was the happiest child and rushed out of his bedroom to show his mummy and daddy what Santa had brought for him. The puppy was duly named Sunny and Chris played all morning with him.

In the afternoon Grandma and Grandad Campbell came for lunch and Chris couldn't wait to show them his special present. Gloria and Howard were ecstatic that they had been the ones to find out the secret wish, and that it had all come together. Life was really good for this little family. After lunch Chris wanted to show his Grandma and Grandpa how he could play his violin. Of course, he could only play a scratchy version of Twinkle, Twinkle, but it was recognisable and everyone clapped him after his performance. No one noticed Fiona's father as he slumped in his chair, his face deathly white, but not a sound came out of him. No moan or groan, he just sort of crumpled as he sat there. Peter was the first to notice and knew immediately what had happened. He didn't want to scare the child so he picked him up and took him, with the puppy and Luke out to the garden, on the way telling the grandmother to go have a look at the old man. From the garden Peter could hear the phone call for the ambulance and the crying of Fiona and her mother. He knew there was nothing he could do, but entertain young Chris and keep him out of the way. The ambulance men came and took Grandpa away, never to be seen again. The child was curious. "Where is Grandpa?" But no one told him the awful truth.

Chris was at play school on the day of Howard's funeral. It was a very sombre affair attended by over a hundred friends and relatives. It was agreed that Howard's beloved Ave Maria be played with Charlotte Church singing followed by Mahalia Jackson singing How Great Thou Art. Being British, Howard had always preferred British artists, but he just loved Mahalia Jackson, an American Gospel singer and played her CDs over and over. Friends of the family sat at the back of the funeral parlour leaving the front seats for the close relatives.

At the back, Luke recognised and saw Marilyn and his heart flipped over, but he told himself, "Don't be stupid, you know she's married, don't look at her – look down to the front, to the coffin and the beautiful flowers." He couldn't help himself though and kept glancing across to where she was sitting. He looked over the other mourners to see if her "hulk" of a husband was close by. He couldn't see him and just the once Marilyn looked up and smiled shyly at Luke, and then back at the hymn sheet she was holding. After the ceremony and after the hearse had taken Howard away everyone congregated on the lawn and had nibbles and drinks. Luke was very careful, looking to see if Marilyn was alone and not with her husband, and when he had assured himself that the brute wasn't there he moved over and through the crowd to where she was standing.

"Can I get you a drink or a sandwich or something?" he asked innocently.

Marilyn was shy and quiet but she recognised him and knew that he had come through the crowd deliberately to seek her out. She wanted him to know and so, brazenly answered him with, "I'm not married anymore!"

He opened his mouth, and was lost for words for a moment. Then a smile lit his face up and her dimples showed quite distinctly as she also broke into a big smile too, and they both laughed with relief and recognition of their mutual attraction.

A funeral is supposed to be a sad and sombre affair but for Luke it was the best day of his life. When everyone started to leave, having given their commiserations to Gloria and the rest of her family, Luke asked Marilyn if she would like to go for dinner. He took her to a tiny Japanese Restaurant where he knew it would be quiet and secluded. They talked endlessly, getting to know each other. She told him of her terrible marriage and how she had been abused, both physically and mentally, but eventually was able to get out of it when he was jailed for assault. The divorce was no problem and there were no children to worry about. Luke listened to her story of abuse and held her hand on the table when she became emotional. She told him, "It's really a long story and I'll tell you more about it one day, but that's enough for now."

Luke himself, was of a gentle nature and just couldn't understand how a man could get pleasure from abusing such a beautiful creature as Marilyn. He also didn't know why any woman would stay with an abusive husband, but he realised it might just be more complicated than that and he hoped she would tell him more some day. He swore to himself that if he could win her for himself, for life, he would make it his job to care for her and look after her. He took her back to her house and then went home a very happy man. That night was the last night that Luke spent alone. The two were inseparable after the funeral and Marilyn agreed to give up her house, which had so many bad memories, and move in with Luke. They were married three months later and one month after that proudly announced that they were expecting their first child. Luke was the happiest man alive.

A few months after the funeral Fiona asked Peter, "Pete, you know Mum's getting quite old now, maybe we should start to think of what we might need to do once she gets older, and maybe frail. What would you think to maybe her coming here to live with us? I mean her house is quite large and the garden too much for her really. I could look after her and if she needed nursing we could get someone in to look after her. What do you think?"

Peter was apprehensive at first, but he got on well with Grandma Campbell and they both thought it would be good for Chris to have her close by. So they put it to her and at first she stubbornly refused, wanting to maintain her independence, but a few more weeks passed and then it became obvious that whilst she could manage on her own now, it wouldn't be too long before it all might become too much for her. The garden was getting overgrown, and the house needed things doing to it, the patio needed painting and with the windows not being cleaned and the paths not being swept the place started to take on a neglected look. She could have employed someone to do this work but she didn't want strangers coming to her house. Peter wanted to help but with work commitments and a child at home he was just too busy. Grandma Campbell was healthy enough but there were little things like, she just couldn't open jars, or bottles herself – her arthritis didn't allow the strength that was needed. At length she agreed it would be better if she sold the house and moved in with Fiona and Peter, which she did. Their house was large enough to give her a room to herself, and an en suite also. Chris adored his Grandma who spoiled him with treats and outings. He loved being taken to the zoo and to the large underwater aquarium at Hillary's Boat Harbour.

A few more weeks went by and Fiona heard from Alan that after months of negotiations the Japanese company had been awarded the contract to build the resort at Du Pont and was almost ready to commence development. He was only telling her for sort of gossip nothing more – they had done their work and had no real interest in the ongoing development. She relayed the news to Peter, and was surprised to see a frown furrow his forehead as she was telling him.

She then asked, "What's wrong, why does that news trouble you?"

He shrugged his shoulders and tried to look unconcerned, but she wasn't fooled and pressed him for an answer. "Come on, spit it out, I know you and there's something on your mind."

He couldn't tell her about his concerns for his mother and so just vaguely waved one arm out in front of him and said, "But it's such a beautiful island, it's a shame to spoil it – and if it's a resort, only the rich will be able to use it."

She wasn't fooled but let it go at that.

CHAPTER 27

DU PONT CHICKENS

The four little chicks turned out to be three chickens and one rooster. Their names were Bossy; the rooster, Whitey; because her feathers, as a chick were paler than the others; and Laurel and Hardy – because they were comics, as chicks, always falling over each other and fighting for food. As they were growing they became quite tame and would sit on Sally's arm, like a tame raptor would. They gave her a lot of fun and a focus for her attention and connection with another living creature, much like one would have with a pet dog or cat. Now they were all grown and Laurel and Hardy produced eggs faster than Sally could eat them. It didn't matter to her that the chickens had been given male names and not female, and she didn't think the chickens themselves minded at all. Bossy and Whitey had escaped when they were only about six months old and had obviously enjoyed a happy married life as there were chickens all over. Sally tried to catch a chicken now and then, but they were too fast for her, so they just multiplied and laid their eggs in the heath and long grass where she couldn't see them. "No matter," she told Joe, "there's plenty of food to go around."

After a few months Sally decided that with so many chickens around she really ought to catch one and have it for dinner – she didn't want to eat the chickens in the coop, producing eggs – only the wild ones running free. Roast chicken sounded good, but how to do it? She tried the obvious, just running after one, but chickens can run really fast when they want to, and it's especially difficult if a person is bent double trying to catch hold of the bird. She realised she was not going to get one that way. She sat and thought about it and pondered on the possibility of making a trap, but she dismissed that idea as being just too difficult. No – there had to be an easier way – but which way? As always she decided to sleep on it, her best ideas always came to her when she was in bed.

The next morning she had it. A plan. She went looking for two pieces of strong wood that could be used as stakes. She went back to the little boat wreck at the end of Windy Cove and, armed with a hammer, broke off two lengths of wooden decking. She took these two wooden struts and hammered them into the soft ground at the edge of the marsh. She hammered and hammered until they were well in the ground, side by side with a gap in the middle of about two inches. She tested the strength of the struts and proclaimed them to be perfectly stuck in the ground. Next she went back to the yacht and to the sail locker where there was still plenty of good flexible rope. She took a good length, about ten metres and laid out a trap for the chickens. She made a hangman's noose and laid it on the ground open for a chicken to step into. Following that she trailed the end of the rope, through the gap in the planks and back to where she could sit and watch a chicken get caught. The chicken had to have an incentive to stand in the noose's circle and Sally had collected a young corn cob, taken the seeds off and had laid a trail leading to a little pile of corn in the centre of the noose. All she had to do was sit back and wait for a chicken to take the bait and get lassoed when she would pull the rope tight around its legs. It didn't take more than ten minutes before a passing chicken spotted the corn and followed the trail leading to the little pile in the centre of the rope noose. When the chicken stepped into the circle Sally gave a yelp of victory and pulled the lasso tight. She had to keep the tension on the rope as she approached the trapped chicken. When she got to the chicken she wrapped some of the rope around its legs and when the poor thing was completely helpless she laid it on its side and left it there whilst she went back to the yacht, to the little pile of flotsam rope she had, and unravelled a length. With this she went back to the chicken and tied its legs firmly together before detaching the larger rope that had held it fast. Feeling like a gladiator who had fought a mighty battle, she brought her poor victim home to be dealt with at her leisure. The chicken was surprisingly calm and didn't wriggle at all as she carried it, upside down, by the feet, back to the yacht. She had a drink and some lunch and just sat, thinking, and looked at the poor chicken feeling a bit sorry for it – but memories of roasted chicken overruled her sympathy for her victim. Now for the worst part; how to kill the poor thing. She didn't have an axe but she did have a hammer and a very sharp carving knife. She apologised to the chicken, but assured the poor thing that it wouldn't hurt – much! She laid the chicken down, and it just lay there, quiet and calm. She took the hammer and gave it a good wallop. The chicken actually jumped a foot off the ground, and flapped its wings furiously, but couldn't run away as its feet were well and truly tied together. The blow hadn't killed the chicken, only given it a bad headache. No, she decided that wasn't the way. No... a different approach was needed. She sat and thought about it for a while and then had an idea. She took the chicken and whilst she was in a sitting position on a rock she held the victim between her knees, with it facing forwards, away from her. Taking hold of the chicken's head in her left hand, stretching it upwards and backwards, and with her right, holding the carving knife, brought the blade across its neck, cutting to the bone. The chicken shivered as blood spurted out from its artery and eventually went limp. Sally felt a little sick, but, "You can't back out now," she told herself, "the job has to be finished."

Sally hung the chicken up by its legs on to a branch of a tree. It bled for quite a long time and only when the bleeding became a slow drip did she take it down and, squinting sideways at it, cut its head off.

She had another drink and pondered on her next move. Feathering. This was not going to be easy, it would be messy, but what else could she do? It had to have its feathers taken off. She sat on the rock and started on the back end. She held the chicken with her left hand and plucked and plucked with her right hand. There were feathers everywhere. She tried to remember the very funny Pheasant Plucking song, she had known many years earlier and had sung at a concert. She couldn't remember all of it but she hummed the tune and sang bits of it as she plucked away.

"I'm not the pheasant plucker, I'm the pheasant plucker's mate

And I'm only plucking pheasants cos' the pheasant plucker's late.

I'm not the pheasant plucker, he has gone out on the tiles,

He only plucked one pheasant and I'm sitting here with piles.

I'm not the pheasant plucker, I'm the pheasant plucker's son,

And I'm only plucking pheasants till the pheasant pluckers come.

I'm not the pheasant plucker, I'm the pheasant plucker's friend,

And I'm only plucking pheasants as a means unto an end."

That was mainly the chorus and she couldn't remember all of the verses, but she did remember the last verse and chorus and sang them over and over:

"Me husband's in the woods all day, a-banging with his gun,

If he could hear me heartfelt cries, then surely he would run,

For I've fluff in all me crannies and there's feathers up me nose,

And I'm itchin' in the kitchin' from me head down to me toes.

I'm not the pheasant plucker, I'm the pheasant plucker's wife,

And when we pluck together it's a pheasant plucking life!"

She was having fun now – plucking with gay abandon – and the feathers were flying everywhere, it was a windy day and although she had tried to contain the feathers in her bucket, it was useless. The wind just took them and scattered them far and wide. Once the feathers were all off Sally knew the worst job of all was next. – worse than gutting the fish, this was gutting a chicken – a much larger, more disgusting exercise. She had learnt her lesson from the first fish gutting session, so long ago. Don't make all that mess either in or near the yacht. Take the mess far, far away. She decided to go up on to her fishing rock and do the gutting there at her fish gutting table. That way all the innards could be thrown into the water for the crabs, or whatever. So where to start: first of all cut around its anal opening – a big way around, and then pull out all its stomach, and intestines. "Oh my God, what a mess… Oh God! Oh God!"

Sally's face was a picture of revulsion and torture. She had to put her hand right into the stomach cavity to scrape out the innards. She felt sick and revolted – but the job had to be done, so like the trooper she was, she got on with the job until the stomach cavity was clean and empty. Little fish were biting at the offal as Sally got down from her rock and took the carcase into the water to wash it clean. The feet were still attached to the legs and Sally had a memory from her childhood seeing her grandmother dealing with a chicken when she returned from the market. In those days her grandmother bought the chicken plucked, but with its feet still attached and when her grandmother cut off the feet she would give the child the feet to play with. The grandmother showed Sally how to pull on the tendons and make the feet work. Pulling on the tendons, opened and closed the feet of the chicken and amused the child who took it to a friend to show her how it was done. Sally remembered all this and had a bit of fun with the feet, once she had cut the feet off the legs. It actually wasn't so easy cutting the feet off, she had to get the hacksaw to saw through the bone – but after that it was all a bit of fun. She pondered the job she had now completed and contemplated whether all that effort would be worthwhile and would she ever want to do it all again.

So the reward. It was getting late so Sally made up a fire and thought how she was going to do the cooking of this mighty effort. Without an oven it would be difficult she thought, and over the fire if she tried to do it all in one go, the inside may not get cooked properly. So she decided to cut up the chicken and have it in pieces. If she cooked the pieces all at once they would keep longer than if it wasn't cooked. The carving knife allowed her to dissect the legs and wings and she cut off chunks of the breast to cook separately. The carcase she decided she would keep until tomorrow when she would try and make a pot of chicken soup. Once the fire had died down and the rocks and ashes were red hot, she took the skin off the carcase and cut it up and put it into a pan over the fire with some coconut rubbed on the bottom of the pan. She didn't have any oil but she reasoned that she could render the skin down, giving her the oil she needed. Once the fat in the bottom of the pan was hot she put the pieces of chicken in. The smell was intoxicating, she was really hungry after her day's exertions and the first cooked chicken leg was bliss, delicious. "Oh my goodness, gracious me, but that's good."

With each mouthful she groaned with pleasure and then told Joe, "Oh, Joe, my love, I don't care if it is a lot of hard work – I'm going to catch all of those chickens – this is the best thing I ever tasted." She went to bed that night, replete, exhausted and very happy.

The next day she cut up the carcase and put it in a pot with lots of vegetables and some of the couscous and barley and made a really good chicken soup that lasted for days.

CHAPTER 28

TRANSPORT

One day whilst Sally was up on the headland she saw a boat, well a ship really. It looked quite small at first on the horizon but as it got closer she could see it was huge. It eventually dropped anchor at Turtle Bay and first of all a small launch brought some people on to the beach, after that the back of the ship opened up and she was surprised to see landing craft emerge and start to transport heavy equipment and materials on to the beach and upwards on to the heath above the beach. The ship had some Japanese writing on the side and in English the words Monyo Maru. Some men were on the beach and supervising others transporting bulldozers, trucks and earthmoving equipment of all different kinds, most of which she didn't recognise. There were also piles being made of long lengths of iron and other materials which were wrapped in blue plastic sheeting. Everything was stowed up on the grassland well away from the beach. As it started to get dark she wondered if they would set up camp, and in time start to come across to Peaceful Bay and end her Shangri-La existence. She went to bed with a heavy heart and wondered what tomorrow would bring.

It became a daily ritual, she would go up on to the headland with the yacht's binoculars in hand and watch the men at work. At the end of each long day the workers would get into the launch and return to the ship. "These Japanese labourers sure work long hours," she said to Joe. "They are obviously very disciplined, hard workers, yes, very impressive. I'm really surprised not one of them has ever wandered off, away from the site to explore the island. No one has bothered me and it doesn't look as if they ever will. I can't imagine Australian or English workers being so disciplined. Can you?" Joe didn't answer.

It became obvious that they were making a harbour and deep water jetty. The machines were going backwards and forwards building up a harbour wall, and an approach from the shore to the beginnings of a jetty. It was very interesting and kept Sally occupied watching the men. At first she had been careful to keep herself hidden from their view, but after two weeks she realised none of the men had attempted to leave the work site. They were a hard working lot, these Japanese; well disciplined. At the end of three weeks the ship, with all the workers, left the bay and headed out to sea. The equipment was left on the shore and the materials covered with blue tarpaulin and tied down.

A few days later another ship appeared, this time bearing the name Kake Maru. The work continued in the same fashion and the workers never ventured away from the work site. It was fascinating to watch them and Sally had got over her fear of being found and actually looked forward each day to seeing what progress was being made. The workers had installed a very large fuel tank above, and away from the beach and they refuelled the machines each day. She couldn't distinguish one worker from another as they all wore the same overalls and safety helmets, and anyway, she laughed to herself, all the Asians look alike to us. There was a regular three weekly turnaround of the two ships and eventually the deep water jetty was finished and the Monyo Maru was the first to tie up alongside. This enabled work to proceed much faster and the harbour wall was taking shape. The island was a sort of triangular shape with Windy Cove being on the north west, Peaceful Cove and Turtle Bay being on the southwest side and cliffs taking up the last third on the east side. The work on the harbour wall extended from the centre of Turtle Bay to the far end, where the cliffs started and a building at the base of the cliffs was being built. Bricks had been brought in from the supply boat but the base of the building was utilising local rock. Sally watched as little Bobcats collected the rocks and wondered if they would come around to her bay when they ran out of rocks on the site and needed more. As she watched she felt a movement, a slight earth tremor and she was glad that she was sitting down, as she felt the movement of the earth might have knocked her over. She could see the men stopping the work and huddling together in groups – probably discussing what to do, if anything. There was no damage that she could see, and no one looked as if they had been hurt. Work continued and she sat and watched. As normal, all the workers retreated to the supply boat at the end of that day. What was not normal was that all the earthmoving equipment was mobilised and taken back on to the ship. The Monyo Maru had only been tied up for two weeks, not the normal three. Once all the heavy equipment was taken into the cargo hold of the ship, it untied from the jetty and left the bay. Sally was puzzled, why had they left early?

The next morning Sally felt; sensed something was wrong. She ran out and climbed up the headland facing west, overlooking Windy Cove and was shocked to see the cove and hundreds of metres inland covered with water. The sea had invaded the island on the west side and was threatening to come over the dunes to where the wreck was situated and where Sally called home. Just in time it stopped short and rolled back, taking with it trees, bushes and a large amount of undergrowth. She stood and stared for a long time. It was frightening, but the water had invaded the northwest side of the island, and thankfully, her "home" as well as the harbour work had not been affected. The boat and the workers never came back. Weeks went by and nothing happened. The jetty was there and quite a long, harbour wall, but no one to use it – strange! What Sally didn't know was that a major tsunami had hit the eastern seaboard of Japan and had completely washed away the offices and warehouses of the building company which had been commissioned to develop the island. The company had their offices in Ishinomaki and Kesennuma, and these buildings were completely washed away and everyone with them. The development, building, and the company itself, ceased to exist. Sally actually missed her daily routine of watching the workers and now, with some caution, started going across the beach to see, at close hand, what they had been doing. She could see out to the horizon and no ship had appeared for weeks. Brazenly now she started to use the jetty, it was brilliant for fishing. Deep water meant bigger fish, and with the pull-along that Peter had given her – it was easy to take her fishing tackle out to the end of the jetty, leave it there and just bring her daily catch home in the trolley. Life was easier and Sally was happy again. She told Joe she just couldn't understand why the Japanese had gone to all this trouble and not finished the job. The jetty was serving no one but herself. However she was grateful for it. The garden was producing so much that Sally was able to feed the two chickens in the coop quite easily. She always kept some seeds back for replanting and it was a continuous rotation of crops that kept repeating season by season. Kitchen waste was dug back into the soil especially waste from the fish, and this way the soil was kept rich and able to keep producing. There were supplies Sally could do with, like new shoes, more toothpaste, a new toothbrush and more books, but on the whole she was satisfied and quite happy. She talked to Joe, but he didn't have much to say back! After a few days of going over to the jetty Sally decided to see if there was anything in the piles of materials and sea containers that she could "borrow". It wouldn't be stealing, she reasoned with herself, just borrowing. There were stacks of different boxes and packs, all covered with tarpaulin. All the packs and boxes were labelled in Japanese and so it was impossible for Sally to recognise the writing and discover what was in all the packs. Some were just too heavy for her to move but some she could open a little and find out what there was. There was a large amount of wood, and a whole container load of cement in not too large packs, but they were very heavy. There were many boxes of tools and metal bolts, angle iron and steel rods. Sally made a mental note of these "'goodies" and thought she might be able to use some things to make her home more comfortable. At the back, and in between two piles of boxes there was, to her surprise, a small Bobcat, and with the keys in the ignition. "Oh, what a find," she told Joe. "Maybe I could borrow it for a while – that might be a laugh."

She asked Joe, "Hey, my love, how you drive these things?"

As usual, he didn't answer her. She looked around to see if anyone was there – which was stupid she knew, as there was no one there and hadn't been anyone around for weeks now. She felt guilty, but daring. She'd only ever driven her little Hyundai at home. She stepped up into the driver's seat and had a good look at the handles and levers. There were no pedals on the floor which was a bit perplexing. "Not to worry", she said to herself, "if men can do this, so can I, how hard can it be?"

She turned the key. The engine burst into life and just idled. "Now what?" She looked at the levers and hadn't a clue as to what did what. There was a lever on her right so she tried to move it forward and nothing happened, but when she pulled it back the bucket at the front moved upwards. "Woops!" So she put it forwards again. "Okay –

so that lever is for the bucket – how do I get the thing moving?"

She liked talking to herself – it was comforting, but no one ever answered, not even Joe. She tried the lever on her left next. At that the engine roared at her and scared her but she experimented with it moving forward and backwards, with each movement the engine either roared or quietly idled. "Okay – so that's for power – but how do I get this thing moving?" She had a lever in front of her now and pulled it towards her. The Bobcat moved backwards and crashed into one of the stacked piles, then promptly stopped. "Right ho! Let's try forwards." At that the machine shot forwards and crashed into another pile of materials. "Whoops! Okay what happens if I move the lever to the left?" Nothing, it was stuck on the pile in front of her. Slowly Sally worked out that if she moved the central lever to the right the machine went that way and the same for all the directions. Manoeuvring the machine, first to the back, then to the side, back and forward and sideways she could get out of the tight space it had been parked in. "Got it!" she shouted out loud. "Now for some fun!"

She manoeuvred the machine out of the storage area and decided to take it for a joy ride. Over hill and dale now, having a whale of a time. Occasionally crashing into trees and rocks, but the Bobcat ploughed through everything. Now Sally had transport and could take the Bobcat from home to the jetty in no time flat, and go to the end of the jetty taking whatever fishing tackle she liked. It was far easier than walking and she was really enjoying the ability to cover a lot of ground in a very short time. Sally wanted to leave her fishing tackle at the end of the jetty but was a bit worried that the wind might blow everything off the jetty and into the water. She needed a box or some sort of storage. She decided to go to the storage area, examine the sea container, and empty one of the boxes and then she could have the box for her own use. She had a look at the boxes at the shore end of the jetty and decided to look into some more of the sea containers. The doors all opened quite easily and when she looked into one of the containers she saw it was half full of packs of some unknown powder, boxes of large bolts, nuts, iron fittings of all sizes, and boxes of "stuff". She had no idea what some of the "stuff" was. Everything again was labelled in Japanese which didn't help at all. She selected the smallest box she could find which was about the size of a kitchen chair and emptied the contents out. There were packets of some yellow powder, but as she couldn't read Japanese she just discarded them. The empty box was heavy, but not too heavy and Sally was able to push and pull it into position so she could lift it into the Bobcat's bucket. Once there she drove the machine out on to the jetty and to the end where she pulled it out of the bucket and set it into the top corner of the jetty. She realised the box could still be blown away in a strong wind, so she went back to the store to get something heavy so she could weigh down the box. She realised that if she manoeuvred the bucket of the Bobcat she could get things into the bucket and then transport them to wherever she wanted. Once she got the hang of that, it was easy to collect a couple of rocks, into the bottom of the bucket. Now she had to lift the bucket slightly and take the rocks out to the box at the end of the jetty. Positioning the Bobcat so that the bucket was over the box was not easy. She released the bucket lever too soon and the bucket tipped forward and out rolled the rocks, missing the box completely and falling into the sea. "Oh bugger!" she spit out. So, minus the rocks she had to return to the shore and collect some more. The second go was better and one rock went into the bucket, the second rock missed and fell on to the jetty. "Oh, tough titties! That will have to do," she said to no one in particular. After turning the Bobcat around, and in the process gently banging into the side of the jetty, she bounced along, taking the Bobcat home in time for her evening meal. On the way, there was an overhanging branch of a large tree, she misjudged it by two feet and it neatly ripped off the roof of the little cab. "Oh bugger!" she cried, but undaunted she carried on having a great time.

The next day she had a ball, bouncing the Bobcat over the sand dunes to Windy Cove to see what damage had been done by the invading water and to collect some mussels, if they were still there. Mussels are very tough she decided as they were still there, sticking to the rocks quite firmly. She had made herself a sort of carry bag out of a pair of trousers, knotting the legs at the bottom. It was an easy job to put the mussels into the bag – and from there into the Bobcat's bucket. Once home again she left some mussels in the sink, ready for her evening meal, and took fishing tackle, mussels for bait and a jumper and jacket as it was quite cool and windy. "This is great," she thought to herself, "easy peasy." As she drove past the fuel tank it occurred to her that the machine might need petrol, or diesel, or whatever it was that fuelled this thing. So she stopped by the pump and had a good look at the contraption for filling her "new car"! It didn't look too complicated and after taking off the cap of her petrol tank she was able to squeeze the trigger and get the nozzle to release its bounty. It was a good job she didn't smoke as the Bobcat's tank filled and spilled out. "Oh bloody hell!" she swore, but was able to stop the flow and put the nozzle back on its hook and turn off the release switch. After getting everything out to the end of the jetty she had a great day's fishing, and caught three large – something or others – she didn't know what kind of fish they were, but they looked really good, clean silver sides, a bit like a small tuna she thought. Life was good, she admitted as she trundled her "new car" over the grass towards home. Sally had taken to singing – out loud. She used to love singing, years ago – and had been happy in the senior chorus of the local theatre group. They did pantomimes each Christmas and usually a musical in the middle of the year. Sally just loved the camaraderie and their "esprit de corps". She didn't have a good voice, but she had a loud voice and could sing in tune; and now she could give vent to it – singing, just for herself, for the sheer joy of singing, at the top of her voice. *"Oh, what a Beautiful Morning"* was her favourite, from the stage show Oklahoma.

Far from being lonely, Sally was having a ball, she actually loved the isolation and the freedom to do whatever she pleased.

"Hey, Joe," she called out loud. "Guess what – I can drive a truck! And no parking problems here." After honing around for an hour or so she parked it up on the headland looking out over the most spectacular red/gold setting sunset – she climbed precariously up on to the driver's seat and, balancing there shouted out, "Look, world, I'm an old woman, but I can do anything!"

CHAPTER 29

PLANS FOR REVISITING THE ISLAND

The seven o'clock news on television reported that a magnitude 9 earthquake shook north eastern Japan causing a massive tsunami. The wave extended eastwards across the Pacific Ocean, decreasing in power as it went. Some islands in the Pacific were swamped and some received only minimal damage. Peter read the newspaper reports and watched the television horrified at the devastation. His thoughts were for his mother, but he was helpless and couldn't even divulge his thoughts and fears to Fiona. She sensed he was worried about something; he sat all afternoon with his head in his hands, looking really depressed. She let him sit quietly all afternoon and all evening. He hardly said a word at dinner. Eventually she could stand it no longer and questioned him that night. He had to keep his promise but he desperately wanted to go back to the island to see if his mother was alright. He just couldn't divulge his knowledge of her survival, and it hurt him to lie to Fiona. She had suspected his mother might still be alive, and suspected that he knew this, so she looked him straight in the eyes and said, quite deliberately, "Look, Peter, just tell me for once and for all, is your mother dead or alive? The truth now."

He looked away from her and said, "I'm just upset at all this devastation, that's all."

"No," she said "it's more than that, isn't it? I'm not stupid you know."

Peter looked at her now, not wanting to lie to her and with tears in his eyes stated what was on his mind. "Look, Fiona, I don't want to tell you any lies, I love you dearly and you are the world to me but I just feel I want to go back to the island and see if my mother is alive or not. I can't honestly say if she is alive – she could have died in the last few years. We know now that the Japanese company have started developing the island and I'm worried that the work will interfere with my mother if, and I stress if, she is still alive. The tsunami is just another reason why I feel I have to go back there."

Fiona shook her head and held his hand as she asked him, "Yes, I understand, but was your mother alive when you went to look for her?"

"Fiona," Peter pleaded, "please don't ask me much more, I'll tell you what I can, just trust me."

Fiona took a deep breath and realised that she wasn't going to get any definitive answer out of him.

Peter went on, "Look, even if she's not alive I really want to see the wreck again and photograph it; keep it private, as a sort of memorial to my mother. I also would really like to take Chris – even though he's only four now – so that in the future he can be told the story of his grandmother's miraculous survival and he would know that he had been there. Photographs are the best record as memories fade. I want Chris to know what happened and where, and to photograph him there at the wreck – for future posterity, for his future when he is old enough to be really interested in his grandmother's story."

Fiona tried reasoning with him. "You realise if we make a trip back to the island it may all have changed and the Japanese company may not even allow us on to the island – it could be a really futile pilgrimage, not to mention quite costly."

Peter put his arm around her shoulders and after giving her a tender kiss pleaded, "I realise it may be a futile exercise but please, my darling, indulge me – it's something I really want to do."

Fiona took a deep breath and, realising there would be no peace until this matter was settled, gave in saying, "Well I'll have to check on work commitments."

That was the answer he wanted and he held Fiona in a tight embrace as he murmured in her ear, "Thank you, darling, thank you – you don't know what it means to me – I just have to know – well everything."

Fiona got them both a cup of coffee and picked up a pen and notebook. She started making notes and then asked Peter, "Alright, if we're going to do this we need to plan carefully. First of all how are you fixed at work? What projects are you working on and can they be left for a while if we take a holiday? And can we afford it – how much will it cost? Another thing, as I said, the Japanese company may not allow us on the island and you know it's privately owned and prohibited to the general public, so that is probably going to be a problem and anyhow, how are we to get there? As far as I know there's no commercial boat service."

Peter acknowledged all the difficulties, nodding his head, but stated, "Look I'll do some research and see if we can fly out to Manila and then get a charter boat to take us to the island, if we don't actually tell anyone we're going on to the island, well they can't stop us if they don't know we're going."

Fiona laughed and handing him the notebook and pen told him, "Well you'd better start to make a list of what you need to do. Meanwhile I'll put in for some holiday leave entitlement and leave the rest to you."

As neither had taken leave for over a year, asking for holiday time off was not a major problem. Harry asked that Peter finish the current design he was working on and all the structural details and then he was free to go off for a few weeks. Chris hadn't started school yet so there was no problem there.

CHAPTER 30

LUKE AND MARILYN

Luke and Marilyn had decided, since finding out that Marilyn was pregnant, to sell his apartment and buy a house, not too far from Peter and Fiona. They looked around and they found an old weatherboard on a large piece of land. The house was neglected and the garden was almost non-existent; land, yes, but could hardly be called a garden. It was a wasteland waiting for some loving attention. The house itself was a fire trap, Sheoak wooden shingles, which are rare these days. All the floorboards were in polished jarrah, well, would have been polished if anyone in the last fifty years had actually polished them, and a kitchen made out of polished jarrah too. There was so much wood that Luke thought he could bring it all back to its former glory, but it would need extensive renovations and would need to be well insured. It was agreed the contractors would come in and start work in the next week, after all the contracts had been signed. As Luke and Marilyn were going to be virtually homeless whilst renovations were happening in their house it was agreed all round, that they move into Peter and Fiona's house as a temporary arrangement, and they also agreed to look after Sunny the puppy. Everyone was happy.

Luke was working on a large project with the glass company, making stained glass windows for a new office block in the city. He had completed many large commissions over the last few years, and was making a good living with his glass making, slumping and blowing. He was a gifted artist and just loved his work, and considered himself so lucky that he could make good money doing the thing that he loved so much. Marilyn had worked for the same hospital for ten years. She had trained as a State Registered Nurse, and had risen to the post of Administrator before being fired for taking too much sick leave. That was three years ago but she was back working now, but in a different kind of environment, that of Women's Refuge. It was only one week after Peter and Fiona had departed that Luke and Marilyn moved into Peter's house. They had only been there four days when Scott Manners, a friend and neighbour, living directly across the road from them, who worked for the Police Department rang her to tell her that Hans, Marilyn's former husband was being released from jail, having served his time. Scott was very familiar with Marilyn's former case against her husband and had read all the records about his prosecution. Luke and Marilyn were not unduly worried as there had been no previous threat but they didn't know that Hans had been harbouring terrible thoughts about his ex-wife since the divorce, and intended seeking her out to get his revenge. It was not too difficult with his connections to the drug and criminal world to find out where Marilyn was now living. He discovered that she and her new husband had bought an old house in South Perth. Of course he didn't know that Luke and Marilyn were actually now, temporarily, living in Peter's house – awaiting the contractors to arrive to start renovations. He was so full of venom and hatred for the woman who had rejected him and divorced him, whilst he was powerless in jail, that he meant to put an end to any happiness she may now be having with a new husband. He had a need for domination and he was frustrated in jail as he knew he had lost that domination over his wife. There was nothing he could do about the divorce. Vengeance is a terrible thing and Hans was blinded by it. Luke and Marilyn had deliberately left the bedroom light on in the old house. Scott lived across the road from them and, being in the Police Department, advised them that when leaving a house for a few days, or weeks, it was a good idea to leave a light on, that way, discouraging thieves and robbers from breaking in. Anyone, now passing the house at night would assume that someone was living there, and was home.

Luke and Marilyn hoped the renovations would all be finished before Peter and Fiona returned. They had only been in Peter's house four days when they got a call on their mobile from Scott their neighbour, who was so relieved to hear that they weren't actually at home. Apparently Scott had seen someone acting suspiciously around Marilyn's home, he didn't realise at first that it was Hans. He couldn't see clearly through the trees what the man was doing but Hans had poured petrol around the outside of the house, and had stacked up cardboard boxes to the wooden doors and windows and was setting the whole house on fire. By the time Scott realised what was happening the house was on fire. He and other neighbours heard the roar of the flames and the banging as the internal beams gave way. Scott rang Marilyn straight away on her mobile, worrying that the pair may still be in the house and was so relieved to hear that they were staying at another house. He immediately rang for the Fire Brigade. Stupidly Hans had stood back from the house and was enjoying seeing it go up in flames, he had got his vengeance, or so he thought, and was relishing in the knowledge that his ex-wife was now suffering. Scott saw and recognised him then from the dossier he had been reading only a few days earlier. Some of their neighbours started trying to get into the house as they thought Luke and Marilyn may be inside, but Scott quickly assured them that there was no one home, the fire brigade was on their way, and there was no use putting themselves in danger, for no good purpose. The police were quickly on the scene too. Scott had recognised Hans and was witness to the arson attack and although Hans had fled the scene the police knew they would be able to pick him up in due course. Following the phone call Luke and Marilyn rushed back to the old house, but it was just a dying ember now. Hans was picked up a few days later and charged with arson, assault and attempted murder. As the police tried to arrest him he fought and screamed abuse at the arresting officers. He resisted so violently that they had to Taser him and physically restrain him in handcuffs. He was taken into custody and the police assured Marilyn and Luke that the lunatic would go down for at least ten years, probably twenty. He would certainly not be a threat to them again, not for many, many years. There was to be a full payment from Luke's insurance company, and the house, which was not really worth saving in the first place, was to be rebuilt, they agreed, bigger, better, modern and just what the expectant couple needed. With Luke's artistic ability and vision, a new house would be wonderful. Luke also thought that when Peter returned he would probably be glad to have some architectural input into the new building.

A few days after the fire Luke took Marilyn and the puppy down south for a few days' rest, relaxation, and recuperation. It had been a stressful event and they needed a break and a few days to get over the drama of the fire. Luke hired a four-wheel drive campervan and they went down south to Wellington Dam for a camping trip. On the way down they stopped at Harvey and called in to the Lemon Grass Café for a cup of coffee, Luke had been there many times before and wanted to show Marilyn this little oasis of art in the middle of a country town. The café had a wonderfully eclectic collection of art work, souvenirs, and collector's items displayed for sale. They spent ten minutes just looking at the paintings and pottery. The coffee was good and hot and served in large ceramic mugs. They chatted a while to Kevin Francis the owner and discussed the possibility of Luke having some of his work displayed there. Kevin was only too happy to accommodate and display some of Luke's artwork and after much discussion helped them with directions to a secluded spot on the Collie River. They sat at the back of the café where it was nice and quiet and as Marilyn was now starting to relax Luke thought it might be a good time to ask her questions that had been bothering him about her past life, with Hans. Marilyn wanted him to know everything, but said she found it difficult to talk about it – but would tell him as much as she could. She started by relating what she thought about Hans when she first met him.

"Hans was a big man. That is," she explained, "large in size, and ten years ago he was a handsome man, in his prime and was kind and considerate. I thought the world of him then, and only slowly did things go wrong.

"First of all, I think he deliberately set out to separate me from my family. He was always making excuses not to go to family occasions and when he did, he would come home criticising my parents and my siblings. I know they have faults, doesn't everyone? But he put them down and slowly tried to turn me away from them. Because he was nasty and belligerent my family kept social obligations with us to a minimum. Whenever my brothers spoke against him, I always came back with the reply 'but I love him!' So that would put an end to any reasoning they had with me. It was the same then with friends. Gradually he started separating me from people I socialised with, especially Sharon and Fiona. We girls kept in touch but each time we organised a girls' night out, or similar, he would insist that he accompany me. If I did manage to get out alone to meet some friends he would fly into a rage and accuse me of having an affair behind his back. The first time he hit me was such an occasion. I had been to lunch with my parents and when I got home he was drunk and abusive and frightening. He hit me so hard I fell over and cut my head. The next day he apologised and swore he would never hit me again. And I believed him; he said it was my fault. However the abuse picked up again each time I did something wrong or something that annoyed him. Little things in the kitchen, too many vegetables, too little salt, not enough sauce, the wrong kind of bread. In the bedroom, sheets were not smooth enough, the house or the windows were not clean enough. It was always my fault. At the supermarket, he said I spent too much money, making the wrong choices and so on and so on, no matter what I did I just couldn't please him. Sometimes he screamed so loud at me I would just cower in a corner, too afraid to even look at him."

Luke shook his head, almost in disbelief. "Oh, my poor darling."

Marilyn continued. "Because he had virtually cut me off from friends and family I had no one to turn to for help or advice. Hans shouted at me so much I started to feel worthless. I was vulnerable, I know now, but he manipulated me until I didn't know what was right or wrong." Luke put his hand over hers, across the table. She went on, "I really don't know why I stayed in the marriage so long. Hans had taken control, not only of my life, but also of my money. He bullied me into allowing him to set up our bank account, but it was only in his name, he had explained at the time that it was for the best, as he was a better manager than I was. I just didn't feel I had the strength to fight him. I took to wearing thick make-up every day to cover up the bruises and I was too embarrassed to let anyone know that he was abusing me. It all came to a head when he wanted me to help him pass on small parcels to people he knew. He would ask me to go into town to a certain spot and hand over a parcel and receive a small packet in return; I was not to open any of the packets. At first I refused, I really knew it must be drugs he was wanting me to move, but he hit me and accused me of not trusting him. Each time he hit me I was bruised and battered and was taking so much time off work that I was reprimanded by my manager. I had run out of sick leave and also holiday leave but there were days when I could hardly get out of bed, never mind go to work. I eventually stood up to him and refused to take any more parcels to town. He screamed abuse at me and beat me severely. I couldn't go to work and after four more days off I was called into the manager's office and officially fired. Now I was really dependent on Hans for my everything, food, toiletries, everything. It was what he wanted – total domination. He had worn me down to total dependency and utter degradation – my self-esteem was non-existent, he kept telling me how worthless I was, and I believed him.

"I did a few more pick-ups for him and then I realised if I was caught I would go to jail. He wasn't taking any risks, I was doing all the dangerous work for him. I refused to do any more drop-offs and again, he beat me severely. At that point I realised if I didn't get out of that situation he was going to kill me. I then called Sharon. She was running a Women's Refuge and I knew I just had to get out of the house and out of that toxic situation. Sharon came immediately. Hans was out and when she saw the condition I was in she rang for an ambulance. Once the story came out, the police were called in and Hans was arrested and charged with assault, and drug trafficking offences. After I had recovered and Hans was in jail, I filed for divorce."

Luke just held her hand whilst she let it all out, he kept shaking his head, hardly able to believe such appalling cruelty, no wanting to believe how anyone could hurt his beloved Marilyn, such a beautiful creature, and so gentle and caring herself.

"That's really my story," she said. "I was stupid I know, but I was vulnerable, and he took advantage of me and manipulated me, dominating me, putting me down all the time until I really didn't know if he was right, was I worthless, I must be worthless 'cos he kept shouting that at me – he was relentless in his abuse, both physical and mental."

Marilyn stopped her story for a moment whilst she had a good cry. Luke told her, "You don't have to go on sweetheart – I've heard enough."

"No," replied Marilyn as she sniffed into her handkerchief, "let me finish telling you everything, just this once and then I won't have to repeat it ever again. Throughout all my troubles Sharon and Fiona were wonderful – they never deserted me, we had remained good friends throughout my marriage. It took me months to regain my confidence, Sharon organised many sessions of counselling for me, and after I had recovered I started to work at the Women's Refuge and then progressed to working for Sharon in her office. We set up two more Women's Refuges, and Safe Houses and it was really good worthwhile work. There are so many women being abused, it's disgusting, but we were helping. What we really wanted to do was to change the way men and women think – to change the attitudes of men who think this sort of behaviour is acceptable, and to change the attitude of women who think they are powerless to do anything about their situation. We started teaching groups, focusing on educating women, teaching those who needed skills for living, skills that would enable them to get a job once they were free of the domination of their partners. We ran classes for bookkeeping, sewing, English Language skills, computer literacy, and so on. You know many of the immigrant women had hardly any English. We had to teach them not to be embarrassed about the abuse they may be experiencing, that they need to talk to someone. 'Don't hide it' we told them, it's not your fault and it's not your 'shame'. We stressed to them, never let anyone tell you that you are worthless, stand up for yourself but, the most important thing for any woman is – don't put up with it – get out of the situation – just leave." Marilyn was on a roll now and went on to tell Luke how they tried to educate the women saying, "We told them that, he'll tell you can't live without him – but that's so wrong – you don't need a toxic situation. There are places, refuges, where you will be welcomed and cared for." She gave a little nervous cough and went on, "Oh dear – I'm up on my soap box aren't I? Sorry – but you did ask."

Luke held her hand throughout the telling of her story and he just kept shaking his head. "Oh, my poor darling. I didn't realise it had been so bad for you. I promise you though, I will never let anything bad ever happen to you. I will look after you, and our child, and I will kill anyone who tries to hurt you – I promise."

"No, please," pleaded Marilyn, "there's been enough violence, and he's been put away for a long time now, so let's just forget him and get on with the rest of our lives, and I've been doing, and will continue doing what I can to help other women going through the same thing. Someone once said, I think, that something good can often come out of something bad, and I think in my case that's true. I have a good job now. I work in Sharon's office, as Campaign Manager, and the Selection Panel at the Labour Party Headquarters have approved Sharon as a candidate and she is to run for the seat of Pearlman. If she gets voted in she'll be a State Member of Parliament and I hope to remain with her as Personal Assistant. She has ambitions to become Minister for Women's Rights and I think her election slogan is going to be, 'NO ABUSE; NO EXCUSE'. Yes, I'm pretty sure that's what we all agreed upon."

The holiday down on the Collie River was just what the doctor ordered. Peace and quiet, swimming in the crystal clear water of the river, playing with the puppy and watching the blue wrens dart in and out of the tall gum trees and they even spotted a bandicoot in the evening foraging for its dinner. A very cheeky possum came down a large tree to see if there was any food going. He was quite large, about the size of a large domestic cat and wasn't afraid of the humans at all. Marilyn took many photos of the possum and thoroughly enjoyed the encounter. No one else was in the forest with them and the tranquillity was just perfect.

CHAPTER 31

GETTING TO THE ISLAND

For Peter and Fiona, flying to Manila was easy to arrange but getting a charter boat was proving to be really difficult. Peter went on to the Internet trying to find a company in Manila who would take them out to the island. No one seemed to be able or willing to go that far. It didn't look promising but Peter was determined. He wondered if the locals in Manila knew about the restrictions regarding that particular island. Having got no joy from his research into charter boats from Manila Peter decided to try and get information from the experts in his home town, Perth. His first port of call was to the Perth Yacht Club. There he met the Chartering Captain, Alistair Conway, and explained that he wanted to hire an experienced sailor who would be able to assist them with; firstly finding a suitable ocean going yacht and secondly, skippering the yacht and navigating to a certain island in the Pacific Ocean. Alistair wanted to know all about the island and why they wanted to go there specifically. Peter had to explain all about his mother's original survival, and told Alistair he thought his mother was dead but just wanted to make a memorial on the island for her. This seemed to satisfy Alistair and he promised to give the proposal some careful thought and would get back to Peter by the end of the week. Three days later Peter got a phone call asking him to meet Alistair in town for lunch. Fiona took some time off work for an extended lunch and met up with Peter and Alistair in town. Alistair was an ex British Naval man who obviously knew all the yachting fraternity in Perth as well as Australia as a whole.

They met in a small busy restaurant and managed to get a secluded table in the corner. After ordering their lunch Alistair started to tell them about his knowledge of the ocean going yachtsmen and who was available at this time. He told them, "You know, Peter, as soon as you put your request to me three days ago, I had in mind a certain yachtsman, but didn't want to say anything until I'd had a chance to talk to the man in question and see if he might be interested in the offer you were making. I know that the man in question would be up to the job but I need a bit more information and then I can arrange for you all to meet, assuming the proposition is kosher and everything is above board."

Peter did his best to reassure Alistair that it was all above board and that they were not planning anything illicit, but found it quite difficult to explain his motives without giving away his mother's secret. Fiona wanted to know all about the proposed yachtsman and asked many questions. "Who is this man? What is his background? Is he really competent? Is he honest and of good character? How old is he? Is he married, and does he have a family?"

There were so many questions and Alistair did his best to answer all her queries and to lay her fears to rest. He told them, "Well, the man in question is Sam Summers, and I can vouch for him personally. He's a forty-five-year-old experienced sailor who is luckily available for the next three months. Sam has been in, and skippered, all kinds of yachts, from nineteenth century replica tall ships, to modern racing maxi yachts. He's very well known in yachting circles and has an impeccable reputation. I couldn't put you in better hands, honestly."

Alistair gave them Sam's telephone number and after lunch left them with best wishes and an invitation to call on him again if there was anything else he could do for them, especially if arrangements with Sam didn't work out. The next evening Peter and Fiona met up with Sam Summers and had dinner with him at one of Perth's best restaurants overlooking Perth Water in King's Park. Perth is blessed with a huge park overlooking the Swan River and across to South Perth with spectacular views further out to the hills of the Darling Scarp. It was a windy night so there was no alfresco dining, but the interior of the restaurant was tastefully decorated and the ambience was just what the little party needed to discuss the proposal. Grandma Campbell was looking after Chris. She was helping him with his letters and she tried to teach him that words have letters. She had a few children's books and pointed out the simple words like "C" is for cat and "D" is for dog. Chris was an intelligent little boy and got the idea very quickly. They went around the house pointing to everything and calling out the first letter. "D" is for door and "T" is for table and so on, it was a fun game and Chris really enjoyed it – to him it wasn't learning, it was just a fun game. Later they watched "Mary Poppins" together on the television, until Chris fell asleep and then Grandma just covered him over with a blanket to await his parent's return.

Fiona liked the look of Sam Summers straight away. He was tall, tanned and she could tell he had a good muscled body, under his smart Ralph Lauren shirt and slacks, but not the exaggerated body builder type. He was relaxed and easy to talk to. Peter explained over dinner, "You see, Sam, we don't have a yacht but I think it would be a good idea if we bought one, rather than charter, and if you're willing, for you to skipper the yacht to a particular island in the Pacific. We'd also need your help in selecting and buying a suitable yacht, as we are no sailors and really have no idea how to go about this little exercise."

"I understand," answered Sam. "But before I agree to anything I really need to know exactly where you want to go and why. I can tell you upfront, I won't be involved in any kind of illicit traffic and will need to inspect everything that has to be taken on board."

Peter stiffened at this suggestion and quickly tried to put that notion to rest by explaining, "Look, Sam, I understand your caution but truly we are honest and decent people who just have a very private and personal reason for wanting to go to Du Pont Island. Of course you may inspect everything that we plan to take on board – we'll fall in with whatever stipulations you make."

At that point in the meeting Sam decided to reserve his judgement on the couple, they certainly came across as decent and honest folk and he decided, in his own mind, to wait and find out more before making a final decision. He took the coordinates from Peter and explained that navigation to that spot would not be a problem. "I'm glad you're asking for my help in selecting the vessel, it will be very important that we get the right kind of yacht and of course, it must have all the most modern equipment and technology on board and available. We'll need to be very careful with our selection and we will need to do some trial runs as well."

Peter went on to confess, "I'll be honest, Sam, we don't know the first thing about sailing, or buying a yacht or even what kind of yacht, what size etc. and whether it's maybe better to get one in Australia and sail it to the island or whether it would be better to fly out to the Philippines and buy one there. What I can tell you is that we will lean very heavily on you for your expertise and advice."

Sam was enthusiastic about this idea and decided that he would trust the two and agreed in his own mind, to undertake the mission. He told them, "I think on the whole it would be better to fly out to Manila, and buy one out there. I have some contacts in the Philippines so I'll make a few enquiries and let you know what there is that may be suitable and available."

"That would be great," replied Peter who was warming to this agreeable, experienced and knowledgeable man.

Fiona then dropped the not so favourable news to Sam, "By the way, Sam, there'll just be Peter and I and we have our four-year-old son we'll be taking with us."

Sam's mouth dropped open, and he struggled with the right words to say. He was none too happy about this – as he explained, "Oh, I'm not too sure if that's a good idea, it's a big responsibility with a child on board and dangerous too."

Peter sat back in his chair and put his two hands squarely on the table saying, "Well it's take the child with us or the whole trip is off – I have a personal reason why I want my son to go and see the island, sorry, but that's it."

Sam shook his head and conceded saying, "Well, alright but the child will have to be in a life jacket the whole time on deck and also attached to a harness. I don't like taking responsibility for a child, it really isn't a good idea, but if you're adamant, well, so be it."

Fiona was agreeable with this stipulation and offered her support to Peter saying, "I know how much Peter wants this so I will take full responsibility for Chris and will make sure he is in his harness whenever he's on deck. I'll look after him if you look after us."

Sam nodded his agreement and Fiona went on to ask about the viability of one person, alone sailing the boat. "As we told you, Sam, neither Peter nor I have ever sailed before or even done any navigation, do you think you will be able to navigate and sail the ship unassisted? Sorry if that's an insulting question, but we really need to know."

Peter cut in at this point. "Sorry if we sound rude but we do need to know if it's a viable operation and not outside your normal expertise. You come with a very good recommendation from Alistair at the yacht club, but we need to know for ourselves if it's a reasonable possibility, that is, buying a boat and sailing to the island. And, as we have said, we don't know anything about sailing, but I am willing to learn and will give any assistance that I can."

Sam laughed and quoted, "The best way to learn about sailing is to get in there and just do it!"

Peter and Sam seemed to get on well together and it was agreed that Peter would assist with the sailing of the yacht when and where it was at all possible.

It was agreed that Fiona would do the cooking and look after Chris. The other stipulation that Peter made was that when they reach the island Sam was not, definitely not allowed to accompany them on to the shore. Sam was a little taken aback at this stipulation and asked, "Why ever not?"

Peter explained that it was a sort of "memorial trip" – a pilgrimage if you like, they were making and that they were worried that a large company developing the island may or may not have interfered with his mother's memorial. He wanted to keep it "sacred".

Sam raised his eyebrows and gave the two of them a sceptical, quizzical look. "Are you sure you're not planning something illegal?"

"No," answered Peter. "It's just that I want to keep my mother's last known living area sort of hallowed, sacrosanct – private."

Sam shrugged his shoulders. Sam agreed with all the financial details and told them that he was sure he would be able to get a boat within their budget and that he was happy with his proposed wages, provided everything was supplied, including flights from Perth to Brisbane and then on to Manila, and also the return trip plus accommodation whilst they were looking at yachts in Manila, and after, later when they return to Manila, taking time to sell the boat on. He explained, "I have some friends, especially one good, reliable old friend who lives in Manila and I'll contact him tonight and see if he's free and willing to assist with all the proposed arrangements. Leave it to me."

After all the discussions it was agreed they would meet again in two days' time when Sam thought he would be able to give them some news of his arrangements. True to his word, Sam made contact with his friend in Manila and suggested they line up two or three suitable yachts for the family and Sam to inspect in two weeks' time. Peter and Fiona took holiday leave entitlements and Grandma Campbell agreed, at first, to look after the house, and the puppy but later changed her mind as she thought the responsibility was too much. Fiona saw through that and discussed it with Peter – she thought her mother was worried for her own health and safety. They agreed to talk it over with her the next day, to see what alternative arrangements could be made. After a phone call it was agreed that Grandma Campbell would go to stay with a good friend in a retirement village not far away. Peter also discussed the house and babysitting the puppy with Luke and Marilyn and, as mentioned before, it was agreed that, as their house was being renovated that they would move in to Peter's house for the duration. Everyone was settled and happy with the arrangements. The puppy was house trained now which was a great relief to Luke. He enjoyed taking the dog with him each morning when he jogged around the park before going to work.

All was well and Peter and Fiona were getting excited about the trip. They met up again with Sam, this time at the Yacht Club in Perth and one or two people there chatted to them about their proposed trip. Sam had much work to do and so kept their meeting short, but it was agreed that

225

everything could be done and they would all be available to fly out to Manila in six days' time. Sam advised them to keep luggage to a minimum and that all food, stores etc. could be obtained in Manila. Provisioning the yacht was not a problem once they were in Manila and he thought the journey to the island wouldn't take too long depending on wind and good weather. Peter and Sam were in constant contact by phone and they had three more meetings to finalise details of the trip.

Sam was worried about the child, but was assured that Fiona would keep him safe by her side at all times. At last the day of departure came and the three of them, plus Chris, met at Perth Domestic Terminal and checked in electronically before wandering around the terminal waiting for their flight. They were to go to Brisbane first and then on to Manila. Chris was so excited as he had never flown before and loved playing with his toy aeroplanes, but this was the real thing and the planes he could see through the glass windows, in the holding lounge, astounded him, he was awed at the enormous size – his imagination had never stretched to these sizes before. Once on the plane the meal was served and within the hour Chris was fast asleep. The two men discussed the course and the trip endlessly. Fiona read for a while but couldn't concentrate, she was worried about Chris and taking him on board a yacht. She wasn't sure if this was really a good idea.

Chris didn't awake until they were landing and Fiona had to sit him up to secure his seat belt. He was sleepy still, but could see out of the small window and was amazed at how the houses looked so small. They were coming in fast and it was a bumpy landing which frightened all the adults, but Chris was ecstatic and thought the bouncing and bumping was normal and it was great fun. The next part of their journey was similar to the first part. They only had one hour to wait for their connection and Chris was having a great time. Everything was new and his daddy kept a tight

226

hold on to his hand, so the child had no worries and being an intelligent little boy, was taking in everything around him. He wanted to know if his violin was safe. Peter had wanted him to bring it along and explained, "Yes your violin is quite safe, it's really well wrapped in its case, and it's with the rest of our luggage in the hold of the plane." Chris looked up to his father with a worried look on his little face and asked innocently, "What's a hole in the plane, Daddy? Won't my violin fall out of a hole?"

"No." Peter smiled and explained, "Not a hole, the plane has a storage area and it's called a storage hold. Your violin is being stored in that safe place."

Chris just held on to his daddy's hand and said, "Good."

Sam and Fiona spent a lot of time and energy discussing storage and stores that would be needed. Sam explained that when buying a yacht it may or may not come with kitchen equipment, crockery, cutlery etc. They would have to wait and see what was available. When they reached Manila and had gone through Customs and Immigration Sam steered them to the Arrivals Lounge where they were met by a tall American whom Sam introduced as his old friend Chuck. He explained that he and Chuck had been part of the crew on many an ocean yacht race, including the Sydney to Hobart Classic. Chuck was an affable, easy going sailor, but Sam had assured them previously that Chuck had a sensible business head on his shoulders and would look after them all, with the business of buying and later selling a suitable yacht for their needs. Before going to see the yachts that Chuck had arranged for them, they checked into the Royal Charter Hotel, just off the main marina wall. Chuck had three yachts lined up for them to inspect. Each was a beauty with clean lines and not too old. Peter and Fiona loved all of them and wouldn't have been able to choose between them, but Sam knew exactly what he wanted. The yacht had to have everything that was electronically possible, and all the technology that modern sailing and communications required. He chose "The Carramar", a Bonatia Oceana 50 priced at $550,000. Price was a consideration as Peter had told Sam of the budget limitations, but as he intended to sell it on after the trip it was alright to spend up to $600,000. "The Carramar" was a 45.5ft 2012 year model with a monolithic polyester hull. The deck material was injection moulded deck in glass fibre/balsa sandwich. It had a beam of 5.1 and a draft of 2.18. There was a sail locker and chart table which became the living room table, also an open bathing platform at the rear of the deck. All the up to date communication systems were in place and the navigation systems had Sam's approval. Fiona was more interested in the kitchen and cabins. The kitchen/galley was L shaped with white laminated worktop, stainless steel double sinks and a front opening fridge. The cooking would be done on a stainless steel 2 hob oven grill cooker. There were three cabins and two toilet/shower bathrooms. Everything was perfect as far as she was concerned. There was a rail around the outer deck and Peter assured her that they would be able to give Chris a harness that would be clipped to the rail whenever he was on deck, and there was plenty of room for him to play and watch his daddy sailing the boat. All the utensils for kitchen use were there – everything was provided except bedding. That was no problem as Fiona was looking forward to going to the local market for food and she would be able to get bedding there as well she thought. Sam insisted on taking the yacht out for two trial runs before he agreed to the purchase. He had taken Peter with him and given him some idea of the kind of assistance that would be needed. Peter enjoyed helping to sail the yacht but was having difficulty remembering all the technical terms for the sails and ropes. Eventually it was agreed that the Elliotts would buy "The Carramar" and Peter and Sam left Fiona shopping with Chris whilst they went into the Marina Office to make arrangements for the sale. Chuck was invited to dine with them that night at the hotel and everyone drank a toast to "The Carramar" and a safe passage to Du Pont Island. Fiona had shopped all day for stores and groceries and Peter had done his own shopping. He surprised Fiona by telling her that he had ordered goods which were to be boxed and delivered to the wharf on the day of their intended departure. He had talked it over with Sam and they had agreed on where his purchases could be stored on the yacht. The largest of his items were two gas bottles, and a cast iron camp cooking pot. Peter had given some thought to his purchases and he had tried to imagine what his mother might need and he thought of her cooking over an open fire each day and assumed that the pans she had been using would probably be ruined by now, so a cast iron pot would be ideal for continuous use over a fire. Sam was intrigued to know what Peter intended doing on the island with these things, as no one lived on the island. Peter wouldn't and couldn't explain, he just asked Sam to trust him, nothing illegal was planned, but it was a private pilgrimage he had to make, and there were some things he wanted to take with him. He also reminded Sam that it was agreed that Sam would not go ashore once they reached the island. Sam was not too happy, but as he was being well paid could not think of a reasonable argument.

Peter's purchases included toiletries, gas kitchen lighters and batteries, CDs and batteries for a small CD player. Some books for reading and some puzzle books. He bought two large wax covered rounds of cheddar cheese and a Prosciutto ham. He bought long lasting small goods i.e. cabai, chorizo, pepperoni. He had plastic wrapped sugar, flour, herbs, spices, chocolates, nuts and packets of seeds for planting. He put in his parcel some pain killers and a pair of his mother's sized shoes. When Fiona saw the receipt for these goods she knew he intended them for his mother – it was obvious. She challenged him again. "Look, Peter, it's no use denying it – I'm not an idiot – you're taking this lot on to the island for your mother – she must be alive. Well is she or isn't she?"

Peter squirmed and looked very uncomfortable. "Look, Fiona I really don't want to tell you any lies, the truth is I don't know – can we leave it at that please?"

It was four days later that the little party left Manila Marina and headed out to the harbour entrance. Sam was highly experienced and knew how to handle the yacht, and with Peter's help they turned north and made for Luzon Straits before turning east and heading for Du Pont.

CHAPTER 32

ON THE ISLAND

The first part of the journey was a nightmare for Fiona. She was seasick from the first day. Peter had to help Sam sail the boat, as the first few days sailing was tricky and complicated, so he was not much help to her. Chris was terrified of the waves and the noise of the sails. He also couldn't understand why his mummy was laying down and sleeping so much. He tried playing with the few toys he had there and looking at some of the picture books but he didn't like it on the boat at all. He lived in Perth, so was often taken to the beach, but the waves there didn't frighten him by making such a terrible noise and the local swimming pool water kept quite still and didn't make a noise at all. He hated the harness and he wanted to go home to his puppy, his swing and his Grandma and all his toys. Fiona had packed sufficient toys and books for the child but he became irritable and didn't want to play with them and he wouldn't eat, which worried Fiona. She struggled through those first few days, trying to be brave and not frighten the child, but it was difficult and she couldn't keep any food down and so had very little energy. She also had to cook for the others and just the smell of the cooking nauseated her.

Eventually though, she got her "sea legs" and was able to play and entertain Chris as well as she could but still the child was not responding as much as Fiona would have liked. He was not really a happy child.

Peter on the other hand was having a great time, he had never been sailing before. He'd been on the boat with the surveyors and Skipper and Chip but he hadn't been asked to assist with the sailing, he'd been too busy in the galley with Cook serving meals. This was exhilarating, exciting and a challenge. He started to learn all the terms for the different sails, knots, roping, and sailing manoeuvres. He decided once they were home again he and Fiona might take up sailing – it was a great sport. He might even consider not selling the yacht if Sam would consider sailing it all the way back to Perth. He did a little homework and thought if he sold the apartment that he was renting out, he could afford to keep the yacht. He thought he'd better not mention that idea either to Sam or Fiona; not just yet anyway. No good spoiling a good thing, either of them might not agree to his new idea. Sam had done this sort of thing before, many times and he loved it. He loved the life at sea and would have done it for nothing actually, but as he was being well paid he was more than happy. Fiona was a good cook and was now doing splendidly in the little galley, with only two burners and a small oven. Peter was a good and enthusiastic student and it was a pleasure teaching him how to sail. They also had good discussions about the world in general, politics, world health, global warming and theology. Sam could see though that the little boy was really miserable and Fiona was none too delighted either with an unhappy child to entertain. He wondered if he could help and after a few days decided to see if he could assist in getting Chris acclimatised to the waves and the water. The back of the deck could be utilised for a bathing platform and on the first really calm day he decided to approach the child and try and tempt him into the water for a swim. Of course the harness would have to be kept on but

Peter had already told Sam that normally Chris loved his swimming lessons. Sam talked it over with Peter and they agreed that Peter would go for a swim first and try to encourage Chris to put his feet over the edge into the little pool. Chris wasn't having any for quite a while, but as it was a warm day and the wind had dropped he slowly let his feet dangle into the pool, followed by his legs and with Peter's encouragement finally slid into the waiting arms of his daddy. The water was cool, and it tasted funny, but it was a lovely sensation being in the boat, but in the sea at the same time. After that it was an everyday pleasure for Chris and Fiona, and Peter spent many hours playing with him in the water. He was a changed little boy and once again became the good natured, placid child; he started eating again and had roses in his cheeks. He was learning to read and both his parents took infinite patience teaching him his letters and the sounds of words. Chris already knew and recognised all his letters, except "b" and "d" – he always got them the wrong way round. They put cards all over the cabin marked, CUP, and BED, HAT, etc. and when he could read these they put labels on each person. Sam was called in to help with this game and he was the first to wear his label which spelt out SAM, Peter and Fiona had labels too spelling out MUM and DAD. From there they progressed to IS THIS and IS THAT. It was fun for Chris and he soon got the hang of changing words around so that now he could read out IS THIS SAM or change it to THIS IS SAM. They all played this game with him going through the cabin marking those objects with simple letters, like TAP and LEG. He learnt to read YES and NO so they could play the game for hours, making up simple questions for him. They drew him pictures of animals and then wrote a question under saying, "IS THIS A CAT?" Sometimes they got quite silly and drew a figure and asked him to read the question which might say, "IS THIS A FAT DOG?" or "IS THIS A THIN MAN WITH A FAT LEG?" The sillier the question the more the child responded and enjoyed the game. He had his violin and practised his one tune over and over again, he now could play the tune straight forward without the rhythm – and he could play it on all four strings too. For Sam it was agony listening to the same tune being played repeatedly, but for Fiona and Peter it was a relief that their little boy was back to normal and enjoying his music.

The island came into view one day and everyone was excited at the thought of getting on to dry land, except Sam who had agreed that he wouldn't go ashore, but was at a loss as to know why he wasn't allowed off the boat. Peter and Fiona were quite surprised as they approached the island and saw the jetty sticking out – it hadn't been there before. Sam brought the yacht from the west across Peaceful Cove, (although he didn't know that was its name) and across Turtle Bay to the new jetty. There was no activity on the jetty and they couldn't see anyone moving at all, no machinery, no work being done. Nothing. Sam motored slowly up alongside the jetty and Peter tied up the yacht. Everything was quiet and still, only the lapping of the small waves against the boat and jetty could be heard. Peter recognised the bay and knew that his mother's wreck was at the back of the cove that they had passed. If his mother was alive, he thought, she would, in all probability be aware that a boat had moored up against the jetty and invaded her little island. She would be hiding and not show herself, even to Peter if someone was with him. He reminded Sam of his promise not to go on to the island and then collected Fiona and Chris. He asked Chris if he would bring his violin with him as he wanted him to play Twinkle Twinkle on the island. Chris was only too happy to bring his violin but wanted to play on the sand and on the rocks. Making sure Sam stayed on the boat Peter took Fiona's hand and they both crossed Turtle Bay and then climbed up and over the headland to Peaceful Cove. Chris was happy to be released from the dreaded harness and ran up and down the beach following his mummy and daddy up the small hill and around the headland. When they came down on to Peaceful Cove Peter took Chris to the centre of the beach and then stepped back and took Fiona's hand. The four-year-old with the golden curls, looking just as Timmy would have looked, did as his daddy asked and took out his violin. Peter explained to the little boy that he wanted him to play his violin because Peter's mummy used to live on this island and if, and he stressed if, she was still there Peter wanted his mummy to hear Chris playing the violin. Chris asked Peter many questions about why he hadn't seen this other Grandma before, and what was she like, and would she like him, and love him like Grandma Campbell did. Peter answered all his questions and told him that if Grandma Elliott was on the island she would just love to see Chris and to hear him play his violin. He also told Chris that if Grandma Elliott was there she would be quite small and have white hair and she might be very quiet – but she would love Chris, he was sure.

The strains of Twinkle Twinkle echoed across the cove. The haunting tune being played by a child on a tiny violin wafted back to Sam who knew there must be someone out there that this performance was being played for, but it was private and he understood he wasn't to be part of it. Chris played it over and over to his father's encouragement. Fiona didn't know what to expect but Peter did. He was watching the break in the shoreline where he knew the wreck was and there, slowly, slowly, he saw a white headed figure appear. Slowly she moved towards the child, who looked to his daddy for reassurance and he kept playing over and over Twinkle Twinkle Little Star. Tears were running down Sally's face as she recognised, and knew it was Peter and this must be his son and she recognised Fiona from when she had seen her on the beach four years earlier.

The tears were flowing now and Sally cried softly, "Look, Joe – it's Timmy come back to us."